Son

Alexan Gilchrist

SONG OF THE STARS

First edition. March 25, 2023.

ISBN: 979-8215632161

Written by Alexandra Gilchrist.

~Praise ye him, sun and moon: praise him, all ye stars of light.~
Psalm 148:3

Prologue

The invaders had taken the last citadel of Vistke 12. Only a handful of defenders survived to land their jump pods at the landing platform anchored below the asteroid that housed the colony on Vistke Prime. The usually polished, reddish hulls of the tiny, single-pilot vessels were scorched and pitted. Instead of the parades and fanfare of heroes, they were met by only the techs necessary to repair their vessels for the next battle, and the medics necessary to heal their wounded. Such as they were, the Vistkian army was far outmatched. Most who fell to the outworlders simply did not return.

Creator, Father will be devastated. Prince Belenos's automated ladder failed to disengage all the way to the ground as he climbed down from the lead vessel, leaving him drop the rest of the way with a wince. He pulled off his helmet and shook his narrow head at a medic shuffling toward him. There were others who needed the attention far more than he did. His injuries could wait until he reported to the emperor.

As he took the lift through the center of the asteroid to the palace topside, he tried to figure out a way to soften the blow his news would bring. The cluster colony of Vistke had circled their trinary star for fourteen generations – nearly ten since their mother planet's decaying orbit had forced their citizens to seek new lives on the asteroids at what had been the middle orbit of their solar system. Vistkians were above all else proud of their advanced technology that had saved them from the fate their home planet suffered. How could he tell them that their technology was not going to be enough to save them now?

The attendant topside bowed with his hands clasped in front of him as the prince exited the lift and stepped onto a waiting hover disk. He nodded his acknowledgment to the attendant grimly as he sped toward his father's quarters. How could he tell the families he'd sworn to protect that by the end of their next orbital cycle, every surviving Vistkian would be a slave to the brutal alien beings that had already taken eleven of their sister cities? He clenched a clawed fist in hopeless determination. His life was already forfeit – he would lead his armies back into battle defending their last outpost and die beside their last warrior – he just wished his efforts to fulfill his vow to his people had not been so futile.

Belenos's hover disk stopped in front of the door to his father's quarters and he pressed a series of symbols on the wall beside the door. The wall was the same polished reddish metal that his vessel was made from, that everything, including the asteroid beneath him was made from. The door slid aside silently, opening to an opulent chamber decorated with a blend of natural antique remnants of their past and bright synthetic tapestries of the present. The gaudy decor soured his mood further. The destruction of Vistke 12 had destroyed this year's larvae farms. If the farms on their last outpost fell, there was no way they would be able to produce enough food to feed even the remnant that remained if by some miracle they could fend off the outworlders. What good were heirlooms and tapestries, or even all the technologies in all the galaxies if their young were to starve to death? He shuddered. Dying in battle would be a much more pleasant death than his failure would guarantee the most helpless of his people.

"Father has been worried sick." His younger brother Timir waited for him outside the council chamber. He wore polished black armor, a treasured family heirloom salvaged in the escape from their homeworld. It was more ceremonial than practical, fitting his brother's role of advisor to the emperor. "I told him you had more lives than a Trakelian Flame Cat."

"The Creator showed His favor to me yet again." Belenos unconsciously rubbed at a broken collarbone he hadn't stopped to get looked at. There would be time for that later.

"It seems He might have forgotten the rest of us." Timir grumbled as he tapped out the symbols beside the door that announced his entry. "We haven't had good news in months, and I highly doubt you're bringing any now."

Belenos wasn't, but there wasn't any need to repeat it twice. The door slid open to reveal a sparsely decorated room with a throne at one end and chairs lining the side walls. The floor was an elaborately enameled star map of their galaxy, with their star system at the center. His father sat in the throne at the far end, while his advisors sat in the chairs along the sides of the room. The chair nearest his father's left hand was empty, awaiting his brother's return.

Emperor Regulus had been considered handsome in his prime, and old age had been very kind to him. His green-gold eyes were as attentive and shrewd as ever, and the scales that covered him from his forehead, down his back, arms, legs and tail were as strong as ever. Even the fading of the fur that covered the front of his body from golden brown to starlight white had only served to give him the appearance of wisdom and maturity. He'd been a great warrior in his youth, and though the robes of leadership he wore now appeared archaic compared to the glistening armor both his sons wore, they were backed by generations of power and respect.

"I bring a report from the battle, oh Majesty." Their family relationship was laid aside for a moment as Belenos performed the role of commander traditionally demanded of the firstborn, a role the emperor had played in his own youth. He clasped his hands together and bowed low. "I am afraid it is not good. The battle for Vistke 12 has been lost. Only a handful of my fleet have returned to Vistke Prime. The enemy has suffered significant losses and dropped back to the edge of our star system to regroup, but time is not in our favor. To stand would mean sure defeat. We must evacuate as many people as we can. My fleet will hold them off as long as we can to allow you time to escape."

"That would be suicide, Commander." Emperor Regulus looked at him grimly, as if the news had not been unexpected, and it probably wasn't. "What if there was another way?"

"Father, that's just theory." Timir leaned forward in his chair in protest. "We're decades away from testing on an actual Vistkian."

Emperor Regulus waved him silent and turned to Zosma, his chief science advisor, instead. "You told me you were ready to try?"

"If the elder prince is willing to submit to the process." Zosma pointedly avoided looking at him, his black eyes darting to the door instead, as if seeking an escape of his own.

"And you believe he's a good candidate?" Emperor Regulus pressed.

The scientist droned on about military service records and psychiatric evaluations and other things of no interest at all to Belenos, instead he looked to his younger brother and mouthed, *What are they on about?*

I'm sorry, Timir mouthed back with an apologetic shrug. "Father, perhaps we should show him and let him decide for himself."

The emperor and Zosma glanced at the brothers, then at each other. The scientist nodded, then started for the door he'd been eyeing. The emperor followed and the brothers fell in behind.

"What is this all about?" Belenos whispered as they wove their hover disks toward the science complex.

"Some new crackpot scheme to save the star system." Timir flashed him a lopsided grin. "If it works, we'll be gods. If it fails, we're dead. At least, you'll be dead. I'll just be driven mad. Stars, you might be dead either way, I don't know, but isn't that what you were looking for anyway? A heroic death in service to Vistke? If heroic, historic, and crazy is your thing, we've got you covered."

"That doesn't sound very promising." Death in battle was far preferable to death as a lab experiment.

"That's the thing. It's just crazy enough it might work." Timir shrugged. "It's going to be your call. All the risk is on you. If you can survive what they have planned for you, my part will be a walk in the star deck. Just a warning, refuse and you'll be the one they blame for the enslavement of our whole race. No pressure, though."

"Thanks, you're such an encouragement. Like always." They'd reached the science complex and were whisked by their father's lead scientist into a sterile room filled with computers, medical equipment, and things he'd never seen before. This was a medical facility, not a military tech lab. Belenos slowed. What was he getting into?

Zosma turned and bowed anxiously to them, his eyes on the emperor as he wrung his paws. "We've developed a super-soldier armor technology. The armor provides a nearly impenetrable shell, regenerative healing powers, and enhanced strength and senses. We've been looking for a test subject..."

Armor he could handle, but Belenos got the distinct sense the scientist was hiding something. Maybe it was the fact that he still wouldn't meet his gaze. "Why hasn't it been tested yet?"

Zosma cleared his throat and still kept his gaze fixed on the emperor even as he answered the prince's question. "We couldn't find a suitable subject."

"Which I apparently am." Belenos waved a frustrated paw. "I got it. Why me, and what's the catch?"

"Your military training and psychic profile make you considerably more stable than our other volunteers." Still no eye contact, and Zosma's clear agitation was increasing. "The catch..."

Timir sighed loudly and pushed off the wall he was leaning against. "You have to *become* the armor. That's the catch. They rip out your soul and upload it into the armor instead. I wear you into battle, and we're invincible. Instant revenge."

Belenos blinked and took a sharp breath. The implications of what his brother was suggesting crashed over him in heavy waves. In order to save his people he would have to give up everything, his entire life, his future, to become little more than an AI tethered to a high tech weapon. *Creator, you know I don't fear death, but this... this is living death. I will never take a mate, never sit on the throne.* Peace pushed back against the waves of terror. "You said you haven't tested it. How do you know it will work?"

"We, er, don't." Zosma shifted his feet. "We've checked and double checked the science, and we're reasonably sure this will work."

"No one will force you to take this risk, my son." His father laid a clawed paw on his shoulder. "Your bravery and sacrifice have been proved over and over again. The choice is yours."

"Yeah, it's not like anyone will remember if you don't." Timir laughed harshly. "You'll go out for your final flight against the invaders and die as a hero and the rest of us will be dead in six months time." His voice hardened bitterly. "You and I both know there isn't a choice. It's not like I'm looking forward to having you inside my head for the rest of our eternal lives."

"What do you mean?" Belenos looked from his brother to the scientist.

"The armor only functions with a host." Zosma gestured to the younger prince. "Once he puts on the armor, you would be bonded physically and psychically. You would share thoughts, feelings, needs, pain – and be able to sustain each other indefinitely."

"Eternal life, infinite power, the lives and undying gratitude of our people." Timir scoffed and his voice took a sarcastic tone. "How can we possibly weigh our own free will against that?"

Belenos stood up straighter as he stared at the medical bed, complete with ominous looking restraints. His brother's tone was clear. He was being given the choice for both of them. He briefly wondered whether his brother was wishing for the experiment to succeed, granting them both immeasurable power at the cost of slavery, or fail, leaving them both to die in freedom. In the end, his brother was right about one thing. There really wasn't a choice.

He blew out a long slow breath. "I will do it. My purpose is to do everything in my power to protect our people. My power has failed. May my life be the ransom for all Vistke."

His father's hand tightened reassuringly on his shoulder and his brother just grunted in resignation.

"Your majesty, you might want to..." Zosma cleared his throat, bowed low, and tried to address the emperor again.

"Belenos will need to be conscious for the procedure to work, but we will medicate him to dull the pain. He won't be able to respond to you until the procedure is completed."

Say goodbye now. Everyone in the room knew that's what he meant. Even if the procedure worked, would he be able to respond freely to his father through his brother? His brother had always resented the closeness of his relationship to the emperor, so he doubted highly he'd facilitate any open expressions of affection.

"My son. I have always been proud of you." Emperor Regulus took one of Belenos's paws in his own and laid his other paw on Belenos's shoulder. His teary eyes met the prince's steadily. "Your sacrifice here will be remembered in the songs of our people for as long as Vistke remains, no matter the outcome." He pulled him in for a tight, desperate embrace. "But I fully expect you to win this battle with the same skill and grace as you have always conquered our enemies. With your tactical skill and moral code and your brother's cunning and political acumen, I will be able to confidently retire to the throne room of the Creator and leave Vistke in your paws."

His father released him reluctantly and Belenos turned to face Timir.

"I'm counting on you to not die here, brother." The gruff bravado in Timir's voice did little to mask the fear in his dark eyes. He punched his older brother in the arm and forced a grin. "We both know this is my only chance to be a hero. Don't screw this up for me."

Belenos rolled his eyes and embraced his brother anyway. If he survived, they'd soon be closer than ever. If

11

not... His brother might be a bit prickly, but he wasn't going to leave him without a goodbye. Instead of pushing him away, his brother relaxed and returned an awkward hug.

"Is there anyone else you need to take leave of?" Zosma prodded as the princes separated. "A mate or lover, perhaps?"

Belenos shook his head. The queen mother had passed peacefully before the war had even started, and romancing the females was more his brother's department. Part of him regretted that there were no young to carry on his name, but most of him was just glad to not be leaving a grieving widow and orphans behind. Even if the experiment succeeded, he would be dead to any family he may have had. "My soldiers are all I have, and if you succeed I will be seeing them again soon. I'm ready."

Zosma looked all at once relieved and gleeful as he motioned a claw to a pair of large orderlies.

"My assistants will make you as comfortable as possible, your highness, while I prepare the armor to receive your soul." Xosma poked the prince's battered armor with one claw. "This will have to be removed. Please disrobe."

He complied, removing his cape, armor, and robes without hesitation. With all he was about to sacrifice, a little dignity was a small added tax.

The assistants took the cue to help him onto the table and strap his wrists and ankles securely. His tail was tucked between his legs and also strapped down. The acrid smell of antiseptic filled the room as they prepped his scales and hide for the procedure. On a pedestal beside the bed sat a multi sided orb made of the same reddish metal as his armor, each side engraved with a symbol representing a word in their language. Wires trailed from the orb to the large computer Zosma was tending, then out again. He dropped his head back against the soft bed and closed his eyes as they attached wires and electrodes to his bare chest and neck. He played the Song of Pleiades through his head to distract from the panic that welled up inside him, begging him to fight for survival. The song thanked the Creator for his care and pleaded with Him to ease the transition to the afterlife.

A heavy helmet was strapped to his head, and tightened so tightly he barely could move his jaw. Something at the back of the helmet clamped onto the base of his skull, piercing the thick scales painfully. He screamed and nearly passed out as it penetrated to his brain stem.

Numbness flooded from the penetration site downward, spreading through his body and extremities. The panic in his chest screamed against the awareness that his body was dying. He tried to pull against the bindings holding him to the bed, but his arms and legs no longer responded. Senses he took for granted, like the rhythm of his own breathing and heartbeat, faded ominously. The song in his head changed to the Song of Orion, a song of desperation and a cry for salvation. *Creator, I beg you, for the sake of my people, do not let me die here!*

The sounds of the busy scientists, calling to each other urgently with the panic in their voices echoing the cry of his own fears, faded. They were losing him. The transfer had to happen now. His father cried out his name. He felt for all the world like he was becoming disembodied, existing somehow outside the dying shell that lay on the medical bed. The feeling was disorienting and unpleasant, but not painful. He was cold. Isolated. Even the pain of the needle in his brain was gone. His only conscious feeling was the song that still threaded through his consciousness. Was this death? Had he failed?

Then, he could feel again. It was dulled, clinical, as if he were flying strictly by sensors without any visual reference. He could see, but not quite. The room was as clear to him as a digital readout, sonographic outlines moving frantically about the room. The placement of the others in the room was different in reference to himself than they had been. He'd moved, and now he could see the outline of himself – his body at least – strapped motionless to the bed beside him. As far as he could guess, he was resting on the pedestal that held the orb, which meant that he probably *was* the orb now. That much of the experiment had been a success.

The chief scientist spoke, his voice recognizable, but muffled. The shape Belenos recognized as his brother started, then crossed the room slowly. He reached out a hand toward the platform and stopped less than a claw's width from touching the orb. Even at this distance, Belenos could feel his fear, with almost as much clarity as he was used to hearing or seeing. At a word of encouragement from the chief scientist, Timir thrust his hand forward to rest on the orb.

Immediately, Belenos was flooded with sensory information. Not only could he access his brother's physical senses, he was granted access to the eddy of feelings raging in Timir's head. Fear, anger, resentment, jealousy, and desire beyond any he was used to or even knew his brother harbored washed through him, foreign in spite of his place in his brother's head.

Starfall! Timir's voice swore in Belenos's own mind. *We all thought you were dead. Father nearly died of the shock.* He hesitated. *Can you really read my mind?*

I can read everything about you. Belenos prodded gently deeper, curious how far he could reach into his brother's mind, but hit a memory of a recent tryst and backed off.

A silent laugh echoed between them. *You always were a prude.* Timir tested his ability to probe Belenos's mind. The memory of his recent loss crossed in vivid painful detail. Belenos winced at his inability to mask the grief and humiliation of losing so many good men, or the graphic nature of the deadly battle. Being open and raw to someone was going to be very difficult.

"Can you sense him?" Zosma fussed around them, waving a scanner of some sort over the orb, then up the younger prince's arm.

Trembling in rage, Timir picked the orb up in both hands. *Together we can avenge our people.* "He's here. Tell me what we need to do to make those monsters pay."

Zosma rubbed his paws together eagerly. "Yes! All you have to do is press the runes on the orb in the proper order: Faith, Honor, Justice, Protection, Peace, Family, Duty."

The six points of the Vistkian star, engraved on the six cornerstones of the palace and symbolized by tiny bright yellow stars at the points of the larger white star on a field of blue on their flag. A rather obvious code, and a pledge to use their powers to uphold Vistkian values. Belenos impressed on his brother the need to take the pledge seriously.

"When this is over, and the invaders are dead, can I leave my brother behind while I celebrate?" Timir intentionally remembered the tryst, lingering over the lurid details to make his point that Belenos did not want to be bound to him always.

"The bond is permanent." Zosma shook his head, his black eyes wide in horror. "Separating you, or worse, severing the bond once it is complete will have untold mental and physical consequences. Madness is nearly certain. Death isn't out of the question."

Wonderful. Both brothers grimaced at the shared thought.

We will manage, Timir. For the sake of Vistke. There had to be a way for them to work together. It'd just take time to figure it out.

"For Vistke. Faith, Honor, Justice, Protection, Peace, Family, Duty." Timir touched the runes in order, each lighting up at his touch. When he touched the final rune, the whole orb lit up and began folding over his arms like scales spreading across his body. For Belenos, it was like becoming Timir's skin. Every sense became his own as the armor he now inhabited covered his brother. Timir's heart rate spiked and his breathing became shallow as the scales spread over his chest and toward his throat. If Belenos could feel Timir's terror as his own, perhaps he could also influence Timir's feelings. He concentrated on feelings of calm and confidence, willing them to his younger brother. He was rewarded with an immediate relaxing of Timir's muscles and easier breathing.

"Timir initiated the bond, Belenos, I need you to complete it." Zosma took their armored hand. *Timir is scared enough. These instructions are for you alone. I will walk you through it.*

I am not yet skilled enough to hide my thoughts from him. Belenos was intrigued to find that he could hear and read Zosma as well, as long as they had some kind of physical connection.

I can hear you both. Timir's panic rose, even though he tried desperately to hide it. *I'm no more scared than is to be expected. Just get it over with.*

Use the training you received for torture resistance, Zosma advised.

Belenos understood *that*. He focused his attention on his favorite Song of the Stars, a holiday carol celebrating the birth of the Son of Redemption. He wove memories of childhood holidays and happier times into the lyrics.

Good. Zosma seemed impressed. *You will need to penetrate his brain stem just as the procedure did with you. You can use the connection you already have to dull the pain so that he doesn't notice.*

Remembering the still-fresh pain from his own procedure, Belenos was pretty sure Timir would notice, even if he did dull the pain, but he didn't dare talk back and lose concentration and his control over Timir. Working carefully to mute the signal of the nerves beneath the scales protecting Timir's neck, he pressed a sharp tendril of the armor's metal to the spot Zosma indicated.

Timir barely flinched.

The moment Belenos made contact it was as if a map of Timir's body opened up to him. Every capillary, every cell – even a cluster of multiplying bacteria Belenos quickly eliminated – were under his control. He realized instantly the power he had over his brother and vowed to take care not to abuse it. Even their thoughts were no longer two foreign beings sharing one small space, but now each consciousness faded into the other naturally.

"It is done." Zosma let go of their hand and stepped back. "You are now Tianyi. May your great power free Vistke and your wise leadership keep her free."

✳ ✳ ✳ ✳ ✳

How did they get to this point?

Tianyi was being honored today for the one hundredth anniversary of their rule. Three generations of peace through power culminated in... this. A one hundred foot statue of them in the most recent iteration of their armor, set up in the center of Vistke Prime for all to see and adore. Belenos felt elation, pride, entitlement, as well as shame and deep guilt. Through the years it had stopped being "his thoughts" and "Timir's thoughts" as their bond deepened and they truly became Tianyi, but the thoughts and feelings that originated with himself had a different tone than the ones he shared with Timir. He suspected it was the same for his brother, who ignored his attempts to amplify the conviction that what they were doing was wrong.

Mercurios, Tianyi's harbinger, was whipping the crowd into a frenzy as they stood in the wings in full armor. Their russet armor was polished and fashioned into an elaborate pattern of spikes down their head and neck. They hadn't publicly appeared without full armor in over a generation, and by the things Mercurios was saying, Tianyi doubted that the people of Vistke even realized they were from this world.

"The All-Powerful Tianyi came from the stars to save Vistke in our darkest hour!" Mercurios gestured to the huge statue as Vistkians added to a massive pile of flowers and other gifts at its base. "They destroyed the threat from outside our stars system, then united all Vistke under their just and benevolent rule."

This is too far, Timir. Belenos froze them in place so that his brother would listen to reason. *We can still change course. Our response to Mercurios's praise will establish the tone of our reign for the next century.*

I intend for it to. Timir looked in the mirror and smirked at their imposing presentation. Not satisfied, he morphed the armor covering their arms to include razor sharp spikes.

I know what you intend. Is ruling a star system too little for us that we must claim the honor due the Creator as well?

We claim our due, brother. There has been no invader, no crime, and no lack–

No freedom.

Timir continued without comment, *– on Vistke for longer than anyone but us can remember. We are god of this star system. It is only fitting we should take that place in our people's hearts.*

I will not stand by and allow you to bring judgment to our planet.

As always, you don't have a choice.

The crowd outside was screaming their name. "Tianyi! Tianyi!"

Release me, or you know what happens, Timir threatened.

We do not even deserve to rule a barren asteroid, much less a star system. Belenos released his brother bitterly. Timir had learned quickly that he couldn't physically hurt Belenos, but that Belenos would do nearly anything to keep him from hurting others. Petty squabbles resulted in a juvenile response, such as creating messes for the staff to clean up. Open defiance ended with a servant being lashed mercilessly.

Vistke survived, and has enjoyed a renaissance of prosperity and wealth ever since Tianyi had taken the throne. Belenos wasn't sure whether that was his brother's voice or his own trying to assuage the loathing he felt for himself, Timir, and Tianyi.

The roars of the crowd rose frantically as they crossed the balcony to stand beside Mercurios. With a gentle wave of their paws, Tianyi silenced the crowd.

"We accept your gifts and are pleased with your tribute." They gestured to the massive statute that towered over the palace. "We also accept our place as your god and appoint Mercurios as our high priest. Serve us well and peace and prosperity will continue in Vistke."

"Bow before the Immortal Tianyi!" Mercurios set the example by kneeling and bowing with his muzzle to the floor.

Creator, forgive us. Being bound to his brother for a century had been one of the hardest things he'd ever done, but he hadn't truly regretted it until this day.

"General Mars, is there a problem?" Tianyi pointed a metal clawed paw at a uniformed Vistkian standing rigidly in the middle of the crowd.

Timir, don't do this. General Mars was the commander of the Vistkian army and a direct descendant of Belenos's own right hand man back when he commanded the army himself. *He's a good man.*

He cannot be allowed to defy us. "Mercurios, bring the General to us."

Mercurios obeyed eagerly, and soon the defiant general stood on the balcony in full view of the murmuring crowd.

"Let's try this again, Mercurios." Tianyi addressed the high priest, but kept their cold eyes on General Mars.

Timir gave the mental command for his gauntlet to change form into a blade to intimidate the general. Belenos refused. Their bond may have advanced to the point that Tianyi had complete control of every aspect of their shared physiology, but Belenos's will was stronger and he would not allow them to become a murdering despot.

"Citizens of the Vistke stars system, bow in reverence to the immortal, omnipotent Tianyi!" Mercurios's voice echoed across the courtyard. None dared disobey, but none dared take their eyes off their new god either.

"I will not bow to you, Tianyi." General Mars responded loud enough for everyone to hear his reply. "I serve the Creator, not a misbegotten robot created out of desperation in the labs of Emperor Regulus."

"It would have been well for you if we had been a robot." Tianyi stepped toward the steadfast general, straining to force the armor to form any weapon at all. *The darkest star curse you, Belenos, cooperate or the baker receives fifty lashes.* "You cannot offend a robot like you can a god."

21

Stand down, or I will recall the armor to stasis and leave you naked in front of your followers. Belenos could play that game just as well as his brother.

"You are no god." General Mars spat on the balcony tile. "You are the worst parts of the young princes Belenos and Timir, cursed to an eternity of–"

Tianyi plunged their armored claws into the soft chest of the rebellious general and drove them into his heart. It happened too fast, an impulse of rage that Belenos couldn't react fast enough to stop. Worst of all, the physical contact with General Mars allowed him to feel not only the soft pulsing, then rupture, of his heart, but also General Mars's feelings of defiance, shock, and terror as death took him.

Murderer! His cry of anguish was as much an indictment of himself as his brother. How could he allow this to happen? Before the General's lifeless body hit the terrazzo, he kept his promise to Timir. The scales of Tianyi's armor swiftly retreated to form a wide, collar necklace over Timir's heart even as he sent a shockwave to Timir's brain that rendered him unconscious.

Both bodies collapsed to the floor of the balcony and lay exposed to the crowd.

✳ ✳ ✳ ✳ ✳

Tianyi had a migraine. Belenos's shockwave had kept Timir unconscious for three hours, prompting a horrified Mercurios to order the servants to carry them to their bedchamber, where they had slept off the effects. Yes, Belenos could heal them, but he wasn't going to. They deserved far more than a headache after the nightmare of the previous day.

They were awake now, wearing a plush robe because Belenos still blocked his brother's access to the armor, keeping it locked in the stasis form they'd used for over a century. That would be less effective once his brother recovered and his hunger for power returned, and Belenos wished there was some way for him to take Timir's control of the armor permanently. Some way other than severing the bond completely. Timir had sought a way to remove him from the armor several decades earlier and the scientists had been quite clear. Only completely severing their bond could separate them, and would most certainly destroy their minds if it didn't kill them. Belenos wasn't a murderer. Tianyi had been a despot for some decades, but not a murderer, before yesterday. The guilt ate at him, as did the vivid memory of General Mars's dying thoughts.

Creator, forgive me. Cleanse my hands from bloodguiltiness. He recalled the Song of Antares, a mournful tune begging forgiveness for a terrible sin and played it back in his mind.

Ugh. He had to die. We could not allow such a challenge to our power to go unaddressed. Tianyi stood and rang for a servant. *We have better things to do than mope for that traitor.* The houseboy bowed low seven times as he entered the room. "Send us our breakfast. And tell Mercurios to see us. I'm ready to select from his candidates for priestess."

Really, Timir? Belenos didn't have the patience for this today. General Mars's death and Tianyi's unexpected illness had canceled the much anticipated beauty pageant to select young females to serve the needs of the immortal Tianyi, in spite of the fact that they already had four mates. *Must we continue this ill-fated ceremony? Isn't it enough?*

It is never enough. "And send me some Orian Brandy," they called after the retreating houseboy. "I have a headache."

Mercurios arrived first with the candidates. Thirty-six eager, nervous young females from the best Vistkian families, dressed in the finest clothing Vistke could import, all vying for the "honor" of serving Tianyi lined up across their quarters.

Tianyi sat up in their plush chair, their headache all but forgotten, as Mercurios began to introduce the candidates and showcase the attributes that made each suited to serve their new god.

Resigned, Belenos returned to his song. After one hundred years, at least twice that many females, and no real companionship, Belenos had learned to passively endure Tianyi's empty trysts. Timir complained that the Songs of the Stars distracted him, but today, petty or not, Belenos simply didn't care. General Mars's mate would sleep alone for many nights to come, his murderer did not deserve to enjoy female company while she grieved.

Breakfast and brandy arrived somewhere after candidate twenty, carried by the baker and his daughter. They bustled quietly beside Tianyi, preparing them a plate of food as the pageant went on. Tianyi's attention strayed to the simple beauty of the baker's daughter. Her face was not made up, and her scales were not gilded as the candidates were, but her caramel fur was brushed sleek and her flour coated apron only accented the shape of her bosom.

SONG OF THE STARS

"Immortal Tianyi, I present to you Cassopi." Mercurios's voice was disapproving as he pushed the next candidate forward. Her scales were dotted with jewels from the middle of her forehead to the slender tip of her tail and heavy makeup accented her black eyes and narrow muzzle. Instead of an apron, she wore an elaborate web of silk, coins, and tiny jeweled pendants that glittered as she preened for her god.

Tianyi barely offered her a glance. They pointedly ignored the pageant for the oblivious servant girl.

Belenos stopped singing and focused his attention as well. He recognized the long familiar rise in desire and longing for power in their gaze. He knew the baker well enough to doubt the baker held ambitions for his daughter to be Tianyi's next mate, but his brother had prided himself on being irresistible even before he became an all-powerful war god, and eternal life had done little to alter those charms, so the baker's daughter may have other ambitions.

Tianyi grabbed the female's wrist. "The beauty of this daughter of a common baker surpasses that of all your candidates, Mercurios." They smiled at her gently as she looked up at them in surprise. "What is your name?"

"Tislit, my lord."

Belenos couldn't feel her emotions unless the armor itself came in contact with her, but her eyes conveyed innocence and meekness, rather than the cunning and ambition of the candidates. He found himself agreeing with their assessment of her beauty. *Slow down, Timir.*

Only 'slow', not 'stop', brother? Timir laughed silently. *After more than a century, have you finally found a female that interests you?*

After more than a century of your lechery, I don't know what I feel. I just know she's not one of your candidates, so perhaps you should look elsewhere. By the stars, he did find her appealing, which made Timir's lustful attention toward her that much more infuriating.

"Tislit is a name for a goddess." Tianyi lifted her chin gently with a cupped claw when she looked down in embarrassment at their compliment. "Have you ever wished to be a goddess?"

"My– my lord?" Tislit stammered and looked to her father for help.

"My lord, the candidates." Mercurios stepped forward to protest. "Surely one of them–"

"Your candidates will all make fine priestesses." Tianyi waved him off carelessly without taking his eyes off Tislet. "Choose the best and prepare them for when I call."

"But my lord–" Mercurios cut his final protest short at Tianyi's threatening glare and hastily started herding his candidates toward the door.

"Goddess Tislit sounds nice, doesn't it?" Tianyi stroked her cheek with his claw. "You will live in the palace as my queen and rule at my side. Your father will never need to work again, and your family will have everything they could ever want." Tianyi stood and held her at arm's length, his gaze sweeping over her as he imagined her dressed in the elaborate costumes of the females who had just left. "All Vistke will worship you as they do me."

At his last statement, Tislit threw a panicked glance at her father.

Terror lit the baker's face as he bowed seven times, and stayed down the seventh. "My lord most merciful Tianyi, we are most grateful for your generous offer, but we are only a family of simple servants, pleased to serve the royal family since the days of Emperor Koiea. We're not suited for this honor."

He was rejecting Tianyi's proposal, even after seeing the punishment defiance earned General Mars. Belenos tensed, every sense alert for a signal that his brother would respond in rage like before.

"I am your god, I can choose who to honor." Tianyi took both her hands in theirs. "I choose to bestow this great honor on your family and will not be refused." *Why is he refusing?*

I cannot read her unless our armor is touching her somehow. Belenos could think of many reasons the baker would not want his daughter bound to Tianyi, but didn't wish to speculate for his brother.

Tianyi tried to activate the armor, but Belenos withstood his brother's will firmly.

Nova take you, put on our armor and read her. Tianyi tightened his grip on her hands and fought Belenos's control.

So we can murder her or her father like we did the general? Not a chance in the stars system. Belenos withdrew all his usual monitoring of Tianyi's physiological input and focused only on their intent and keeping the armor in stasis.

With a vile internal epithet, Tianyi took one of Tislit's paws on both of theirs, kissed it gently, then held it to his chest over his heart. "I ask you from the bottom of our heart, beautiful Tislet, will you bestow the honor of your companionship on us as our goddess?"

Fear flashed across the necklace beneath her paw to their mind. Tianyi had figured out how to circumvent Belenos's precautions and her reservations were now clear. Her family served the Creator and would not bow to Tianyi as god. The general's murder had terrified them, yes, but had steeled them in their decision.

Rage filled Tianyi's heart and contorted his face as he released Tislit's paw and the terrified female scrambled to her father's side. The strength of his anger challenged Belenos's refusal to allow them to activate the armor, which only increased his rage. *May the Creator reject your armor bound soul, Belenos, stop fighting me.*

I will never stop fighting you, Belenos responded with quiet determination.

"Kneel before us, both of you," Tianyi demanded as he took the sharp knife the baker had been using to slice the bread in his paw. "Pledge your loyalty to us alone, or face the same end as General Mars." *I wish you had died on that table, brother.*

So do I. Belenos grimly decided his course. Tianyi was a monster that should never have been born. *Creator, accept my sacrifice and allow our reign of terror to end this day.*

Faith, Honor, Justice, Protection, Peace, Family, Duty. Belenos severed the bond with his brother and the necklace fell from Timir's neck. It hit the ground as the multi sided orb and rolled to the baker's feet as Timir fell to his knees with a scream of agony that echoed inside Belenos's mind. As the bleak realization that he had condemned them both to an eternity of lonely madness sent a black icicle into his own soul, Belenos cried out to the Creator for the relief of death, but was answered only by silence.

ALEXANDRA GILCHRIST

Chapter 1

An acapella cover of "Mary Did You Know" blasted through Isaac Anderson's earbuds as he ducked from lab to lab emptying garbage. He sang along softly in the barren hallways, reasonably confident no one was there at two in the morning to care what he was singing, or how badly off key he was. Even if Doctor Jonathan Judah in the Star Songs department had lost track of time again, he'd get a good laugh to hear him singing Christmas songs in October. If anything it was Dr. Judah's fault. His collection of European Santa figures lined the wall of the lab behind his desk year round, and dusting them every night had put Isaac in the mood to sing.

His job as the night janitor at SentryTech had been a godsend. He'd been a struggling college freshman at SoCal even before he'd married. A wife and baby later and he'd needed something better than working the drive through at BurgerWorld. Tech gave him decent pay, benefits, and a very low stress job – pretty good for a twenty-two year old with no college degree. Coordinating his schedule with Becca's was a bit of a chore, but they were managing, and Becca only had one more year before she graduated with her law degree.

A noise down one of the halls caught his attention. Probably a science geek putting in some night hours. No one in this wing kept regular hours. Isaac chuckled. No one in this whole place kept regular hours. He'd even seen Steve McGuiness, SentryTech's founder and top geek, poking around the labs well after he'd arrived to clean. Isaac intentionally turned down the Area 51 hallway instead. It was mostly storage rooms and dusty artifacts, and he didn't need the distraction of a chatty space scientist tonight.

The noise clarified to footfalls, and his curiosity got the better of him. Leaving his cart parked beside the door to the first lab, he went back to the corridor intersection and rounded the corner. Three men were near the main offices at the entrance to the wing, heading up the main corridor toward him. They weren't security, even though they looked as if they were heavily armed.

Isaac ducked back down the hallway and frowned. As far as he knew, StentryTech's military visitors only came during the day, though he supposed they could be there about some top secret project. He'd overheard conversations about some of them, so he knew they existed, but something felt off. He pulled his phone and started to text Don, the head of security. *Better safe than–*

A muffled explosion shook the building. Isaac jumped, screamed in surprise and terror, then ducked behind his janitor's cart and looked down the Area 51 hall with wide eyes. The hall used to dead-end after the storage rooms; now two more armed men crawled through a jagged, smoldering hole. Smoke and dust billowed into the hallway around him. He scrambled back toward the main corridor and the exit, but shouts and gunfire blocked that route of escape. Desperate and too scared to think of anything else, he ducked into the first lab and jammed his fist into the button that slid the door closed behind him. He fumbled with the hightech lock, hoping the men who crawled through the rubble hadn't seen him, but knowing they probably had. *They don't need me. There's nothing valuable in here. I'll be safe.* He tried to convince himself, even though he knew deep down that he had no earthly idea what those men wanted or what they were willing to do to get it. Still, he ducked behind a platform that looked like a cross between a food service table and a hospital bed that supported an object he didn't give a second glance to. If they got the door open and looked inside, at least they wouldn't see him immediately.

The shouts in the hall turned to screams, then stopped. Hope calmed his anxiety. *Don and the rest of the security guys got them. It's over.*

A second explosion ended that illusion. Isaac shielded his head as plaster and large bits of the equipment suspended from the ceiling fell around him. The largest piece of machinery fell on the table itself, cracking the table, shattering the object on top, and sending a football-shaped orb rolling into his lap.

That was definitely *not* the security guys. Fear squeezed Isaac's chest. He curled into a tight ball and unconsciously hugged the orb to his chest, hoping to make himself as inconspicuous as possible behind the remains of the table. If they found him back there, he was dead.

I'm never going to see my family again.

Panic sent a cascade of terrible thoughts through his mind. Images of Becca and Aster filled his memories. Would they ever know what happened to him, or would the government cover up his death? How would Becca finish school without him? Would she remarry? Would Aster even remember him?

An unfamiliar scene and a soft voice flashed into his mind. *I can help.*

Isaac jerked away from the strange orb and sent it rolling from his lap. The vision vanished as soon as he broke contact with the object. He looked at it more closely. It was a multi-sided prism about the size of a football made of a polished rust-colored metal. Each side was engraved with a strange symbol unlike anything Isaac had ever seen. Whatever it was, it was clearly the object the platform had been built for, and probably what the attackers were after.

I can help. He remembered the voice in the vision and chewed his lip. Voices and clattering nearby indicated someone was shifting the rubble from the blown-open door. If it was security, he was fine. He highly doubted it was security.

He touched the artifact again, sucking in a deep breath and holding it against the vision. The explosions and gunfire mirrored the present situation, but the setting was a glistening alien city with three suns and barren reddish mountains in the background. The voice began again, gently, *I've battled their kind before. I can help you now.*

"What are you?" Isaac whispered as he took the artifact into both hands. The thing seemed to absorb his fear and replace it with steady courage.

SONG OF THE STARS

I am a who – Prince Belenos of Vistke. I traded my body for this form to save my planet. We can use it to save you.

"You're a person? Not... Like an AI or something?" Voices at the door distracted him for a moment. "Forget it. I don't want to die. My family needs me. Tell me what to do."

I am a symbiote and a weapon. If you allow me to bond with you, I can protect you.

"Bond?" Isaac squeaked and fumbled the artifact. "You can unbond or whatever, right, it's not permanent."

The vision changed to an image of a strange being that looked like someone used a pangolin for a D&D paladin and the artifact infused the image with heartbreaking grief. *A superficial bond may be broken. There is no harm in separating after a short time.*

A shout sounded in the hall, followed by running footsteps. Alien symbiotes were the stuff of nightmares, but the guys in the hall just blew up the lab and probably gunned down some of his coworkers. Which was scarier?

✳ ✳ ✳ ✳ ✳

The explosion had freed Belenos from his prison, but without a host, he was vulnerable. The pod his brother had banished him to had done little to protect him from the prodding of his captors, who he guessed to be some primitive scientists, and freedom in the violent attack left him weak and damaged. He used his limited energy reserves to begin self-repairs as he prayed to the Creator that... What? He didn't even know what to pray anymore. After so much time, he'd given up hope, and had begun praying instead for death. Hope meant finding a miraculously perfect host. The gunfire and screams of dying beings coming from the areas beyond him did not bode well for him being rescued by a suitable host. He wasn't about to make the same mistake as last time. Death would be better than creating another war god.

Creator, Spinner of Universes, allow me to find my place with you in the heavens before I fail you like that again.

Freedom from the stasis field of the pod allowed him to sense his environment clearly for the first time. The room was sterile, if chaotic from the explosion that freed him, and the being in the room with him was alone, and – unless these beings had unheard of powers – unarmed.

The explosion had also cast him into the arms of the being. He prodded gently and carefully, not wishing to alert the being to his existence in case the race was hostile.

Surely his scans were wrong. He paused and repeated his scans as thoroughly as he dared. The being was not just unarmed, he was *horrifyingly* defenseless. His body was pale, with only a tuft of nearly as pale fur on the top of his head. Even his eyes were a pale blue. He was soft, and scaleless, without even his own natural fur to cover his body. The clothing covering him offered no defensive protection and only little protection from the elements. His claws and teeth were short and blunt, completely worthless for defense. Perhaps this being was prey to whatever it was outside? Did sapient beings hunt each other on this world? How could a race clearly intelligent enough to create clothing and scientific facilities not at least provide armor to its defenseless members?

Belenos stopped repairs and quieted all systems as he probed the being's mind. Even without a bond, he could feel the oppressive depth of terror that gripped the being. This was not a combatant, though his suspicion that the being was prey was becoming more likely. The being clutched his artifact closer to himself. It wasn't just fear, it was fear for his family. The being was intelligent, his feelings and thoughts no different than a Vistkian noncom would be in his place. Distant memories resurfaced in Belenos's mind of discovering laser scorched grub farms and shelled office buildings, their workers dead in place as they tried to salvage their livelihood or flee – workers who had perhaps felt in their last moments not much different from how this being felt now. With the memories he relived the helplessness and agony of knowing he hadn't been able to save them. That had been the primary driving force to push him to take this form to begin with. Now, by the creator, he could at least save this one.

I can help, he told the being.

The being jerked back and broke the connection.

What am I doing? Belenos didn't want another host. Well, he did, but he needed time to find the right one. But he could help, and without his help, this being would surely die. He hadn't sensed corruption in the being during their brief connection, but then his brother hadn't been corrupt until they'd bonded.

What would happen to this being's family if bonding made him a war god as well?

The being touched him again, fear of the aggressors breaching the room surpassing the being's fear of him. He couldn't just let the being die. He gave him a vision of a victorious battle on his home planet and pushed courage into his mind. *I've battled their kind before. I can help you now.*

"What are you?" the being whispered. Belenos probed his mind subtly looking for corruption or any sign that he would be a dangerous host. He couldn't risk probing too deeply, or he might begin the bonding without the host's permission. He may be a war machine, but he wasn't a monster.

I am a who. I traded my body for this form to save my planet. We can use it to save you.

"You're a person? Not... Like an AI or something?" The voices outside grew louder and the being paused. "Forget it. I don't want to die. My family needs me. Tell me what to do."

I am a symbiote and a weapon. If you allow me to bond with you, I can protect you.

"Bond?" The being's fear spiked and he fumbled the artifact. "You can unbond or whatever, right? it's not permanent."

Memories of his brother transferred to the being across their connection, along with his own heartbreaking grief. *A superficial bond may be broken. There is no harm in separating after a short time.* No need to worry the being about the effects of breaking a lifetime bond. He wasn't going to get that close to the being.

A shout sounded in the hall, followed by running footsteps. He wouldn't force a bonding on the frightened being, but if the being didn't decide soon, they were both in serious trouble.

✳ ✳ ✳ ✳ ✳

"I'll do it. Just until we're free." Heaven help him. Isaac knew what happened to Spiderman in the comics, but surely a short time wouldn't hurt.

The image in his head changed to a sequence of symbols matching some of the ones on the artifact. Isaac quickly touched the matching symbols in sequence. When he touched the final symbol, light filled all of the engravings. The artifact opened, and its sides folded over each other like a Jacob's Ladder toy, rapidly engulfing his hands and leaving them sheathed in the same reddish metal. Isaac clenched his teeth against a muffled scream.

I will not harm you. My purpose is to protect. The voice in his head was stronger, a second consciousness he could feel beside his own.

"Are you dangerous?" It was a little late to ask that, Isaac realized as the artifact unfolded over his arms and across his chest toward his heart. This was *far* worse than the mercenaries. What had he done? Would the alien take over his body and imprison him in his own mind? Panic screamed in his mind. He pushed back against the presence in his mind and the creeping artifact retreated.

I can only protect you if you trust me. Please, the warriors in the hall have defeated your last ally and are breaching the door at this moment.

"Answer me!" Panic shrilled in Isaac's voice. *Being killed by a bullet is better than being possessed by an alien.*

Isaac felt the presence in his head flinch. The artifact shrank back on itself and the presence retreated from his head. His immense relief was only slightly tempered when one of the mercenaries in black pushed his way through the rubble into the room.

Yes. I am dangerous. I am a weapon. The voice sounded sad and the images of the battle in the alien city returned. *But I will not possess your will, and I will not consume your own personality. I am a companion, not a master.* The voice became more distant and the artifact stopped glowing. *I will not violate your independence or force an unwelcome bond.*

The artifact was quiet, but Isaac could still feel its steadying courage seeping into him as he held it. A companion, not a master. That didn't sound too bad.

If it was telling the truth.

"The thing's broken," the mercenary called back into the hall.

Isaac curled up closer to the backside of the platform. If they got too much closer, they'd see him and the artifact. There was no doubt at all that they would kill him for the artifact. A brief temptation crossed his mind to throw the artifact at them and run.

I am dangerous. I am a weapon, the guy in the artifact had said. But he'd also said his purpose was to protect. Isaac highly doubted the guys who murdered SentryTech's security guards had protection in mind. How powerful a weapon? Could the artifact be used to take over the country? The world? He'd ask, but the mercenary was coming closer to examine the shattered pod that had housed the artifact and Isaac was afraid to even breathe. Alien tech was always that strong in the movies.

"You! Stand up!"

He'd been discovered. Isaac flinched and clutched the artifact closer to himself as he obeyed. If he died, the bad guys got the tech. The artifact didn't seem to be able to do much to protect itself.

"Thanks for keeping it safe for us." The mercenary gestured with his huge gun at the artifact. "Hand it over and I'll let you go home."

Ha, right. Isaac knew he wasn't walking away from this. "What do you plan to do with it?"

The mercenary laughed meanly. "We're getting a ton of money for that thing. It's not my business what my buyer does with it."

The artifact went cold in his hands.

The mercenary fired twice in rapid succession. Both bullets slammed into Isaac's chest like fists. The first knocked him back, the second knocked him to the floor behind the cracked platform. Fire burned in his chest, making it hard to breathe, but ice crept up his hands and feet. He looked down at his uniform shirt to see two small tears and a rapidly spreading patch of warm blood. He was dying. His shock-disoriented mind was confused that he wasn't already dead, and could only partially focus on two things: the first was how much his family would miss him, the second on how important it was to protect the orb. In the back of his mind he was aware he couldn't keep them from taking it now, but after what the mercenaries had said about their buyer, he had to try.

He awkwardly felt for the orb with a bloodied hand, finding it under the table where it had rolled when he fell. As soon as he made contact, he was hit with a sense of urgency.

I can heal you. The symbols flashed again quickly, backed by grim determination. *I would rather take my chances with you than be turned into a war god by their master.*

Isaac hesitated, but only for a moment. His brain felt sluggish, and decision making was hard. *I'm not ready to die.* He wasn't sure if he was more afraid of being turned into a monster or dying, but he didn't have the time or energy to argue with the artifact. The mercenary that shot him had rounded the table and was raising his gun for the kill shot. Touching the runes quickly, Isaac closed his eyes and dropped his head back in exhaustion as the scales swept over him, creeping beneath his shirt and covering his body.

Screaming an expletive, the mercenary squeezed off a shot at his face.

Chapter 2

The bullet never hit, the armor covered Isaac's whole body now and deflected the kill shot. The places in his chest where he'd been shot burned like a hot pad had been pressed against it, and the pain was fading. Strange, soothing music played in Isaac's head as the pain faded and his mind cleared. The mercenary was trying to empty his gun into Isaac, but the armor stopped every bullet without Isaac even feeling the impact.

Confused and disoriented now more by the surreal events rather than blood loss and shock, Isaac pushed himself to his feet. He was vaguely aware that the mercenary scrambled back around the table to where his partner had also squeezed into the room, and that the mercenary had stopped shooting at him, but it mattered so little it barely registered. He held his hands out in front of him and flexed his fingers. Jointed scales made of an unfamiliar reddish metal covered his hands, ending in clawlike points at the tips of his fingers. He could see his sort of reflection in the polished metal of the lab equipment. He looked like a cross between an astronaut and a medieval knight.

The sound of the mercenaries reloading finally got his attention. *They hurt a lot of people. How do we stop them?*

Point and fire. The alien voice was in his head again. Soft, but fierce.

Point what? He thought back. He waved his hand. *I'm not... armed?* A bizarre looking gun formed in his hand. *You're not going to* kill *them, are you?* Both mercenaries were now shooting at him, but since the alien artifact covered his entire body, he didn't care.

I'm going to return their projectiles to them. The alien returned dryly. *Will that kill them?*

Yes.

Then they deserve it.

The gun in his hand glowed with the symbols on the sides of the artifact.

"Wait!" Isaac cringed when he realized he spoke out loud.

Everyone in the room froze. The mercenaries looked at his hand with wide eyes.

"I don't control it." Isaac cleared his throat and infused boldness into his voice. "Surrender or be shot." *I don't want to be a 'war god' either.*

They killed your allies and would have killed you. Justice is not the same as interplanetary conquest.

Are they an immediate threat?

No. The alien sounded slightly disgusted by that thought. *They are of no consequence.*

"The alien weapon wants to kill you." Isaac told the hesitating mercenaries. "Please surrender."

Point at the pod that was my prison. The alien turned his attention to the shattered pod on the platform.

Isaac did, and an energy charged bullet blazed across the room and vaporized the remains of the pod.

Both mercenaries immediately laid their guns down, laced their hands behind their heads, and got to their knees.

We'll need something to tie them up. Isaac kept the gun trained on them, but after that demonstration, he doubted they would move. Frankly, he was a bit terrified himself.

Perhaps the wires that powered my prison? The alien voice conveyed a bit of glee at further dismantling the platform that had housed the artifact.

The gun folded away at the thought, and a polished sword formed in his hand instead, its blade the same reddish-brown metal that the armor was made from. It sliced through the hanging wires effortlessly, leaving him with fistfuls of scraps plenty long enough to make sure the mercenaries didn't move before the security guards got to them.

The sword disappeared, leaving him free to tie them tightly with a knot he had never seen before in his life.

"Are there any more of you left?" Isaac asked the guy who had tried to kill him. He'd seemed to be the leader anyway.

Of course, the mercenary just glared at him.

I sense three other beings like you within the compound. I cannot tell without visual contact if they are friends or enemies.

I know most of the security guys. Let's go take a look. Isaac rolled his shoulder. It barely ached. Maybe he was unconscious, having some fever dream in the ICU right now. This was too weird for reality.

The alien consciousness seemed amused by his thoughts, but didn't comment.

Together, they entered the hallway. A pair of security guards lay in a spreading pool of blood in front of the door to the lab. Isaac knelt beside them grimly, and laid a gauntleted hand on the nearest one. A readout of the man's vitals appeared as an overlay on his visor. He was very dead, as was the second. Nausea and grief gripped Isaac's stomach. He'd seen both of them when he'd clocked in this evening, and had talked to them about their plans for the weekend. Now they were both dead, and he had nearly been dead like them. Why had he survived?

I was a military commander in my star system. Death is always hard. When we stop being upset by death, we become the monster we are trying to fight. The alien sympathized and calmed his stomach, but also urged him forward. *We cannot help these, but we can prevent more victims.* An infrared overlay showed two men assaulting a door to a room down the main hallway, with a third man curled up in a ball inside.

That's my boss's office.

Steve McGuiness rarely stayed late. Usually all Isaac saw of him was as he arrived first thing in the morning. Even so, he was always friendly enough to greet him by name. There was nothing he could have done about the security guys, but he wasn't about to allow something to happen to his boss when he could do something about it.

Isaac ran down the hall and turned sharply, fascinated by the fact that the armor didn't seem heavy or to slow him down. *I need to be intimidating.*

We are intimidating. Trust me.

I don't want to have to kill them, even if they are bad. Not if I can avoid it. I want to scare them into surrendering.

The alien laughed silently. *You are nothing like my last host.*

Spikes erupted from the armor covering Isaac's arms and shoulders, and the shape of the mask changed. He barreled around the corner just as the mercenaries breached the office.

I recommend caution. The occupant of the room is unarmed. We do not want to encourage them to harm him.

Voices reached Isaac's ears as if someone had turned up the volume on a headset.

"Take us to this artifact or we'll blow your head off."

"Ha. I can't help you. Do you think I keep track of every collectible in this facility?" Mr. McGuiness's voice sounded clear and strong. If he was afraid of them, he was hiding it well.

They'll shoot him. Isaac crept to the edge of the door and waited.

Not if they think they can get what they want from him.

In other words, Mr. McGuiness is asking them to kill him.

The alien seemed frustrated. *Yes.*

Let's do this then. Butterflies fluttered in Isaac's stomach, but the alien calmed them almost immediately. Isaac wasn't sure if he appreciated it or if it just reminded him of how much control the alien already had over his body. He decided that Mr. McGuiness's life depended on his not thinking too hard about that right now. He swallowed against a dry mouth. *Dramatic entrance?*

The alien reacted with confusion for a moment, so Isaac concentrated on a memory of a cartoon superhero making a grand, explosive entrance.

Will an electrical show work? The alien was amused still, confused at Isaac's reluctance to kill, but humored by him all the same. *We will need an energy source to recharge if we wish to maintain functionality. You were too injured for me to use your own electrical energy.*

"Listen here, smart guy." The mercenary in the next room growled at Mr. McGuiness. "This isn't one of your cheap trinkets. It's a highly powerful space weapon. Use your computer to find it, if that's what it takes. You've got three minutes."

Space weapon? Well, he's half right. Isaac tried to mimic the alien's amusement. The artifact they were looking for was so much more than just a weapon. He looked down at his clawed hand, then at exposed wires beneath the wall switch where the mercenaries had torn up the door to get in. *How much can we handle?*

A direct lightning strike. Do it.

Cupping his hand to aim the razor sharp claws at the wires, Isaac plunged his hand into the wall, tore the live wires free, then held the bare copper in his hand.

The alien armor began to glow radiantly, and a sword made from a bolt of lightning formed in his left hand. A sense of strength flooded through him, and the alien consciousness seemed relieved to recharge their power.

His hand still tangled in the wires, Isaac turned to stand in the doorway. Swinging the sword in a lingering arc, he thundered, "Drop your weapons."

Everyone in the room froze, including Isaac. He sounded like an action movie character. This was definitely *not* actually happening. He just hoped that didn't mean he was dead.

He pulled his hand free of the wires and stepped into the room as another electric sword formed in his right hand. The mercenaries looked like they were going to wet themselves. Mr. McGuiness started shifting from one foot to the other with a look of sheer excitement. The mercenaries did not, however, make any motion to drop their weapons.

"If any harm comes to Mr. McGuiness, I will make sure you pay with your lives." They were almost within reach of the first mercenary, who panicked and began firing his automatic weapon at them.

The armor absorbed the bullets until Isaac brought the sword down on the barrel, slicing it clean off. The sword in that hand disappeared. *Touch the attacker. I can share some of our excess energy with him.*

Not too much, okay? The last thing they needed was some mercenary exploding all over the office. That'd be a nightmare to clean up. Isaac grabbed the guy's wrist between his sleeve and glove. The charge from the radiant armor electrocuted the mercenary, who crumpled to the floor with an agonized scream, then lay still.

"I–I'll kill him!" The remaining mercenary grabbed Mr. McGuiness by the arm, pulled him close, and jammed the nose of his rifle into the soft flesh beneath his chin.

"Kill him and you never get the artifact." Isaac paused. *You're the military commander. What are our options?*

We cannot use electricity to incapacitate him, or it will harm his captive. The alien grew tentative. *Sacrificing his life to save your friend may be our best option.*

Or we can give him what he wants. Isaac let his arms go limp to his side. *Can you return to your original form?*

I strongly advise against this course of action. Panic threaded across their connection.

Just do it. Trust me. Isaac focused on confidence and reassurance, hoping he could share it with the alien the way that the alien did with him.

He felt a shudder, then the armor folded back to the multi-sided orb in his hands, though now the runes glowed brilliantly with the remaining electrical energy they had absorbed.

"This is what you want. Let him go and I'll give you the artifact." Isaac held it out as an offering, being careful to stay just out of the mercenary's reach. His boss's eyes went wide with recognition, but he thankfully didn't call out his name.

"Done." The mercenary shoved Mr. McGuiness away from him, slung the rifle over his shoulder, and held out his hand. "If this is a trick, I'll put a bullet in both your heads."

Isaac concentrated hard on the next part of his plan as he gingerly set the artifact on the desk, hoping the alien got the hint. He stepped back as Mr. McGuiness scrambled to his side.

The mercenary kept one eye on them as he reached out with both hands and picked up the artifact. As soon as his hands closed on the glowing orb, his eyes went wide with horror, and the remaining electrical charge discharged into his body. He screamed and shook for a long moment, before the electricity cut out and he collapsed over the desk.

"Isaac?" Mr. McGuiness stared at him, his eyes tracing the remains of his tattered, blood stained uniform and his fresh red scars. A wide grin split his face. "You saved my life! My janitor is a superhero!"

Isaac didn't actually *feel* like a superhero. He felt like he was going to be sick. It had all really happened. All of it. His stomach rolled. How was he going to explain any of this? "No, no. I'm not a superhero. It was all the alien in the artifact. You're not going to tell anyone are you?"

"Oh. Of course not." Mr. McGuiness frowned. "I'm going to have to explain it somehow. The police will have questions. Maybe I can tell them we were testing a new security feature and Don..."

The color drained from Mr. McGuiness's face and he sat down hard in his chair. "Why did you save me instead of my security guards? Are they–"

Immediately, Mr. McGuiness was back on his feet, grim determination on his face and his cell phone in hand as he rushed into the hall, presumably to assess the situation.

Exhausted, nauseated, and horrified, Isaac leaned back against the wall and dropped his head back. He didn't want to go assess the situation. Maybe he was a coward, but he didn't *want* to see anymore of the security guys he talked to every night lying dead or wounded on the floor. He wanted to go home, to sleep, and to forget this whole terrible night ever happened.

One look at the artifact made him realize that the last one, at least, was never going to happen.

Chapter 3

Isaac dragged himself to the suburban split level he and his wife shared with his in-laws. Frank, his father-in-law, had hurt his back falling off a ladder cleaning gutters just a couple months before Becca had found out she was expecting. With his in-laws struggling to make ends meet off their savings and he and his wife wondering how on earth they were going to afford both rent and childcare, Frank and Alice's offer to share their home had seemed like a godsend, even if Isaac wasn't sure he believed in God any more, thanks to an aggressive college philosophy professor. They'd given him and his wife the two bedrooms, bathroom, and family room on the lower level. They shared the laundry room and the entire ground floor, and his in-laws had the upper level. He parked in the garage and entered through their entrance quietly, hoping not to wake anyone at this time of night – especially not Aster.

He tiptoed past both bedrooms and straight to the bathroom. The blood staining his clothes and the tears in his shirt were a surreal reminder that the events of tonight weren't a nightmare. He shoved his uniform deep into the bathroom trash can and took a long shower, trying to wash the dried blood – and the memories – down the drain.

As clean as hot water and soap could get him, Isaac crept into his bed and snuggled close to his wife.

"Isaac?" She murmured, then sat up startled. She leaned over and tapped her phone to look bleary-eyed at the time. "It's two in the morning, why are you home?"

"The place was robbed and they let me go home." He shuddered. "I wasn't feeling well anyway."

"Robbed? Are you all right? Was anybody hurt?" She sat up straighter and squinted at him in the dark room.

"I'm... fine." He sighed. He wasn't sure if that was true at all. "People died, Bec." He remembered the bodies of the guards he stepped over, then the sharp impact of the bullets and the realization that he'd almost been one of those bodies on the floor hit him nearly as hard as the bullets. Suddenly he wasn't fine at all. He pulled her close, buried his face in her hair and stifled a sob.

"Died? Oh, baby, I'm sorry." She hugged him tightly and didn't shame him for his tears. "It's okay. I'm here. You don't have to talk about it until you're ready."

He wasn't sure he'd ever be ready to talk about it, but for the moment, in her arms, in the safety of his own room, he felt better.

* * * * *

Isaac nearly called in sick for work that night. The desire to see the alien again was uncomfortably strong, like walking past his favorite food truck after Becca had decided they both needed to go on a diet because she needed to lose the baby weight. He really hadn't been successful resisting that temptation, as his bathroom scale testified, and he was pretty sure this wasn't going to be any different. Besides, he was nearly certain he'd have to answer questions he didn't have answers for. He even peeked out his window to make sure there weren't reporters sitting on his front porch waiting for him. There weren't, so he sucked it up and left. He needed this job. Before last night, he *liked* this job. He couldn't afford to risk it over the one night thrill of alien armor.

The facility was quiet when he pulled into the lot, though a bunch of new security guys greeted him at the door with a metal detector wand, ID check, and pat down – things he'd never had to deal with before. It was a reminder that his world had changed in a way he was certain he wasn't going to like.

He clocked in with a sigh, and froze with his hand on the machine as a horrifying thought struck him. He'd been so worried about having to face his role in what happened last night, that he didn't stop to ask who was cleaning up after last night. His hand shook as his mind flashed back to getting shot the night before. Debris and drywall dust he could handle, but blood – especially his own blood – was a hard nope. He swallowed back the bile in his throat and took a shaky step toward his boss's office. He had to ask, otherwise he might just turn around and not come back.

His boss's door was still a gaping hole, with a smaller hole beside it where he and the alien suit had put their fist through the wall to charge up. The memory was way more pleasant than the other one, but somehow equally terrifying. Isaac sighed. Maybe he *should* look for a different job.

"Isaac! We were just talking about you." Mr. McGuiness swept toward him and ushered him into the office. Gorgeous mahogany shelves lined the walls and were filled with models of famous TV spaceships, like the Enterprise, the Millenium Falcon, the Serenity, and even a couple others Isaac hadn't recognized. Isaac made sure to dust the shelves and the models especially carefully each night.

"Mr. McGuiness, sir, I needed to talk to you, too." Isaac swallowed and tried to work up the courage to ask about getting a bioremediation specialist to clean the building. His hesitation was just enough to allow his boss to continue.

"Call me Steve." Steve directed him to a plush chair in front of the polished mahogany desk. He nodded to a scowling blond in the other plush chair. "This is Dani Apryl, head researcher in our Galactica division."

Isaac wasn't looking at the scientist. The alien artifact sat on the desk, as lifeless as it had been before he'd touched it, but it somehow still seemed to call to him.

"I think you probably know why we were talking about you." Steve rounded the desk and sat in his own black leather desk chair, then put his feet up on the desk and leaned back. "We understandably think you might be able to help us answer a few questions about last night."

"Steve, he's the *janitor*. Just give my techs a little more time." The blonde leaned against the desk. "We need to finish the spectrum analysis, bring in a linguist to analyze the symbols..."

"Dani." Steve made an impatient gesture. "It won't help and you know it. That pod has been passed round from one science facility to the next for longer than any of us have been alive. Someone wanted it badly enough to attack now, after all that time. We need to know more, and we need to know fast. Besides, *he* made it work without any of that."

Dani sat back in the plush chair with her arms crossed over her chest as Steve turned back to Isaac.

"You've been with us since you left college. You do excellent work, you're never late, and you respect the things we have here at this facility – from my frivolous little collection to the billion dollar lab equipment. I need you to tell me everything you know about this artifact here."

Isaac passed a dry tongue over even dryer lips. Being in the same room again with the artifact made the temptation to put the armor back on even stronger. "I ducked into the room housing it last night to keep from getting shot. The guys who broke in last night were looking for it. I... kept it away from them."

Dani made a scoffing noise, but Steve cut her off with a wave. "No offense, but you were unarmed and those mercenaries had already killed three MPs and five of my own security team. How, exactly, did you keep it from them?"

He looked from the artifact to his boss. "Uhh. That's kinda hard to explain."

"Let me tell you what we know so far." Steve picked up a piece of paper off his desk and started reading from it. "The mercenaries told us they thought they'd killed you, but that the artifact 'opened up and swallowed you.' Then you 'stood up like a copper paladin and attacked them.'" He stopped reading and looked up at Isaac. "Unfortunately, the mercenaries cut the security cameras before they began their assault, so we're not exactly sure how you did it."

Isaac's hand unconsciously went to his chest where the symbiote had healed him. They were never going to believe him, not unless he activated the symbiotic armor again, and he wasn't sure the symbiote would agree to that.

"Strange thing is that there was a lot of blood on the floor in that lab, and there weren't any wounds on the guys we took in." Steve jerked his head toward Dani. "We're more than willing to take a sample to compare yours to what we found."

"N-no, that's okay." Isaac held up his hands in protest. "Look, I'll tell you everything, but there is no way you're going to believe me."

"Try me. I'm way more open minded than you might think." Mr. McGuiness smiled encouragingly and relaxed into his chair. "I saw you in here last night, when you saved my life. *That* we have on camera. Call it a personal interest if you like, but I really want to know how you did it."

Dani's expression conveyed that she wasn't quite as open minded as her boss.

"I ducked into the lab to escape the gunfight in the halls, not realizing that was the lab they were after." Isaac's hurried words stumbled over each other as he relived the entire attack. "I accidentally touched the artifact, which had fallen off the table in the explosion that had blown out the lab doors. It... talked to me. Well, thought to me, anyway. It told me that it was an alien symbiote and it could protect me." He looked to Mr. McGuiness for understanding. "I've seen the movies. I didn't want any alien symbiotes taking over my mind. The symbiote hadn't seemed all that eager either, honestly, talking about not wanting to be a 'war god' again. But then the mercenaries arrived. I knew the symbiote would be a super weapon in their hands, so I tried to keep it from them."

He fell silent as the memory of getting shot overwhelmed him for a moment. The force of the bullet hitting him. The pain and blood. The knowledge that he wasn't going to see Becca and Aster again. In everything that had happened, he hadn't really stopped to process it. Now the backflash made him feel like panicking.

"They really did shoot you?" Mr. McGuiness actually sounded excited, like this was one of his sci fi movies. "Somewhere harmless like the leg?"

"Getting shot in the leg is not harmless, Steve," Dani said with exasperation as she gestured at Isaac. "And he is clearly fine. The blood probably came from one of the MPs."

"Chest, actually, straight through my left lung." Isaac whispered as he closed his eyes and fought to push down the panic and steady his breathing. "I dropped the artifact. It just hurt so much and the blood..." He coughed and shook off the memory. "I somehow managed to get the artifact back. The mercenary who shot me was going to finish the job and the symbiote was begging me to let him save me, so I did as he asked. He covered me with this reddish brown suit of armor that looked like Iron Man went to a Renaissance Faire, stopped the next bullet, and healed the gunshot wound. As you can probably guess, taking down the mercenaries was pretty easy after that."

He opened his eyes and looked at his small audience for their reactions. Mr. McGuiness looked like a ten year old who'd just found out that Santa was real, while Dani looked like she suspected him of being the biggest con man in the world.

"If you want to take a sample, you'll see I'm telling the truth." He offered her his arm, fully realizing that getting up from a mortal gunshot wound was probably not the least believable part of his story.

"That won't be necessary." Steve waved Dani off. "Can you make it work again?"

"Maybe? Like I said, the alien inside had some kind of trauma in his past and only responded to me because it was an emergency." Isaac *wanted* to give it another shot. He wanted the symbiotic connection. "I doubt he's going to just perform to prove a point."

Steve glanced at Dani, who just rolled her eyes. He shrugged and leaned forward. "I'm going to lay this all out here. The attack on this facility last night was the fifth one in the last two months. Each time, the mercenaries targeted some arcane artifact with no clear purpose. Each time they have been successful. Until you stopped them."

"That wasn't me." Isaac interrupted and pointed at the artifact. "That was *him*. I was just trying not to die."

"You more than succeeded." Mr. McGuiness looked at the artifact warily. "The scientific value alone of what you did is incalculable. Half a dozen of my staff – Dani and I included – tried to recreate it, but the artifact was just as cold and dead as ever." He stroked one of the runes on the artifact disappointedly. "Beyond that, though, is the looming threat posed by whoever hired the mercenaries. If this artifact is a terrible space weapon, there's no telling what the other things he already got his hands on can do. We need some of that power on our side."

Isaac looked down at his hands. He didn't want to be a science experiment. He wasn't even sure he wanted to be a hero. He just wanted to mop floors, collect his paycheck, and go home to his family. But he didn't like the idea of letting the nut who hired the mercenaries who'd nearly killed him actually use the stuff he'd collected either. Or worse, make another try for the symbiote. He sighed and took the artifact in both hands. The runes on its sides immediately started to glow. "I'm not sure he'll agree, but I'll ask."

I will be no planet's war god. The symbiote's immediate response was accompanied with a vivid memory of nodding to worshipful crowds, carrying out public executions of strange pangolin-like beings, and conflicting feelings of bloodlust and self-loathing.

Horror and revulsion brought tears to Isaac's eyes as he realized the source of the symbiote's reluctance. *Were you the war god, or was your host?*

The symbiote responded with surprise, then thoughtfulness. *I am power. Power corrupts. My brother could not resist the corruption and it destroyed him and nearly destroyed our people. I would not wish to destroy you or your kind.*

His own brother? No wonder a new bond scared him so badly. *I don't want to be a war god, but I need to stop one. Can you sever our bond if I begin to abuse your power?*

Yes, but not without damage to both of us. His reluctance wavered. *A superficial bond like we shared when I healed you carries less risk of corruption or of damage if the bond is broken, but still allows enough functionality to stop your planet's war god.*

Isaac did wonder at what would constitute a deeper bond, since all he could think about since bonding with the alien was bonding with him again, and what more functionality that would bring, since they had been more than powerful enough to take down the mercenaries. However, the alien didn't seem interested in responding to his casual speculation.

I am a protector, I would love to serve that purpose again. The alien's reluctance faded to the same firm confidence he had the previous night as the sequence of symbols flashed through Isaac's mind.

I'm just a janitor, but I don't want to see the things you've shown me happening here. I'm afraid that's what the man who tried to steal you has planned.

Isaac opened his eyes to see Dani and Steve watching him intently.

"Well?" Steve gripped the edge of his desk and leaned forward eagerly.

"I managed to persuade him, but with a few caveats." Isaac remembered the pain of being shot and the horror of the symbiote being forced to execute his fellow aliens by his corrupted brother. "First, we're protectors, not some kind of war machine. We will not be the aggressors, and I highly doubt an intergalactic symbiotic prince is interested in earth politics."

"Global threats and super criminals, check." Mr. McGuiness agreed with a short laugh. "It's not like I can make you do something you don't want once you put that thing on anyway."

"And I need assurance that, no matter what happens to me, my family is taken care of. Those guys last night nearly killed me already, and I'm messing with a power we don't remotely understand."

"How's double your current salary for as long as you're participating in the 'experiment', plus a one million dollar insurance policy if you are in any way unable to continue to care for your family as a direct or indirect result of the experiment?" Mr. McGuiness stood, leaned over the desk, and offered Isaac his hand. "I'll get my lawyer to write up an official contract first thing in the morning."

Isaac tucked the artifact in the crook of his elbow and hugged it to his chest as he shook Mr. McGuiness's hand.

"Steve. Before lawyers, signatures, or insurance policies, don't you think he should at least show that he can deliver?" Dani tapped the artifact. "So far we only have his word and the word of three terrified mercenaries that he can turn this thing into anything more than a multi-sided Rosetta Stone."

Are you ready? The alien's question threaded with a strong dislike for Dani, which amused Isaac, since he didn't particularly like her either.

Yes. He wasn't, and he blushed when he realized the alien knew he was lying.

It's okay. I understand. The alien's calm confidence seeped into him, easing his fears. *This will be easier if you remove your shirt.*

I didn't last time. Isaac's face burned hotter. Taking his shirt off in front of Dani and Steve was humiliating.

Last time preserving your life was more important than preserving your shirt. The memory of his blood saturated shirt, split at the seams by the alien armor flashed into his mind. *It is your choice whether preserving your pride is more important now.*

The alien's amusement was clear, and only grew as Isaac actually considered the question for a moment. *Fine.* He set the artifact on the desk, turned his back to the others in the room, and quickly unbuttoned his uniform. He took a deep breath and pushed aside his discomfort and self-consciousness. He didn't get to the gym anymore since Becca got pregnant, and his torso was soft and painfully pale. He reminded himself that this was way more important than his self-image issues, and put his shirt over the back of his chair. He turned back to see Dani with her hand on the artifact and a wide-eyed look of horror on her face. He took it from her quickly, and she sat down hard on her chair.

"Dani, are you okay?" Steve looked at her worriedly, then back at Isaac. "What did it do to her?"

"I– I'm fine." Dani shook her head, and the skepticism that had contorted her face since Isaac had entered the room was replaced with a grudging respect.

I simply showed her a taste of what her staff have subjected me to since I was brought here. The alien sounded just a little vindictive, leaving Isaac just a little curious about what Dani had done to him. *She resents that I chose you instead of her. I showed her one reason why.*

Yeah, we'll need to answer that question of 'why' at some point. Isaac shook his head. *At the moment, I think we have a promise to keep.*

Isaac touched the symbols in the order he now had memorized. He drew a slow, deep breath and held it as the artifact folded over his arms, more gently than before. Small, oblong, hexagonal scales spread over his body, the leading scales still lit with runes, leaving russet scale armor in their place. Beneath the point of his collarbone, a large rune continued to glow, even after the scales had moved up his throat and down over his pants.

What does that mean? Isaac touched the rune and was surprised to realize he could feel it through the armor. He flexed his hands and ran his thumbs across his finger tips. He could *see* the metal covering them, but it *felt* as if they were bare.

I can share my sensory perception with you – or take yours, like I did with your pain last night. The alien was in his head again, like he'd somehow been given a second internal narrative. *Your language is unwieldy. This is 'eternal protector' in mine, to signify what we are. My name is Belenos, together we are Gemini, unwavering protector of the Solar System.*

Steve swore in amazement and Isaac realized the transformation was complete. The visor covering his face lent him a clear one hundred eighty degree view, overlaid with rolling data in both peripheral fields of vision.

How do you get used to the sensory overload?

I can monitor any input you find excessive, and only report if it needs your attention. The rolling data disappeared and the feeling that his senses were dialed up to eleven faded back to a vague feeling of clarity. *The longer we are connected, the more natural it will become.*

But the deeper the bond will become, too, right? One of the many conversations they were eventually going to have to have. Isaac already had a feeling they were lying to themselves about the likelihood of avoiding a permanent bond.

To a point. The alien hesitated and Isaac felt a gentle prodding as if the alien was reading his mind. *Do not be afraid. A lifetime bond is not an accident. Without it, even a connection of many decades may be broken with minimal risk.*

Dani was on her feet, scanning him with a large handheld device and muttering to herself while taking notes on her phone.

"You certainly look impressive." Steve reached out tentatively and touched his scaled arm. "What can it do?"

Isaac looked down at his arm where Steve still touched him and almost missed the question. He could feel what his boss was feeling. Awe, excitement, and a little jealousy, but no animosity passed through him where his skin touched the armor.

Tell him he would likely rather we demonstrate outside or in a less fragile environment.

"Um, Belenos – the alien – says that if you don't want your office destroyed, we probably should take the demonstration elsewhere." Isaac cringed at the thought of having to clean up the beautifully decorated office, or being responsible for breaking Mr. McGuiness's collectibles.

"What are we waiting for, then?" Mr. McGuiness shot out of his chair and was at the door before either Isaac or Dani could move. He tapped out a message on his phone as he moved. "I'll reserve the R&D demo lab for a private session. This is going to be great!"

SONG OF THE STARS

Chapter 4

Belanos could already tell Isaac was a superior host to his brother. The realization both relieved and saddened him. He had been willfully blind to his brother's flaws until it was too late and had no intention of repeating that mistake. While anger and lust were his brother's motivating emotions from the moment they bonded, Isaac's seemed to be family and a deep sense of morality. Even the very strong fear that was the first impression Belenos had gotten from their initial contact was tempered by those two core values. Time would tell if a deeper corruption lay within, or if the power Belenos offered would corrupt his new host as well.

Perhaps it would be best if we didn't walk the halls dressed like this. Belenos prompted his new host. It was a bit of a test, honestly. Tianyi never went in public without their armor. Their image was bolstered by the 'otherness' the armor provided, an intimidating reminder of their power to all their people.

"Um, Mr. McGuiness, er, Steve, sir, do you really want the whole compound knowing this," Isaac waved a gauntleted hand at himself, "is me."

"Of course! How could I overlook that." Mr. McGuiness actually looked apologetic as he stopped in the doorway.

"You've got a family to think of. You figure out how to take it off without disconnecting from the alien symbiote, and your secret is safe with us."

Ms. Apryl rolled her eyes and folded her arms over her chest. "Steve. My lab techs need to know who and what we're working with here. Isaac's obvious lack of any military or scientific training will have to be considered when organizing the testing."

SentryTech's chief science officer resented his choice of Isaac, and was determined to make sure Isaac failed. Belenos had seen that in her mind when she had presumptuously laid her hand on the artifact that housed his soul. His host thought she was a jerk, and was quite content to agree with Belenos's feelings about her without probing for more information.

His host was a bit too trusting.

Tell her I was the commander of the entire Vistkian army and crown prince of the Vistke Stars System. I ruled the twelve thrones of Vistke for a century. My experience will more than cover any lack you may have.

Embarrassment flooded to him from Isaac. *If I tell her that, she may fire me.* Images of his wife and kid rose up in his mind. *I can't lose this job.*

Belenos laughed. *We are the job. She doesn't have to like it, but she does need to understand it.*

"The symbiote –" Isaac began.

Belenos, or you may call us Gemini. For whatever reason, the term 'symbiote' was pejorative in their language, as if he were a leech or a vampire. He was not a parasite, he was a companion. It would be good if they learned to use his name.

"Belenos," Isaac corrected happily, "said 'I was the commander of the entire Vistkian army and crown prince of the Vistke Stars System. I ruled the twelve thrones of Vistke for a century. My experience will more than cover any lack he may have.'"

Mr. McGuiness barked a laugh while Ms. Apryl's face burned red. Confidence was contagious and Belenos felt Isaac's lift.

How do I take off the armor? I can't, right? What are my options? Isaac touched the rune on his chest. *I can't go to Walmart looking like this.*

It is better if we do not separate, but we can do this. Belenos gently retreated back to the broad collar necklace shape he used with Tianyi. It allowed him contact with both Isaac's heart and nervous system so that they could maintain their connection.

"Let me grab my shirt and we're good to go." Isaac snatched his shirt off the chair he'd thrown it on and dashed out after the other two.

This superficial bond was awkward and inefficient. Things he took for granted with Timir were inaccessible. Thoughts and feelings were not automatically shared, which meant he either had to probe Isaac's mind for the information he sought – and risk deepening the bond – or wait until Isaac intentionally shared the information with him. They had proved they could make it work with the mercenaries, though. Their synergy was undeniable. Every moment with Timir had been a conflict between his morals and his brother's lusts. In the short time he had worked with Isaac, the human had shown time and again that he was a moral being that valued life. Belenos still harbored a nagging fear that the lure of his power would corrupt his new host as well, but over a century of reflection had opened his eyes to the truth that his brother had never been a good person. Perhaps that crucial difference would be what saved them now. *Creator help me, I need this to work.*

Ms. Apryl led them to an empty, wide open room that reminded him of a starship hanger. After imperiously ordering all the lower scientists out of the room, she locked them and Mr. McGuiness into the room.

"Alright you... two, let's see what you guys can do." Mr. McGuiness rubbed his hands together eagerly.

I can form anything from my scales. Belenos prompted as they engaged their armor. *Just tell me what you want.*

Uhhh... You're the soldier. I'm just along for the ride. His host took a defensive stance.

Belenos formed a pair of razor sharp blades where their gauntlets had been, and his host obliged by slashing at the air. He pulled the blades back and turned his fists into heavy balls of spikes. Isaac smashed them down into the floor.

I can also use any energy they provide as a weapon. Belenos reminded him of the electric swords. *Just like last night.*

"We can use anything you give us as a weapon as well." Isaac looked around the bare room. "Not that there's anything here we can use."

That wasn't quite what Belenos had said, but since it was technically true he didn't correct his host.

"Oh, yes! Show Dani that thing with the electricity." Mr. McGuiness got excited again. "That you did last night."

"That 'he did last night'? You mean from when you almost got killed?" She flashed an accusing glare at her boss. "Is this all some movie to you?"

"Nah, movies are fake. He – they – actually saved my life last night." Mr. McGuiness grinned at her unapologetically. "It was awesome. You saw the videos. You know it was awesome."

"Steve, you're going to get killed someday." Ms. Apryl groaned. "Fine, what do we need? A car battery?"

"Too small." Mr. McGuiness shook his head. "How much can you handle?"

"A direct lightning strike," Isaac answered quickly. "Or everyday electrical current."

"Can't you just plug into the wall outlet?" Ms. Apryl crossed her arms over her chest.

Can we? Isaac glanced at the outlet uncertainly.

Yes. They crossed the room and formed a plug in their hand, plugged in and absorbed so much electricity the lights flickered.

Glowing radiantly, they stepped away from the wall, formed the same brilliant electrical blades they did the previous night, and advanced toward the others. Ms. Apryl took a step back, but Mr. McGuiness just clapped his hands like an excited child at Christmas.

We can fire an electric bolt. Point your hand away from them.

Isaac pointed one hand away from them and a bright streak of electricity fired from his hand.

"We can also transfer energy to people or things we touch." Isaac chuckled softly. "But we can't really demonstrate that here."

Ms. Apryl just hummed skeptically. "What else can you do? Fly? Shoot lasers?"

I can read her mind if we touch her. Belenos made it clear he was being testy, not actually suggesting it.

I think she already knows that.

Oh. She does. His brief read of her didn't reveal her to be a bad person, just petty, arrogant, and more than a bit jealous that he'd picked the janitor. His last host had been a prince, and that hadn't turned out so well. So far the humble janitor had been a much better choice.

What else can we do? Isaac changed the subject on purpose.

Jump. Run. Lift. Anything your species can do, we can do better.

So Isaac jumped, touching the high ceiling easily, then ran a circle around the large room, ending back in front of the stunned pair, where he picked up a startled Mr. McGuiness and lifted him over his head.

He set his boss back down and stepped back, not even out of breath. *I feel great, Belenos, like really great. I'm not even tired. What's happening?*

I can convert available energy to biological energy as well. It helps increase your stamina and reduces your need for rest and food during battle. When energy is scarce, I can draw from the biological energy your body creates from food and sleep to maintain function.

That's cool, I think. His host was getting a little overwhelmed by everything.

Perhaps that's enough demonstration.

Yeah, sounds good. Isaac willed the armor away and Belenos obliged. The lack of permanent bond meant Isaac didn't have direct control over the armor, one of the distinct benefits of the weaker connection.

"We're practically indestructible." Isaac reminded them as he walked toward them. "The armor not only stopped bullets, but could fire them back in return. And if we do get injured, Belenos can heal me, just like before."

A movement beside them crossed into Bel's sensor range, just beyond Isaac's peripheral vision. He flashed a warning signal into the helmet visor. Belenos's sensors registered it as a large projectile, that it was a threat, and that it was heading toward the three of them.

Armor, Bel! Isaac moved before Belenos obeyed, grabbing both Ms. Apryl and Mr. McGuiness in a two-armed tackle just as his armor swept over his body. *Shield.*

Belenos spread his scales into a dome that covered the three of them just as the object hit them and exploded. His new host froze for just a moment as reality caught up to him. That had been a real grenade. He stood and surveyed the smoke hazed room. Nothing was damaged and no one seemed hurt. *Had that been part of the test, or did someone try to hurt us?*

It was Ms. Apryl. Belenos was livid. His new host was never in any danger, but he deeply resented that the jealous scientist had threatened him. *She was more surprised that we tackled her than that the grenade went off. Ask her about it.*

"What happened?" Mr. McGuiness straightened his blazer and looked around the room in bewilderment.

"Ask Ms. Apryl." Isaac crossed his arms and willed the armor away. This time Belenos didn't listen. *Come on, Belenos. The threat is over.*

No. She threatened us, I wish for her to be reminded that we are also a threat.

"You wanted a test, Steve." She faced her boss and gestured to Isaac. "You want to send a janitor up against a band of mercenaries and murderers. The test needed to be more than extreme gym class. He needs to be ready for an unexpected threat."

"What if Belenos hadn't activated the armor in time?" Isaac fought to keep Belenos's anger from reflecting in his own voice.

"You ask him. Could he put you back together then? What happens if a terrorist blows you up? How far can he protect you?"

The horrified look on Mr. McGuiness's face told her she went too far. She dropped her arms beside her and sighed. "It was remotely detonated. I wouldn't have triggered it if there was a real risk."

Mr. McGuiness scoffed in disgust. "We'll discuss this later, Dani. Right now, you owe Isaac and Belenos an apology."

"I apologize." She held out her hand, looked at Isaac's still armored one, hesitated, then seemed to steel herself. "I... went too far. It won't happen again."

"Make sure it doesn't." Isaac took her hand and shook it, while Belenos prompted him to hold it for a moment longer. He had something else to add.

If you ever try to harm or sabotage my host again, I will personally avenge him. Do I make myself clear?

"Ye– yes." Ms. Apryl pulled her hand free and stepped back quickly.

"Well, if this did nothing else, it proved that you can think on your feet and take care of yourself in unexpected situations." Mr. McGuiness grinned. "Pretty good results for our first test."

The visor at least, please? This time Belenos complied and lowered the helmet. Isaac looked at Ms. Apryl with a challenge. "We can do this. Belenos has both the skill and the experience to find and stop these guys. And I have the personal interest in making sure whoever ordered this attack can't turn our planet into a wasteland. We just need your help pointing us in the right direction."

"Great! I'll have my lawyers get on that contract and my PIs put together a summary of what we have on this collector. I'll handle human resources as well, since you're leaving your janitorial position without notice." He yawned and shrugged. "How about we start keeping more normal hours now that you're on my regular payroll? Why don't we all get a couple hours sleep and meet at my office at ten. In the morning." He looked at his watch. "Today. Heh. We'll come up with a tactical plan then."

✳ ✳ ✳ ✳ ✳

Isaac was more than happy to head home early again. Though explaining it to Becca might be difficult. Unlike the previous night, he was overwhelmed with the implications of his new job and new companion. The testing had made him feel like a superhero, and he had the distinct impression that Belenos was holding back. He still felt jazzed by the energy they'd taken and decided it might be best to clear his head before heading home. Since it was after midnight, walking the barren halls of SentryTech was really his only option.

He touched the hard metal necklace through the thin fabric of his shirt. It looked kind of like the wide collars ancient pharaohs always wore in the pictures, only it was made of long hexagonal segments of the same metal as the armor that widened at one end. The center segment was wider than the rest to accommodate the glowing alien rune. The entire necklace touched the tops of his shoulders on either side, and the middle of his breastbone in the front. There was no way Becca was going to miss that. Figuring out how to explain it to her without freaking her out was going to be a chore.

He pulled out his phone and started scrolling through flower delivery sites. Maybe if he buttered her up a little before breaking the news, she'd take it better.

Who was he kidding? He'd need at least a diamond necklace to make up for this. He searched instead for the jewelry chain in the mall and started browsing infinity necklaces.

What is this device?

My phone? Isaac's answer did nothing to slake Belenos's curiosity. *Uh... It's a communication and research device. I can talk to anyone, buy anything I need, and learn anything I want with just a tap on the screen.*

Belenos observed in silent awe as Isaac went back to scrolling through far too pricey necklaces. Well, he was getting a raise, wasn't he? He tapped a necklace with a diamond infinity symbol wrapped through a gold heart. It wasn't *too* expensive. He opened another tab and checked his bank account. A bit more expensive than he could afford right now. He sighed. Flowers would have to do. He ordered a dozen roses for delivery, and threw a dozen Milky Way chocolate bars into the cart as well. Hopefully, Becca wouldn't be suspicious as soon as she saw the gift.

Can you research your culture and history on that device?

Anything at all, Bel. Isaac remembered a movie he watched where an AI decided humanity was worthy of destruction after surfing the internet, and winced. He pushed the memory across their connection. *There's lots of garbage on there, too, so you have to be intentional.*

I do not need a device to tell me creation is corrupt. Belenos scoffed. *Is there an access port?*

Yeah. Isaac reluctantly turned the phone to the power port. It was silly that he would let an alien access to his brain, but not his phone, but, still, it seemed like a violation of privacy.

Belenos must have sensed his reluctance, because he hesitated. *I would like to know more about your star system. Can you show me?*

Relieved, Isaac directed the browser to NASA's website and just started reading random articles, some at Belenos's explicit request, others just clicking from one article to the next as he wandered the empty halls.

His aimless wandering took him down the Star Songs hall. Somewhere in his subconscious, he was aware that Doctor Judah was working late again, but his familiarity with the bizarre noises blocked them out until Belenos interrupted his thoughts.

I know that song. Belenos seemed anxious about the space noise coming from the open lab door. Even though he only said he knew the song, Isaac could tell he actually didn't like it.

You guys listen to radio star signals on your planet? Isaac stopped to listen. He couldn't understand why anyone would want to do that, much less have such a strong opinion of one.

The stars sing the songs of the Creator. Belenos seemed to wonder why anyone would not want to listen to them, then understanding filled their connection. *You have not translated them yet? How do you know about Him, then?*

We have a book. Isaac felt Belenos's gentle searching and found he was embarrassed that the alien would find he'd never read it – at least not all of it.

Hmm. We must find a copy. Perhaps online. There was no judgment as Belenos continued. *We translated the songs of the stars many generations ago. Each one teaches us about the character of the Creator. My favorite is the song of the star that proclaimed the birth of his Son that came to redeem the broken creation. This particular song is about the coming judgment. I can't say I enjoy it.*

SONG OF THE STARS

Isaac stood rooted to his spot, his mind reeling a bit from Belenos's revelation. The Star of Bethlehem sang about Jesus' birth? And Belenos could understand it? *How – how can I hear that song? The way you hear them. They sound like random noise to me.*

I can translate. While this is not my favorite, I still know it well enough. Timir knew it frightened me as a child, so would play it often.

Your brother sounds like a piece of work.

Hmm. Belenos didn't bother to comment on his brother any further. Considering how terrified he seemed to be of his time bonded with his brother, Isaac wasn't shocked to find his brother was a bully as a child as well.

The Creator returns
The worlds will burn
All He created will be undone
Evil will be consumed
All good transformed
To live forever with the Son

That... does sound horrifying. The words coupled with the eerie music filled Isaac's head with images of vaguely remembered snippets of Revelation.

The verses are worse. Belenos shuddered.

I can imagine.

Isaac was tempted to go straight to Dr. Judah and... what? Tell him "my symbiote can translate your songs for you"? Yeah. Not yet. He wasn't even sure how he was going to tell Becca.

He sighed. *Let's go home.*

ALEXANDRA GILCHRIST

Chapter 5

Coming back in at ten meant a quick word to his wife about his hours changing and a promise for more details after he got off work, but effectively delayed a deeper explanation about his job change and especially about Belenos. Both he and Becca needed sleep too much to deal with it now. He might even have intentionally slept past the time Becca left for class so he didn't have to talk about it at all.

Isaac stood outside the shower in his underwear, staring at the steam rising from the hot water, and tracing the center rune of the necklace uncertainly. *Do I take it off to shower?*

It's probably better if you do not. Belenos's words were mild, but the emotion behind them was firm. He clearly thought it was *much* better if he did not.

Then how do I... Isaac looked at the hot water and sighed. This was going to take some getting used to.

After his shower, he went down to grab a bite of breakfast. Frank and Alice, his in-laws, sat at the table. Frank was reading the news on his phone while Alice was trying to coax Aster to eat some excessively fruity smelling oatmeal. Half of it was on the toddler's hands and bib.

That is your offspring? Belenos regarded Aster with deep curiosity. The baby was creamy brown, several shades lighter than Isaac's inlaws, with tight curls, deep brown eyes, and a happy expression.

Yep, though we would call her a baby. Aster Blaire Anderson. She's nine months old.

She cannot even feed herself? The question seemed to cause Belenos an undue amount of anxiety.

Well, sometimes she manages to get a Cheerio in her mouth. Isaac self-consciously buttoned the top button of his polo. Explaining Belenos to his in-laws before Becca would be a horrible mistake. *Human babies can't do anything without their parents. She just started crawling a couple days ago.*

Belenos fell into horrified silence. Isaac blew a short chuckle through his nose and shook his head. *Don't you know what a baby is? Or are babies that different on your planet?*

Tianyi had a large number of offspring, but never saw them. My brother was adamant that it was his mates' job to care for the young they bore him. This is the closest I've been to any in over a century.

Then you definitely need a refresher.

"Good morning." Isaac greeted his in-laws, kissed Aster on her curly head, and sat beside her. "I can take over, if you like."

"That would be nice, actually." Alice passed him the half empty bowl, being careful to keep it away from Astar's grabby fingers as she crossed it over the high chair tray. "I need to run to the Dollar General really quickly and Frank has a doctor's appointment. Becca said you got new hours. When do you need to leave?"

"Probably about nine fifteen." Isaac teased the spoon of peach baby food mixed with oatmeal into the toddler's mouth. His in-laws were silent and he could see them waiting expectantly. "I got a promotion. I'll be working directly for Mr. McGuiness now, instead of as the night janitor." He shrugged, and dipped the spoon back into the bowl without meeting their eyes. "Better pay, but less predictable hours."

"Will your responsibilities change?" Frank laid the phone face down on the table and focused on him.

Isaac rubbed the necklace through his chest subconsciously. *I don't want to lie to them, but they can't know about you yet.*

Be vague. We don't really know what Mr. McGuiness wants from us.

"Yeah, quite different." Isaac realized he was rubbing the necklace harder and dropped his hand to his side quickly. "I'm supposed to meet with Mr. McGuiness today to outline my new job expectations."

"Well, congratulations." Alice slung her purse over her shoulder and patted her husband's arm. "We'll be back in plenty of time to take over. Aster usually takes a bottle at nine before her nap."

"We'll be fine. See you in a bit." Isaac started wiping the food off his daughter's hands and face as his in-laws left. He usually took a shift with Aster in the afternoon, so this wasn't anything he couldn't handle. Though that was usually when she was getting up from her afternoon nap.

"Hey, my little star baby." Isaac unclipped the high chair tray and Aster responded by squealing with delight and holding out her hands. "Dada's got some time to play with you this morning."

"Da da da da da!" Aster echoed happily as he lifted her free of the chair and held her in his arms. She patted his face with her damp, chubby hands and tried to pull on his nose.

"I think Grandma knew what she was doing." He wrinkled his nose and held his breath. Holding her away from his body, he took her to the living room and laid her on the carpet so he could find a diaper and wipes.

The baby is attempting to escape. Belenos alerted him.

Yeah, I got it. She won't get far. Isaac scooped a diaper and package of wipes out of the basket Becca kept by the couch. When he turned, Aster was already halfway into the adjoining bathroom. He simply turned her over and changed her diaper where she lay. When he was finished, he carried her back into the living room before quickly returning to the bathroom to throw away the diaper and wash his hands. *Keep an eye on her, will you? She pulled up to the toilet last Friday and decided it was her personal swimming pool.*

I can watch. Belenos's curiosity was waning to confusion, and Isaac couldn't help but wonder if the culture shock was overwhelming to him.

Aster decided teething on the edge of the couch cushion was more interesting than the toilet for that moment, which gave Isaac an opportunity to clean up and collect a couple toys to play with her until his mother-in-law got back.

As naptime neared, Isaac prepared Aster's bottle. Becca pumped and refrigerated her milk when she could, all he had to do was warm it up carefully.

Are all babies this... helpless? Belenos's confusion was threaded with anxiety.

More or less, yeah. Humans don't become adults until eighteen or twenty. Isaac chuckled as he handed Aster her bottle and hugged her to his chest. *Heck, I'm barely considered an adult, and I'm twenty-two.*

Where is your mate? Does she not care for your offspring?

She's still in school, studying to be a lawyer. I... dropped out. It's hard to study religion when your philosophy professor debunks the whole thing. Isaac scowled at the memory and pushed it aside. It wasn't that he rejected everything he was raised to believe, it was just... he didn't know, and thinking about it was scarier than just walking away. You couldn't pastor a church if you questioned everything in the Bible. He shook his head and kissed Aster's forehead as her eyelids drooped. *Then Becca got pregnant, and Frank hurt his back, so we moved in with her parents so we could take care of each other.*

Belenos fell silent, but the anxiety remained. Isaac almost asked him about it, but Alice returned and the sensitivity of trading off a sleeping baby drove the thought from his mind.

It was kind of weird going to work in the daytime, out of uniform, while the building buzzed with activity. But then, Isaac's whole life just got crazy weird, and this was just normal weird.

He made his way straight to Steve's office and knocked. The door slid open immediately to reveal Dani and Steve sitting at the desk.

"Isaac!" Steve's face lit up as he entered the office, he gestured to the empty chair beside Dani. "Perhaps you and Belenos can settle this argument for us."

"Oookay?" Isaac lowered himself slowly into the plush chair.

"AI or organic entity?" Steve gestured at Isaac's shirt covering the necklace. "I told Dani the armor *is* an alien being. She says that's scientifically impossible and that he's an advanced AI created by an alien race. Who's right?"

"He said he was a general and prince before he was a suit of armor, so I'm going with alien being, but I'll ask." *Belenos?*

I was a created being as yourself before I allowed our scientists to place my consciousness inside this armor so my brother and I could save our stars system. Belenos seemed distant and the anxiety that had run as an undercurrent in their mind all morning spiked when he spoke.

Dani groaned and passed a twenty dollar bill to her grinning boss.

"We have a mission for you and Belenos." Steve turned to him, still grinning. "I have to go inspect one of the few SentryTech labs that haven't been hit yet. Dani's coming with me to 'help transfer' some of the tech that we housed here before the break in. We're hoping that word gets out and the guys looking for Belenos think we're moving him there. I want you to start work as a janitor at that lab. You will not engage them. We need the guy they mentioned they were going to take Belenos to their boss. Can you and Belenos track the guys back to their boss?"

"That's why we're here, right?" Isaac felt a little relieved that they wouldn't be looking at combat right away. The feeling was echoed by Belenos to an even greater degree. "What happens if we find the boss?"

Steve glanced at Dani. "We'd recommend that you avoid engaging if you can. The existence of Belenos has made us concerned about a risk we didn't consider before."

"How is working with Belenos a risk?" Isaac's stomach flip flopped. He'd made the choice to work with Belenos, and he would stand by it, but that didn't mean all of his apprehension to working with a symbiote was gone.

"Heh. I'm pretty sure we already understood the risks of allowing you to bond with an alien symbiote as well as we could." Steve waved at the necklace. "But if a being... weapon... artifact like him exists and was housed in this facility for years without our knowledge, what else could we have collected without understanding what it was?"

"And there were other robberies and other artifacts stolen." Dani looked grim, and maybe a bit smug. "Other artifacts we understood no more about than that necklace you wear."

"The short of it is, we don't know what they might have." Steve picked a folder up off his desk and handed it to Isaac. "This is the description of everything he took. Make sure you memorize the list. The stuff on it could be anything from a harmless alien child's toy to a blackhole device strong enough to swallow the entire solar system."

Isaac flipped through the pages with a growing sense that he was in over his head. *Do you recognize any of this stuff?*

No, but I will if I see it again. We will not be caught off guard. Belenos's confidence seemed forced.

They can't use any of it, though, right? Not without instructions.

I gave you instructions myself. Belenos scoffed. *We will have to assume it is all dangerous until we determine otherwise.*

"Isn't this enough reason to scrap this foolish project?" Dani slapped her hands down on the desktop and glared at Steve. "Artifact 174A12 could be a death ray for all we know, and they'll both be dead before they know what hit them."

"If Artifact 174-whatever is a deathray and you don't send us out, this guy could just use it on someone else. Or a lot of someone elses." Isaac closed the folder and looked at Steve, swallowing the butterflies trying to escape his throat and forcing himself to sound confident. "This is why I agreed to take on Belenos to begin with. Only alien tech can defeat alien tech. We can do this. Just give us a chance."

"We don't have any other options." Steve gestured at the list of stolen artifacts and swept his arm toward Isaac. "No matter what we feel about it, the alien armor chose Isaac. We have to play this through."

✳ ✳ ✳ ✳ ✳

Explaining to Becca that he was going on an unexpected trip with Mr. McGuiness was easier than Isaac had expected. The excitement over his new promotion hadn't worn away to weariness and suspicion yet, and the flowers and chocolate had put her in a celebratory mood. He was going to have to figure out how to explain his new job to Becca pretty soon, though. Cleaning always gave him time to think. Perhaps it would give him time to figure out a way that wouldn't freak her out too bad. Belenos wasn't helpful at all. Apart from a rising throb of anxiety in the back of his head, the symbiote was uncharacteristically silent.

Dani had given them a blueprint of the facility, which Belenos had immediately memorized, and a list of the alien artifacts housed in the facility. She and Steve toured the facility under the guise of examining the security, then made a show of leaving for the campus VIP housing. Isaac and Belenos's job was clear: clean the hall housing the alien tech while keeping their senses tuned to any threat, let the thieves take what they wanted, then follow them to their boss.

At six p.m., the nervous director of the facility escorted Steve and Dani out for dinner, leaving Isaac and Belenos alone with the few random guards left in the building.

So what do you think it is? Isaac leaned on his janitor's cart and stared at the object Dani had called "Artifact 174A12." He shuddered. It kind of did look like a deathray from a scifi movie.

Its power bank is depleted. Bel seemed as relieved as he was. *Whatever it did, it can't do at the moment.*

So, hey, weird question. Isaac rubbed his temples. *If you can heal a gunshot wound, you can heal a headache, right? Mine's been getting worse since we got here.*

Shame and guilt muted the anxiety at the back of his head as the headache faded. *I apologize. I failed to anticipate your need.*

No problem, it's gone now. Isaac shrugged and pushed the cart down the hall to start cleaning at the intersection.

He wasn't used to feeling someone else's feelings alongside his, but he could have sworn the headache came from the persistent stress he'd been picking up from Belenos. How do you ask a symbiote what his problem was? *You okay? You haven't seemed as, you know, confident as usual.*

Confidence, strained and forced, replaced the negative feelings Isaac had been getting from Belenos. Something was wrong, and Belenos was trying to hide it from him. *Look, I know we're not bonding completely here, but common sense says a team works together best when they trust each other.*

I... fear we made a mistake. Belenos's tone was soft and the thready confidence wavered. *The men we are tracking killed seven men in your facility alone, and nearly killed you.*

You had my back then, you'll have it now. Right? Isaac felt his own confidence waver. *I mean, you're an invincible symbiotic suit of armor. I saw what those guys' bullets and Dani's grenade did, what do we have to worry about?*

I am not invincible, and you have much to lose. A vivid image of Aster asleep in his arms replayed in his memories.

You're freaked out because I have a family? That explained the rising sense of anxiety he'd felt all morning.

Timir and I had little to lose if our experiment failed, but lost everything of value we did have. Nearly to our own souls. The anxiety returned with the force of a migraine. *Even my vast power could not protect us from ourselves.*

"Ugh! Bel, stop!" Isaac pressed his hands to his head and leaned heavily on the cart. The headache faded again. *I'm not your brother and neither are you. Give this a chance to work.*

Belenos's anxiety faded back to be covered by a weird otherworldly song. *'Why are you cast down, O my soul? and why are you disquieted in me? hope in God: for I will yet praise him for the help of his countenance.'* The tune wasn't exactly pleasant, but it was soothing all the same. *I will honor my agreement. We must protect your star system from this threat, then we can see what happens next.*

Isaac went to work aggressively, his thoughts occupied with Belenos's lingering doubts and fears. Not being able to separate his thoughts from Bel's was going to be frustrating.

We have company. Belenos announced abruptly and started to activate the armor.

No. We have to make this look good. We want them to steal the worthless gun so we can follow them. Stick to the plan.

They have Ms. Apryl and Mr. McGuiness.

What? How? That wasn't part of the plan.

Clearly. Belenos scoffed. *We can either stick to the 'plan', or engage our armor and rescue them.*

You've got my back, right?

I swear by the Creator of the Stars that nothing bad will happen to you if it is in my power to prevent it.

Then let's see if there's any way to salvage this without getting someone killed.

Chapter 6

"I'm telling you, I may own these facilities, but I don't work here." Steve was protesting as they neared the corner. "I can't help you find what you want."

"And I'm telling you that you'd better figure it out or you're both dead." A deep voice grumbled. "After all the trouble we took to lure you here you have to be good for something."

The owner of the voice rounded the corner and ran right into Isaac's janitorial cart. He swung his gun around with a cry.

Isaac dropped the bag of trash he was holding and raised his hands over his head. He swallowed hard as he stared into the barrel of the gun, suddenly wondering if maybe Belenos had the right idea after all.

A menacing smile crept over the mercenary's face. He kept the gun pointed at Isaac's face as he rounded the cart. "Ah. Someone who actually works at this facility." He grabbed Isaac by the collar and pulled him closer. "Take us to wherever they keep the space artifacts that just arrived today."

"I haven't seen any artifacts." Isaac trembled with real fear under the threat of the gun, his chest aching where he'd been shot previously. Belenos soothed the pain, but did little for the shared fear. "Please. I need this job. Don't make me do this."

"You're gonna take us to the alien tech, or I'm going to kill you and hold the scientist chick and your boss for ransom to make up for the money we were supposed to get for the tech." The mercenary twisted the fabric of Isaac's collar tighter and shoved the gun against his chest hard enough his ribs hurt.

"Come on! He's a janitor for Pete's sake. It's not like they're giving him access to space weapons." Dani yelled. The mercenary standing behind them smacked her in the back with the stock of his rifle. She stumbled forward and glared back at him when she regained her balance, but fell silent.

Please let me armor you. Belenos's concern was clear, but it was mingled with frustration. *If we touch him, we can find out where his boss is. Our mission is over, and all of us can go home.*

If he even knows. Let's do this right. You can heal me if he hurts me anyway. Isaac whetted his lips. "I– I'm a janitor, not an astronomer. Why would I know anything about alien tech?"

You don't, apparently. Belenos responded caustically to the question he'd asked the mercenary. *I can heal injuries, but I can't fix dead. Please...*

"If you don't, I guess you're not worth keeping alive." The mercenary moved the nose of his gun to the soft point where Isaac's neck met his collarbone. He pushed hard enough that Isaac gagged.

Fear caught Isaac's breath at the mercenary's threat. He sensed a stronger threat from Belenos that he was about to defy him and activate the armor anyway.

"No, wait!" Isaac raised both hands, speaking as much to his companion as his captor. *Come on, Bel, give this a chance to work.* "I'll take you wherever you want to go. Just, please, don't hurt me. I've got a baby at home."

"That's better." The mercenary let go of Isaac's shirt and stepped back to allow Isaac space as he holstered his gun. He gave Isaac a grin that showed far more teeth than necessary. "Lead the way."

I do not need a physical connection to sense his intent. If he touches you again, he will regret it.

Isaac tried not to smile at the protectiveness in Belenos's tone. *Where am I going?* He found himself wishing for the visor's head's up display so he could see Steve's map for himself. He'd have to rely on Belenos's directions.

Second hall, third door on the right. I am concerned they will attempt to kill you and keep Ms. Apryl and Mr. McGuiness whatever we do. This was not part of what we discussed.

Isaac frowned as they rounded the corner. Belenos wasn't wrong. In fact, that was probably the best scenario they could hope for. *I have an idea. What if we let them? You can armor me like a vest under my shirt and make it look like I died, right? Then we just track Dani and Steve back to their boss and rescue them there. Mission accomplished. Everyone walks away.*

I hate that idea.

Do you have a better one? Other than to abandon the mission and battle it out right here?

What if he aims for your head?

Then you have my permission to suit up and we take them down, I guess. But this will work. I know it will.

Belenos made his disgust and doubt very clear, but quickly formed a protective metal vest beneath Isaac's loose fitting janitor's uniform.

Isaac left his cart and led the mercenaries, Dani, and Steve to the room housing the gun he just left. He stopped in the doorway and gestured inside. "This is where they dumped all the crates that came today. I don't have any idea what's actually in the crates, other than the fancy gun they left on the table there."

"Open the first crate." The lead mercenary hit him in the arm with a crowbar to "hand" it to him. He grunted in surprise, but felt little pain. He rubbed the spot anyway as he took the crowbar and complied.

Busy with the crow bar, Isaac had his back to the mercenary when he felt Belenos tense.

May the Creator smile on us. Belenos's familiar determination was back, though mingled with lingering fear.

Something hard punched Isaac in the back between the shoulder blades and he blacked out.

✴ ✴ ✴ ✴ ✴

Dani screamed an obscenity at the mercenaries as Isaac slumped over the crate he'd been trying to open, but Belenos was only half listening. It was harder than he had anticipated to manipulate his host's autonomic functions without being fully bonded. He managed to stop his heartbeat and breathing in case the mercenary came to check if he were dead, but he didn't want to risk permanent damage, so he took the responsibility for blood circulation on himself. He could deliver a steady, pulseless stream for a limited period of time before he would be forced to wake his host. He redirected some of Isaac's blood to the place the bullet struck, hoping the sight of blood would satisfy the mercenaries and keep them from taking another shot, one probably aimed at Isaac's head.

"You two, help carry out the boxes or you'll be next." The mercenary waved his gun at Ms. Apryl and Mr. McGuiness as he none too gently kicked Isaac's body out of the way.

Belenos's anger flared. If all his energy wasn't being used to keep his host in this strange twilight state between life and death, he would have kept his promise to hurt the aggressive mercenary. *By the stars, you will pay for this indignity the next time we meet.*

Mr. McGuiness swore softly and cast a worried glance at Isaac's crumpled form and the growing bloodstain on his shirt, but didn't dare defy the mercenary to check on them. With his host down, Belenos couldn't reassure him unless a physical connection was made. Isaac would have to apologize for worrying them later.

The mercenaries didn't seem to give Isaac another thought, which allowed Belenos to center all his energy on his host, other than the bare minimum needed to make sure no sudden threat arose. Satisfied that Isaac's body was functioning safely, he took a moment to analyze Isaac's bizarre plan. His new host had chosen a subtle path of cunning and sacrifice, rather than the bold, aggressive, glorious path of violent victory Tianyi would have chosen. Belenos couldn't tell how much Isaac's complete trust in his ability to heal him played into his plan, but that wouldn't have mattered to Tianyi in the slightest. Even he himself would have preferred a direct assault to this dangerous plot, but his way would have sacrificed the mission to remove all risk to his host. By the Creator, he still wished they'd done things his way, but if this worked... Being bonded to this human would be a true adventure to say the least.

If he conceded to complete the bonding, that is. He was still determined to separate from Isaac as soon as they tracked down this Collector – before they could become more attached to each other – for his host's sake and for his family's sake. But, Creator help him, he was starting to wonder what being bound to a compatible host would feel like, and every moment he spent with Isaac led him to believe that perhaps *Isaac* was that host. He needed to pray Isaac's plan worked. If they worked together too much longer, he might not have the determination to do what needed to be done.

It took the four mercenaries, Ms. Apryl, and Mr. McGuiness forty minutes to clear out all the boxes. By the time they packed up the gun on the table and cleared the room, Belenos was dangerously low on energy. He risked extending his sensor range to make sure they were truly gone, then sent a quick shock to Isaac's heart to wake him.

Isaac sat up with a gasp. He looked frantically around the room. *Did it work?*

Yes. But if we don't recharge we will lose them. Now that Isaac was awake, Belenos could draw from his bio energy. Unfortunately, his host was also tired, which limited how much he could take without putting both them and their friends at risk.

Yeah, I could really go for a burger and a nap, but I'm guessing that's not going to work for you.

Normally it would, but in combat or emergency we can take a shortcut. He directed Isaac's attention to the same kind of electrical source they'd used in testing. *We're going to need to suit up to track them anyway.*

Okay, just let me take off my shirt. He shrugged out of the uniform and looked at the blood stained hole in confusion. *Bel, how is there blood here? I wasn't really shot again, was I?*

I decided a realistic hole in your shirt was better than a realistic hole in your head. Belenos activated the armor.

I wonder if Steve would authorize an expense account. Isaac grumbled as he wearily pushed himself to his feet and made his way to the outlet.

Belenos formed a tendril out of his scales and inserted it into the holes of the outlet. The rune on their chest glowed brilliantly as he absorbed as much energy as they could safely hold. If the mercenaries tried to hurt his host's friends, they would need the advantage additional fire power would give.

Um, wow, that's even better than a burger. Isaac took a deep breath and rolled his shoulders. *Can we track them now? I'd feel better if we were close enough to intervene if the mercenaries changed their minds and decided to dump them off a cliff or something.*

I know their last direction, but they are now out of range. They don't have so much of a headstart to keep me from locating them if we catch up a little. Ready to run?

Lead the way. Isaac jogged for the door, only to cry out in surprise when Belenos augmented his speed. *This is awesome! How fast can we go?*

I... do not know the conversion factors to frame it in a way you would understand. Some things would be difficult to explain even with a complete bond. Belenos doubted his host had even heard of the necessary conversion ratios, much less memorized them. *Far faster than the vehicle that brought us here.*

Isaac fell silent, concern for the other humans taking the focus of his mind. *You'll tell me when you sense them, right? When you're sure they're okay?*

I will.

They're safe for now at least, right? They want them alive? Isaac chewed his lip as he second-guessed his brilliant plan. *They won't... kill them as soon as they get out of range?*

If they wanted them dead, they would have killed them with you. Belenos soothed Isaac's worry even though he didn't really trust either of them not to do something stupid, especially if they thought Isaac was dead. *As long as they don't do something foolish, they'll be fine by the time we catch up.*

The darkness hid them as they ran alongside the highway in the direction the car had traveled, not that Isaac seemed to care about secrecy at the moment. They had only been traveling a few minutes when Belenos sensed the mercenaries' box truck at the border of his range. He drew Isaac's attention to it silently. It was too far out of range for him to sense if the two captives were all right.

Just a little closer, Bel. I want to make sure they're not in immediate danger, but I don't want the mercenaries to see us.

Easy enough. He brought them within full scanner range and slowed to match the truck's speed. *I sense six people within the transport vehicle. Two in the cabin, and four in the cargo area. The biometrics of two in the cargo area match those of Mr. McGuiness and Ms. Apryl.*

They're okay? Relief poured from Isaac so heavily Belenos shared his feeling.

Frightened. Perhaps angry. But unharmed.

Angry. I'll bet. Isaac smiled. *Dani probably hasn't stopped yelling since they left. How advanced are your sensors? Can we see them? Hear them? Anything at all to make sure the guys with the guns don't decide they need one less hostage.*

Belenos could amplify both Isaac's sight and hearing, but since the other humans were in the enclosed cargo area of the truck, enhanced vision wasn't going to help. Instead, he activated infrared sensors, immediately showing his host two figures apparently sitting on boxes and two standing over them. Isaac responded to the amplification of his natural senses with surprise and pleasure. Belenos reflected the pleasure back at him. His new host was quite easy to impress.

"I'm just saying we wouldn't be in this mess if that idiot Anderson hadn't gotten himself killed." Ms. Apryl was grumbling in a low tone barely perceptible to their sensors. "I told you giving that power suit to a janitor was foolish. He can't even use it right."

"I'm sure Belenos can heal him. He did it before." Mr. McGuiness's heart rate was closer to normal and his voice was steady.

"Yes. I'm sure a centuries old royal general turned space weapon wants to spend eternity playing combat medic to an untrained twenty-two year old mop jockey."

Belenos felt Isaac freeze, forcing him to slow their pace. Confusion and shame filled Isaac's thoughts. Belenos stopped running altogether, a little shocked by his host's reaction to Ms. Apryl's harsh words. While he certainly didn't expect Isaac to demand they punish Ms. Apryl for her criticism, he also didn't anticipate him taking her comments so personally.

Keeping me alive like that was hard, wasn't it? That's why we were both so tired afterward. It was a silly and dangerous plan. A military man like you wouldn't have suggested it in the first place. I'm sorry.

Do not apologize. Do you understand how many military men handled my prison pod before you did? I could have taken any one of them as my host, and I explicitly did not. I will not be another war god. Belenos softened his indignant tone and reassured his host instead. *Healing you is both my duty and my pleasure. She does not know what she is saying.*

Isaac hummed uncertainly and started jogging after the truck. Belenos activated his sensors again. The pair were still safe and Ms. Apryl was still complaining.

Would it be better if I monitored the audio for you so you don't have to hear her? I can still notify you if the situation changes.

No, I know she doesn't approve of you choosing me. Isaac sighed. *I don't really care what she thinks, as long as you think you made the right choice.*

Belenos forced neutrality into their connection. His confidence in his "choice" had nothing to do with Isaac's qualifications, and everything to do with the deadly and corrupting nature of his own power.

"He wasn't breathing, you know." Ms. Apryl's strident tone softened. "I looked. More than once. And the blood was real. The symbiote *didn't* heal him. Maybe the symbiote was damaged by the bullet, I don't know." She took a deep breath. "He had a *family,* Steve. He was the sole breadwinner for his wife, nine month old daughter, and disabled in-laws. Did you know that? Did you even *bother* to check before recruiting him for this stupid mission?"

"I didn't." Mr. McGuiness's voice was nearly inaudible.

Now it was Belenos's turn to take the overheard conversation personally. He *knew* Isaac had a family. He had seen his offspring, seen how the family depended on him. He knew the risks better than anyone. He knew what he and Timir had become. How could he have allowed this to happen?

"Bel?" Isaac was speaking aloud but gently. "What would happen to Aster and the rest of my family if this collector got ahold of you or another weapon like you?" He pushed Belenos's own memories of Tianyi's tyranny back across their connection, but with human cities and human victims replacing Vskian ones. "I don't want that for my daughter, no matter what it costs me." Isaac shuddered at a separate thought he managed to keep to himself. "Just, let's try to keep the worst case scenarios from happening, okay."

Chapter 7

The truck is slowing. Belenos alerted Isaac and directed his attention to a spot in the distance. *Someone is waiting for them.*

Their boss? This was going to be easier than Isaac had thought. Not only were they actually going to face the bad guy, they were going to do it at night and in the middle of the Southern California desert where the risk of collateral damage was nearly zero. *Is there any way you can identify him?*

Belenos responded by magnifying their vision and activating the overwhelming visor display. Numbers scrolled up the side of the display, but slower this time, and Belenos subtly pushed their meanings across their connection. Height, heart rate, estimated weight, respiration – nothing Isaac could use to identify him.

Facial recognition of a being with a mask is impossible. Belenos noted ruefully. *If we get closer, I can try to use ultrasound to get a view of his bone structure. We can at least identify him if we see him again.*

Focus on his teeth, our police use dental records to identify skeletons all the time.

The box truck pulled to a stop near the man, who wore a polo, slacks, and a Darth Vader mask. The area was little more than an empty field, with only the box truck and the man's sports car anywhere near them. It was going to be impossible to sneak up on them. He got as close as he could – behind a copse of overgrown brush – and crouched down to listen.

The driver of the box truck rounded to the back and raised the cargo door. The armed thugs from inside prodded Dani and Steve out and to the side where the new guy was waiting.

"Whatever amount you want, I'll pay it." Steve had his fingers laced behind the back of his head and a gun prodding him in the back. "Double if you let Ms. Apryl go. I already lost one employee tonight and I have no desire to lose more."

The guy in the mask tapped a thin tablet in his hand and turned the screen to face Steve. Belenos instantly magnified their vision to see a grid of bizarre objects, like an alien Amazon page.

"Do you recognize any of these?" The man's voice was distorted, just like Darth Vader's.

Record it anyway, Bel. Who knows what tech Steve's guys have.

Steve examined the screen as the man scrolled. One was the powerless gun from the lab. "This one's in the back of the truck."

The man nodded to the driver, who returned to the cargo area of the truck. "You transported a high profile artifact to that facility. It was important enough for you to accompany it yourself and bring your top scientist along for the ride. I want it."

"I brought a ton of artifacts." Steve shrugged awkwardly. "Your men already proved security at our main lab was subpar. Why would I keep anything important there?"

"It was a multi-sided orb. Each side showed a strange alien symbol. It might have glowed when you touched it." The man tapped the screen and turned it back to show Steve a detailed picture of Belenos's orb. "You give me this, I let both of you go."

Steve leaned forward as if to get a better look, then straightened and shook his head. "That wasn't in the boxes we brought."

Dani flicked her gaze from the screen to Steve in an obvious tell.

Isaac grimaced as the man turned his attention from Steve to Dani.

"But you recognize it. Good." He paused to take the space gun from the thug that had retrieved it. He reached into his pocket with his free hand and pulled out a small, pyramid shaped device that he stuck in the side of the gun. "Ms. Apryl, did your scientists ever figure out what this was?"

"We had other priorities." Dani crossed her arms over her chest and glared at him defiantly.

The weapon started to glow and a different readout started down the side of Isaac's visor. *Translate, Bel. I don't know what any of that means.*

It appears to be a microwave cannon.

The blood drained from Isaac's face. *Do you have any idea what that would do to Dani or Steve if he used it on them?*

Given that your body is seventy percent water, I can speculate.

Can you tell the difference between him just being an intimidating bully and actually a risk to Dani and Steve?

Maybe. Belenos seemed more doubtful than Isaac was comfortable with. Indecision and a sense of deja vu filled their connection, but Belenos didn't offer to share the memory that prompted it. *I would rather not bank your friends' lives on it.*

"This is a microwave gun. From Antares Three, apparently." The masked man stroked the barrel of the gun lovingly. "As a scientist, I'm sure you understand what this would do to a human body, but perhaps you might want to enlighten your boss."

"No! That's quite all right." Steve gave Dani a wide-eyed look. "I get it."

"Let me make my offer clear." He lowered the gun to aim at Dani's chest. "Give me the artifact I seek, and I will let you both go. Refuse, and I boil her from the inside out."

Bel, get ready to move. I know Steve explicitly ordered us not to engage them, but I'm pretty sure he wasn't planning on getting captured at the time. We're going to have to take them down.

Happily. We must take out the leader first and neutralize the weapon. If we can capture it, we can integrate it into our armor.

Isaac shuddered. *No thanks. I have no desire to use it on an enemy and it might be a bit overkill to use it to warm up a slice of pizza.*

Steve stared at the masked man for a long moment, as if trying to make up his mind. He finally took a deep breath and drew himself up taller. "I've seen that artifact in action. I can't do that."

The microwave gun wavered as if Steve's response surprised the masked man. He quickly aimed the gun at a half-filled bottle of soda someone had thrown at the roadside from a passing vehicle and fired. There was a delay as the gun glowed brightly, then the bottle exploded in a spray of steam and boiling soda.

"She's next." The masked man repositioned the gun to aim at Dani. "I want the artifact. Last chance."

Can we take a direct hit from that thing?

Yes. I can convert it to energy like any other–

Isaac moved after the 'yes.' He could feel Belenos's surprise and frustration, but the alien quickly augmented his speed anyway.

Unless we are fully bonded, I cannot reliably read your thoughts if you do not intentionally push them to me.

I'll try to keep that in mind. He's not going to give us up. He thinks I'm dead and you're defenseless. Dani was right about one thing: they would never have given me this assignment if they weren't desperate. They're not going to risk these guys stealing an intergalactic superweapon off my dead body.

Dani swore and spit in the masked man's face. Startled, the man took a step back and raised the gun to her face.

How fast can we go?

There are limits to what your human joints can withstand.

Forget that. Fix it later. Isaac gritted his teeth as he wondered how bad this was going to hurt.

An immediate burst of speed was accompanied by muted pain throughout his entire lower body, throbbing deeper with each staccato step. He'd expected a sharp, tearing pain, and suspected that Belenos was managing his pain somehow. The masked man swore loudly and adjusted his aim. They were almost there, but were still going to be too late.

We're not going to make it, Bel. Divert all our energy to speed. Whatever it takes.

Nova, Belenos muttered the word like a swear word. *I'm sorry.*

They shot forward so fast the scenery blurred. Now Isaac did feel like his legs were being ripped off. He screamed in agony and tried not to black out. As bad as it hurt, maybe it would be better if he did black out.

Dani screamed – or was that himself? – and his visor glowed a blinding, brilliant red. The masked man had fired, and the rush of energy Belenos fed him accompanied a flood of relief. They'd managed to take the shot for Dani. For a moment, Isaac thought he would cry, both from the pain and the relief of knowing Dani was safe.

Belenos shot a tendril from each arm, wrapping one around the gun and the other around the masked man pinning his arms to his sides. He wrenched the gun from his hand and crushed it with the tendril. *Tell him we will do the same to him if he doesn't order his men to release their captives.*

Isaac took a deep breath. The pain in his legs and hips was gone, and he could feel Bel reconstructing his joints, but he still couldn't use them. Bluffing seemed like a good plan. "Order your men to release your captives, or we will crush you like we did your weapon."

The field was silent as every eye stared at them in shocked amazement. Defiance seeped through the weak connection afforded through the masked leader's heavy shirt. If he thought he could get away with it, he'd order his men to kill the captives instead. *Bel, use your free hand to create as threatening a gun as you can.*

Belenos complied gleefully, throwing the mangled gun aside and retracting the tendril onto a massive arm cannon that would have made Rambo proud. They aimed the cannon at the lead thug that had shot them at the lab. *I can redirect the microwave energy at him.*

No. Come on, Bel, we're not like them. Isaac adjusted his aim at a nearby cactus. The gun glowed brightly and the cactus exploded. He pointed the cannon back at the obnoxious thug and addressed the masked man, "I won't say it again. Release them both and give them the keys to the van."

Steve's shocked expression turned to a smirk as he held out his hand for the keys. The thug looked from the massive maw of Bel's cannon to the masked man. When the masked man didn't respond, Bel tightened his tendril enough to make him grunt in pain. Rage trembled through the villain's body as he inclined his head in assent.

"Man, Isa– I mean Gemini – you have no idea how glad I am to see you." Steve closed his hand around the truck keys and grinned at Dani. "You owe me twenty bucks."

"We didn't make a bet, Steve." Dani sounded exasperated, but looked relieved to see them all the same. "But, dang, Gemini, you've got a lot of explaining to do."

"Go home. Call the cops on your way and send them to pick these guys up. I'll explain everything after I finish here." Isaac counted the thugs to make sure they were all accounted for and none of them were waiting in the van to ambush his friends. *Keep an eye on them until they're out of sensor range, will you?*

"Give me the keys. I'm driving." Dani snatched at the keys as Steve lifted them out of her reach.

"Heh, no chance. I've had enough excitement for one day." Steve twisted out of her reach and sprinted toward the cab of the box truck.

"Do you even know how to drive a truck that size?" Their argument continued as they climbed into the truck and pulled away.

Isaac shook his head and turned his attention back to the mercenaries, glad his friends were finally out of danger. *I want to disable the car. Can we target the radiator? If we hit the gas tank we're all going up in a fireball.*

If you tell me where the radiator is, I can target it as precisely as needed.

Isaac directed his attention – and the arm cannon – at the grill of the car. The gun glowed brightly, then a loud crack and a cloud of steam told him the car was immobilized.

"You," Isaac gestured with the gun at the driver, "toss the keys in the ditch. Then all of you get in the car."

The thugs obeyed quickly, leaving Isaac and Belenos alone with the masked man still wrapped in a tentacle. *Can you read his mind? Is he the one we want?*

I cannot probe deeply, but if you ask him questions, I can tell you what he thinks in response. Belenos snaked their tentacle further around the masked man, wrapping it around the bare skin of his neck between his shirt and mask.

"You're going to answer a few questions before the cops get here." Isaac prompted Bel to remove the man's mask, and Bel responded quickly by pulling it off with the end of his tendril. The man was thin, substantially older than Steve, and glaring at them defiantly through steel gray eyes shadowed by heavy gray eyebrows. Isaac was glad Bel could read his thoughts, because he didn't look like the type of guy that would respond to anything other than torture. *We don't do that either, Bel.*

I wasn't going to ask. Bel laughed. *Stars, you're different from my brother!*

I'm definitely taking that as a compliment. Isaac smirked and turned his attention back to the unmasked thug. "Are you the one collecting all these artifacts, or do you have a boss?"

"You're the artifact, aren't you? The one in the orb?" The man ignored his question and looked at him with a mixture of awe and cold assessment.

He's not the collector. He's thinking about how he can make up for failing his boss if he claims us.

"All you need to know is that I can snap your neck with a thought." Isaac was a little uncomfortable with the covetous vibe he was getting through their connection to the man. "Who do you work for?"

"All *you* need to know is that whatever McGuiness is paying you, my boss will pay you double to work for him."

"Ha, not likely. I know what your men have done to secure the artifacts you're hunting. I won't be your victim or your pawn." Isaac only got a confused sense of duplicity and lust from their connection, and Bel didn't offer more, so he tried again. "Tell me who your boss is."

"Hephaestus." The man smiled in spite of Bel's tentacle wrapped around his throat. "And he will have your technology one way or another."

Bel?

Ask him where to find his boss.

"Where's Hephaestus, then?"

The masked villian clamped his jaw shut, but the sense of triumph that came through from Belenos told Isaac they had gotten all they needed. Good thing, too. Isaac could hear the police sirens in the distance.

Hephaestus runs Olympus Art Galleries in town. His mind went directly to it as soon as you asked. We've completed our mission.

Oh, good. Let's get this guy in the car with the others and go home. Isaac relaxed enough to let the masked man breathe easily. *I really need that burger now.*

Chapter 8

"What happened back there, Isaac?" Mr. McGuiness sat at his desk and stared at them over templed fingers. Dani sat in her usual chair, with her usual scowl, and her usual closed posture.

Belenos waited as his host chewed and swallowed a huge bite of his second triple deluxe burger. They were finally seated in Mr. McGuiness's office, debriefing on the mission, and – Belenos expected – giving account for scaring their superiors. Nervousness flooded their connection. His host was afraid of his superiors' reactions, but not sorry for the path he took.

"I knew that guy was going to kill me one way or another. Belenos wanted to gear up and take him down, but that would have sacrificed the mission. I figured if they thought I was dead, they'd leave me alone and give us a chance to track you." Isaac sat up straighter and set the rest of his burger on the wrapper in his lap. "Belenos preferred to abort the mission and take the guys down, especially when that one guy got rough." He looked firmly at Ms. Apryl. "Dani never wanted me to do this to begin with. I knew we could save the mission and you. Bel was willing to give it a try, as long as they didn't aim for my head."

"We saw the blood, Isaac, and you weren't breathing." Dani leaned forward and tapped her index finger where the rune rested beneath Isaac's shirt, giving them a muffled hint of anger spiced with fear. "Either that alien killed you, or he failed to protect you. Whichever it was, I think it's ample proof we need to abort this whole project. Too much is at stake."

Belenos's own anger and indignation rose at her accusation, tempered by Isaac's quiet wrestling over what to say. His host's head was down, and in spite of the turbulent feelings crossing their connection, he couldn't read Isaac's thoughts. Nova, being bonded was easier! He couldn't tell whether his host felt distressed because Dani's bitter words were getting to him or not, but he didn't appreciate the possibility that he might have to persuade his own host that he didn't intend to kill him.

"You're right." Isaac finally answered, but his feelings were more decided and defiant than submissive. "Too much *is* at stake." He looked up and met Dani's glare with confidence. "Belenos is power. I'm not even sure we've scratched the surface of what he's capable of. We're not even fully bonded, but I can *feel* his fear of his own power, and his terror of it falling into the wrong hands. My family's future – heck, the future of the world – depends on Belenos and I stopping Hephaestus, from keeping Belenos out of his hands and making sure he doesn't have something else he can use to take over the world." The fearful thought that tormented his host returned, but Isaac did a masterful job of hiding it from both his friends and Belenos, with only a hint of a shudder crossing their connection. "I know the risks. Believe me. But the risks of doing nothing are greater. You need us. The world needs us. Even if we are unpredictable and unconventional."

Belenos pushed appreciation and support over their connection. *I did not kill you.*

I know. She's just angry.

"You're nuts, that's what you are." Dani grunted and crossed her arms over her chest. "If you insist that you're going through with this, we have to figure out a way to allow you to communicate with us if something like this ever happens again."

Steve nodded as if he knew exactly what to say next. "Even if it's just smooth sailing from here out, we really do need to communicate from a distance. I think R&D has exactly the thing."

"Steve." Exasperation filled Dani's voice as she rolled her eyes to the ceiling. "You already gave this kid an irreplaceable intergalactic suit of armor. Don't you think that's enough? This isn't one of your superhero movies."

"Ha, no." Steve laughed. "If it was, I'd be the one wearing the suit. We're calling this 'an investment into Project Gemini.'" He sobered. "No offense, but we really can't afford to lose track of Belenos. If you had been dead and those idiots had gotten their hands on Belenos, life could have gotten very difficult very fast."

Please remind them that I am a sapient being and am no more likely to bond with their collector than I was with them. Bel conveyed his irritation to his host strongly. *The true danger comes from the other unknown artifacts he already possesses.*

"That's not the risk here. Bel is not interested in becoming a war god. We just don't know if the collector already has another weapon that would make him a threat." Isaac chuckled. "He's actually kinda angry with you both. He resents your insinuations and wants to remind you that he's a... a person. With feelings. He really didn't appreciate you suggesting that he murdered me. Keeping me alive while making those thugs believe I was dead was actually very hard."

That is not what I told you to say.

Was it false? His host was still laughing on the inside, and Bel didn't quite understand why he found this so funny.

"Regardless, we want you to communicate if there is any problem." Steve opened a small silver box and pushed it across the desk to Isaac. Inside was a sleek watch made of a polished cobalt enameled metal with a simple blue digital screen. "This is our latest smart watch technology. We can track you, monitor your biometric readings, and communicate directly to you by connecting directly to our satellite network. Try it on."

Isaac pulled it free from the velvet lined case and snapped it around his wrist, the hidden clasp catching tightly. "So how does it work?"

"It's already programmed to send us a constant feed of GPS coordinates and biometric signals, which may not be particularly useful if Belenos makes you "not dead" again." Dani gave them a sour look and continued. "You can speak with us here by pushing the set button on the side."

Which will also not be particularly useful since I can not talk to them except through you.

I guess I'll be teaching you morse code, then.

"What do we know about Olympus Art Galleries?" Isaac intentionally changed the subject. The face on the watch told him it was getting late and he wanted to get home to his family.

"It's actually a very reputable source for people looking to buy ancient artifacts and priceless art. Mr. Anders Koine – the founder – facilitated the sale of a priceless Minoan vase last month. He looks as clean as can be." Steve passed a thick file folder over to Isaac. "The man himself is pretty mysterious. Known for throwing lavish parties, then disappearing completely as soon as they end. Supposedly he's both obscenely rich and obsessed with anything rare and beautiful."

"What would an art dealer want with Bel?" Isaac started skimming the papers in the file absently. Fortunately for both of them, Bel had been created with the ability to save any input he received.

"That... we're not sure about. Power? Money? Simply being the only guy on the block with his own superhero?" Dani shot a pointed look at Steve. "If he's selling this stuff on the black market, we could be in a ton of trouble."

"So where do Bel and I come in?" Isaac went back to eating his burger warily.

"Well," Steve drew the word out as his eyes glittered with excitement. "I *may* have been invited to the next gala he's throwing, and I *may* have RSVPed with a date and a bodyguard."

Isaac stopped mid-chew, while Dani laughed out loud.

"He's a high tech janitor, Steve, and we're not..." She trailed off when Steve's expression grew serious. She made a choking sound. "Are you asking me out on a *date*?"

"I was, actually, but we can call it a work assignment if you want," Steve responded dryly. "And Gemini has proven themselves more than capable of saving my life, by actually doing it two more times than anyone else has." Dani fell into a stunned silence as Steve turned his focus to Isaac. "I'd get you an appropriate suit, of course, but it will be up to you to figure out how to explore the building to find what we're looking for."

"What if he tries to hurt you or Dani while we're off 'exploring'?" Isaac set the burger back down again.

"Not likely, especially if we stay in the public areas." Steve shrugged. "Besides, that's what the watch is good for. If we need you, we can call you immediately."

Bel? Isaac's excitement over the proposal carried brightly over their connection.

I am not quite as confident that they're completely without risk, but their role should be minimal. Belenos still was somewhat uncomfortable with the thought of placing his host at risk, but respected his reasoning – appreciated it actually. *Our risk is also minimal, as long as we don't get caught.*

Then we'll need a plan for if we do get caught. Isaac pressed his lips in a tight line and nodded. "We're in. We'll do whatever we can to take this guy out."

"Good. The party isn't until tomorrow night. Go home and rest. Dani and I will work out the particulars." Steve didn't meet Dani's eye, and Bel was willing to guess the rest of the conversation was going to get quite awkward.

Isaac stood quickly, nearly forgetting to scoop up his burger before it fell. He popped the last bite into his mouth, mumbled"Good-bye," and hurried from the room.

Bel... Isaac slowed his pace as they neared the parking garage. *If we catch that guy tomorrow, what happens to you?*

Belenos flinched at the question. It wasn't something he wanted to deal with at the moment. His heart ached for a permanent bond with a suitable host, and dreaded returning to his artifact form alone. But he couldn't place the burden of an eternal bond on Isaac. An eternity of resisting the corruption of his power. An eternity of life beyond those of his mate and child. Eternity was a long time to regret taking a symbiote.

There's only two choices, aren't there? Isaac's stomach turned as he shared Belenos's dread. *Make me your permanent host or go back to your artifact form. We can't just go on like this forever, can we?*

Unlikely. I cannot say what the risk of a continued superficial connection would be to your system. Belenos soothed Isaac's stomach. He could, however, categorically say that a continued connection would have decidedly negative consequences for himself. Already, after only a couple of days, he felt his desire for a permanent bond growing and their connection deepening to only short of a complete neural link. Separating even now would be very hard for him. He shuddered as he remembered Isaac's fear of him when they first met, and the hidden fear that still lurked just beyond their connection. *I swear by my hope of the Celestial Heaven that I will not force an unwanted bond on you. I would live an eternity alone before I violated your will.*

"I know," Isaac whispered. His dread and fear eased, leaving only the fear he kept hidden throbbing in the back of his mind. "Thank you."

Chapter 9

I saac parked in the garage beside his wife's Volkswagen and entered through the garage. It was a bit odd getting home in the evening and he found himself looking forward to the prospect of eating dinner with the family on a regular basis. This new job assignment had the potential of being really good for his family, in more ways than just their finances.

The savory smell of Alice's slow-cooked pot roast greeted him as he entered the hall, and the indistinct sound of female voices carried from the ground floor. He placed his hand on his shirt over the necklace. Was dinner the right time to break the news? How did you tell your wife and in-laws you'd contracted with an alien symbiote to be a real-life superhero? Belenos didn't offer any suggestions, just a quiet assurance he would be there to support him whatever he did.

A movement at the end of the hall caught his attention and piqued his heightened senses. His father-in-law pushed open the squeaky basement door with the huge tote of Christmas decorations he was carrying.

Isaac rolled his eyes and bit his lip to keep from rebuking his father-in-law. He wasn't supposed to be carrying anything, much less up stairs, but Frank hated the forced helplessness, so rarely obeyed orders.

"Let me help with that, Frank." Isaac held out his hands to take the box from his father in law.

"I've got this one, there's plenty more down there." Frank jerked his head sharply to the side. "The girls want all the decorations up so they can see what we need for the party."

"So soon?" The in-laws hosted a huge holiday get together the Saturday after Thanksgiving, but that was still a few weeks away.

Dad made a face and set the box down at his feet. "It's going to take longer to get the decorations up this year."

Isaac pressed his lips into a straight line. There was no way Frank could do the decorating, and was especially forbidden to climb anything, so outside decorating was completely out. "I'm here this year. Let me help."

Frank scowled at the box and yanked it up more abruptly than he should have and grunted in pain.

"Look," Isaac took his arm and looked him in the eye. "You guys are sharing your home with us, and watching Aster while we work. The least I can do is carry a few boxes and hang some lights. This is a mutually beneficial arrangement, remember? You cover what we're lacking, and we do the same."

This is what I mean by 'symbiote.' Belenos nudged. *Together we can be more than we are alone. Just as you and your family are.*

Isaac hummed thoughtfully. *Can you help me move these boxes without Frank's help? He's going to hurt himself.*

I can augment your strength, yes. However, we will need to be cautious about lifting anything noticeably beyond your normal strength unless you wish to explain me to him.

Ha. No. Let's not. Isaac scrambled down the stairs and made a beeline for the largest box of decorations. He wedged his fingers under the edge and gave a trial tug. It moved effortlessly. *Well, this is going to be easy.*

Belenos sent an odd feeling similar to an eye roll across their connection. *At least pretend to make an effort.*

Isaac hunched over the box a bit more to make it appear heavy. He set it down next to the one his father-in-law had set down, then jogged after the older man.

"So how's the new job going?" Frank gripped the rail tightly as he navigated one step at a time.

"Great! I love the hours and my... coworkers are really, really good at what they do." Isaac breathed a relieved breath through his nose as he felt Bel's approval, and bent to pick up a box that contained an artificial tree before his father-in-law could.

"What, exactly, do you do again?" Frank's voice took on a hard edge as he lifted a trash bag full of wreaths off the stack of boxes. "Becca said you were working directly with Steve McGuiness, but didn't exactly know what you were doing for him. They aren't having you clean the executive offices during office hours, are they?"

"No, I..." He fumbled the box to cover his distress. *Help me out here, Bel!*

Tell him the redacted truth. Bel pushed confidence and encouragement across their connection. *You interrupted the mercenaries that attacked SentryTech Monday night and Mr.*

McGuiness was so impressed he hired you to participate in a top secret experiment.

Isaac set the box down with a sigh, straightened, turned to face his father-in-law. "I haven't had a lot of time to talk to Becca about it. We keep passing like ships in the night. You heard about the attempted theft Monday night, right?"

The antagonism on Frank's face melted to concern. "It was on the news. Becca told us you were upset about it. Did you know the men who were killed?"

"I did." Isaac took a sharp breath and closed his eyes against the vivid memory of being shot. He clenched his fists and chewed his lip. *I nearly died.* He resisted the urge to rub at the scar in his chest, took a deep breath and looked at the floor. "I managed to interrupt the guys when they tried to hurt Mr. McGuiness. He was impressed enough to offer me a job assisting with a top secret experiment. Better hours, far better pay, benefits, a chance to make a difference – I couldn't pass it up."

Frank processed that quietly as he went back down the stairs for another load. He set another box on the floor, pressed his hands to his arched back, and winced. "The 'top secret experiment', it's not dangerous is it?"

Not any more dangerous than being a night janitor in a place that's constantly being robbed. Isaac bit back a snide retort and opted instead to continue with Bel's advice for vague honesty. "I guess, but isn't any experiment that has the potential to change the world? My team is the best at what they do, and my partner is specially trained to make sure nothing bad happens to me." He couldn't get past the fact that he'd been shot twice in the last three days just being a janitor. "Honestly, I'm far safer on this project than wandering those empty halls alone."

Frank nodded as if satisfied. "I get that you can't talk about it with me. But you are going to explain to Becca, right? She's excited, but worried about you. It's not fair to her to keep her in the dark. She has a right to know."

Frank shuffled off, leaving Isaac with Bel and a pile of Christmas ornaments. His mind went back to the flowers and candy. He wasn't going to dodge this long, and he doubted Becca would settle for the superficial explanation he'd given Frank. Nervousness twisted his stomach. She'd totally understand, wouldn't she?

✳ ✳ ✳ ✳ ✳

After dinner, Isaac's mate went to prepare the baby for bed, while Isaac sat in their living room to wait for her. He kicked off his shoes and popped open a soft reclining chair.

If we're going to have Steve's watch in case of an emergency, you're going to need to be able to communicate with him if I'm not able to. Isaac pulled his phone out and tapped his index finger against a fingerprint sensor in the back. *I figure Morse Code is best. You can make a clicking noise somehow, right?*

I can. Belenos focused on the screen of Isaac's phone as he thumbed through a series of dots and dashes and their rune equivalents. *Steve knows this language?*

He'll figure it out. Isaac shrugged and kept scrolling. *If I'm down he'll have no choice. The question is, can you send a message in our language? Yours looks really different.*

The armor contains an active learning translator. Between it and our connection, I have been able to learn much of your language.

129

You probably should also know what latitude and longitude are, so you can direct him to us in an emergency. Isaac typed a search question and tapped through several more articles.

This device functions as a communication device and accesses all the accumulated knowledge of your world? Belenos pushed his amazement across their connection. *Truly your science rivals our own.*

Isaac laughed out loud. *Your science placed a living soul in an invincible suit of armor. I think that trumps an infinite library and unlimited cat videos.*

Belenos only made a skeptical hum. Desperation fueled ascendance in warfare didn't seem more worthy than the pursuit of knowledge, especially from his perspective. Humans were strange beings.

"Aster's finally asleep." Isaac's mate came up behind them and hugged them from behind. Her body pressed against Isaac's neck and captured all of his attention. He had taken her words as an invitation and stood from his chair to follow her to the bedroom, the news article forgotten for now.

Isaac closed the bedroom door behind them and took both his mate's chocolate brown hands in his as he admired her. Her brown hair hung in dozens of tight braids that tumbled around her shoulders, framing her heart-shaped face. A short pink dress made of a thin, shiny fabric clung to her curves, cutting low over full cleavage that held Isaac's gaze for a moment before his eyes trailed to round hips and a short hemline. Belenos had no idea what was considered beautiful to humans, but his host found her very attractive indeed.

The feelings of passion shared between mates wasn't new to Belenos. What fascinated him more was what was missing from his experiences with Tianyi. He sensed no pressure to perform, no selfishness in Isaac's lovemaking. Yes, his new host was enjoying himself, but he was also concerned that his mate was enjoying herself, not so that he could prove himself a superior lover, but because he cared for her satisfaction as well. More than that, though, Belenos felt a connection. A natural bond that went deeper than just friendship, nearly as deep as what he currently shared with Isaac himself. Perhaps deeper if his telepathy was factored out. They shared each other wholly, body and soul. Belenos had always despised Tianyi's empty, self-centered lovemaking, but he hadn't realized until that moment that there was an alternative, that the connection he had longed for over a century was possible.

"What's this?" Isaac's mate whispered huskily as she unbuttoned the top couple buttons of his shirt and stroked the rune etched in their collar necklace. The brief contact of her fingers with the necklace revealed the same selfless passion shared by Isaac, interrupted by curiosity.

Belenos' disappointment at the interrupted lovemaking was almost as acute as Isaac's own. *It is only right that you explain. Her claim on you is superior to my own.*

Isaac shrugged his shirt over his head and sighed deeply. "I think maybe you'd better sit down."

Becca sat on the end of the bed and Isaac took her hands in his as he sat beside her.

"You remember the attack on SentryTech a couple nights ago?" Isaac forced himself to look her in the eye.

Belenos could feel his rising anxiety. "A bunch of mercenaries broke into the lab looking to steal alien artifacts to sell to some rich collector."

"Yeah, you told me about it. It was the night you came home sick." She returned his uncomfortable look with one of concern. "Did something more happen?"

"Yeeeeaahh." Isaac's eyes darted aside and his stomach clenched. Belenos responded by calming his nerves and offering him confidence. "I tried to hide from the mercenaries in one of the space labs. It was unfortunately the lab the mercenaries were looking for."

"That doesn't explain this. I know you're not going to tell me you stole it to keep it out of the mercenaries hands." Isaac's mate pulled one hand free and touched the rune again. Belenos felt her fear beneath the confident questions and shared encouragement, calm, and Isaac's love for her through their connection. Her dark eyes widened and she pulled her hand away. "Isaac? What is that thing?"

Belenos, stop it. I've got this, Isaac snapped. His fear was teetering close to panic. *What if she leaves me?* The comment wasn't necessarily meant for Belenos, but the strength of the fear pushed it across their connection anyway.

Creator forbid. Belenos hadn't had enough contact with Isaac's mate to know if that was a possibility, and hadn't really considered that in his risk analysis. That would never have been a problem on Vistke.

"This is Belenos. He saved my life."

"He?" The word squeaked out of a tight throat. Isaac's mate jerked her hand off of the rune as if it had suddenly gotten too hot to touch. "Isaac, please stop, you're starting to scare me."

"He's an alien symbiotic suit of armor. The mercenaries were hired to bring him to their buyer. Once I spoke to him, I knew I couldn't let them have him." Isaac took her hands again, but looked away. His anxiety spiked as his mind replayed the trauma of that night. The least Belenos could do was hold back the trauma and help him get through his story. "They... shot me. In the chest. Twice. I was going to die, and who knows what they would have done with Belenos. I agreed to partially bond with him to keep him from being used to take over the world, and to save my life. Steve – Mr. McGuiness, my boss – offered me twice my salary, better hours, and a one million dollar insurance policy if Belenos and I can stop the collector who attacked the lab."

The stunned look on Isaac's mate's face contorted to anger. She pulled both hands free and stood. "A symbiote, Isaac? What are you thinking? Letting an alien into your head? How could you do that? You know how that always turns out in the movies."

"This isn't the movies." Isaac kept his voice level even though his mate was yelling. Still, the nagging fear of the word symbiote grew in his mind.

Belenos wished he could promise he wouldn't harm his new host, but memories of Tianyi rose in his own mind. Power was a toxin, and he was nearly the most powerful toxin in the universe.

"Don't push me. If I hadn't touched that thing, I'd have thought you were either lying to me or that the trauma of the robbery did something to your mind." The anger faded from her face. "You didn't tell me you nearly died. You just said you were sick."

"I wasn't sure it was real, either." Isaac touched the faded scars. "I woke up and these were still there. I tried to forget Belenos, but together..." He looked up at his mate with eyes that pleaded for understanding. "We can be a powerful force for good, Becca."

"Or just as easily become the monster you think you're trying to stop." Tears swam in her eyes. "Please take it off. Go back to Mr. McGuiness and tell him you changed your mind. It's too much risk. I'd rather be married to a poor janitor than an alien possessed super criminal."

"I'm not sure I can do that." He also wasn't sure he wanted to, but Belenos could already tell that if it came down to a choice between him and his mate, Isaac would take him back to SentryTech in a heartbeat.

"Figure it out." She caught her breath and shook her head. "I'm going to bed."

Chapter 10

What happens if I take off the necklace? Isaac felt for a clasp at the back of the necklace. There wasn't one, but that didn't stop him from searching. *You said a superficial bond can be broken without permanent harm, so what does happen?*

I don't know. I forged a permanent bond with my brother within moments of connection. Belenos shuddered at the memory of the agony following cutting his bond with his brother. *I'd rather not find out.*

One night, Bel. I want one night alone with my wife. Isaac covered the rune on the front of the necklace with his hand. *I need her to see you don't own me. That you haven't changed me. I'm still me.*

An image of a hideous black monster, human-like with teeth of an alligator and tendrils of a climbing vine, flashed into Isaac's mind. Deep rooted fear was attached to the image, along with the definition, *symbiote.*

That is not us! Horror and dismay clashed with Belenos's own feelings of guilt over Tianyi. Were they any better than the monster Isaac feared him to be?

Belenos, no, I didn't mean you, it's just—

Belenos couldn't listen anymore. He had felt his host's fear of him, of *them*. Perhaps time was exactly what they needed. Belenos cut the connection and the necklace fell silently from his neck, returning to Bel's artifact form before it hit Isaac's hands.

✳ ✳ ✳ ✳ ✳

After a restless night that rivaled the first month of Aster's life, Isaac woke up feeling worse than he could remember feeling in his life. His head throbbed and his stomach churned. He swung his legs over the side of the bed and sat up. His hands shook and he felt a sense of anxiety and nameless fear. Becca still slept beside him, Aster nestled in her arms where she fell asleep nursing. They looked so peaceful, the exact opposite of what he was feeling.

He needed Belenos. "No permanent damage" apparently was alien code for "you'd be surprised what you can live through." He felt horrible, not just because of the physical results of the withdrawal, but also because he'd hurt Belenos. They'd only been together for three days, but the nature of their symbiotic bond had allowed him to get to know the alien pretty well. He wasn't a monster. Isaac suspected his brother had been, but if there were two things Isaac had learned about Belenos it was that he cared about doing right and that he was desperate to redeem his mistakes with Tianyi. He wasn't the thing Isaac or Becca feared. He was gentle, thoughtful, and moral.

Isaac hoped he was also forgiving. He cringed. Apologies would have to wait. His stomach rebelled at his upright position and he made a dash for the bathroom.

"Isaac?" Becca called after him.

The noises from the bathroom made it clear he was otherwise occupied.

"It's the alien, isn't it?" Becca's voice over his shoulder was soft and worried as she laid a hand on his back. "Being without him is making you sick."

Isaac's only answer was to vomit again.

"You're sure he's good, Isaac? I mean, really sure?" She crouched down beside him and offered him a warm washcloth to wipe his mouth. "I love you too much to watch you turn into a monster."

"That's the last thing either Belenos or I want, too." Isaac sat back shakily against the sink cabinet and cleaned his face. "We can do good, Becca, and stop someone really bad. But without me, Belenos is just a suit of armor, and without him I'm just a janitor." Isaac remembered Belenos's tone when talking about the Songs of the Stars. All it had taken to shake Isaac's faith was a smartmouthed philosophy professor, Belenos somehow managed to hold strong after everything he'd suffered. "And I think he's more good than I am."

Becca scooted closer and rested her head on his shoulder with a sigh. "I don't want to share, Isaac. I barely want to share you with Aster. But I hate to see you like this, and if you're sure, I trust your judgment. Just, do you think I can talk to him? I want him to understand I'm holding him responsible if anything happens to you."

With a weak smile, Isaac leaned on his wife to stand, washed his hands and face in the sink, then crossed the bedroom to the bedside table where Belenos's artifact rested. He gave Becca a hug and a quick kiss, kept short by the returning nausea, then picked up the many-sided artifact.

The runes on its sides glowed faintly at his touch, but Belenos didn't immediately respond. Turgid emotions swirled inside the artifact, fighting for supremacy with the Star Song Belenos had mentioned as the one that had gotten him through his decades trapped in the artifact.

I'm sorry.

The swirling emotions quieted and the song dimmed, but Belenos still didn't answer. Isaac could feel him though, his now familiar consciousness just on the other side of the runes.

I was wrong. I'm not afraid. That wasn't completely true. He was a janitor, not a superhero. He was terrified of what that meant, but he wasn't afraid of Belenos. *I'm not afraid of us.*

Belenos was silent for a beat. *I... Am afraid of us. I was too quick to grant your request last night, even though I knew the consequences would likely be regrettable, because part of me wanted the opportunity to be free. You are not my brother, but I still struggle with what my part was in creating Tianyi. I am still afraid, but with the Creator's help I believe we can be the great protector Tianyi never was.*

Isaac quickly touched the rune pattern he had memorized and the armor crept over his bare arms and torso quickly, soliciting a gasp from Becca. As the armor covered his body, the nausea and headache faded and the anxiety calmed. When the transformation was complete, Belenos's consciousness beside his own was nearly back to his old quiet confidence with only an undercurrent of anxiety remaining.

"That is Belenos?" Becca squeaked. "All you need is a sword and you'd look like a copper crusader."

Belenos? Isaac smirked playfully as the armor responded to form a shining reddish sword in his right hand. He swung it in a wide arc as Becca jumped back with a tight laugh. Another mental command and it retreated. *Mask too, Bel. I think this would be easier if she could see my face.*

The armor folded back to stasis, leaving just the collar necklace with the glowing rune pulsing in time to his heart. Isaac offered Becca his hand, and pulled her into an embrace. He didn't miss that she was careful not to touch the necklace, though. "I'm still me."

His wife stared at the necklace with a tightlipped expression, then looked up at Isaac expectantly.

Becca wants to talk to you.

She didn't try to destroy me in the night, so that must be a good sign. Belenos responded with his familiar amusement, though some unidentifiable fear threaded his tone. *Tell her to touch the rune.*

✳ ✳ ✳ ✳ ✳

"Touch the rune on the necklace and he can read you by telepathy." Isaac took her hand again and gently laid it on his chest over the rune. Her emotions were a mix of fear, jealousy, and fierce protectiveness.

I am Belenos. I was prince of a distant star system until an unwinnable war forced me to take this form. Belenos relaxed and allowed her to sense more of his personality than he usually would. *Together we are Gemini, the solar system's steadfast protector.*

"I am Becca, Isaac's wife and the mother of his child." Isaac's mate spoke aloud, which gave Belenos the unique opportunity to read her and Isaac's reaction to what she said.

At the moment, it was just pleasure and pride, as if happy they were finally meeting. "I love him more than anything on this earth, and have since long before you got here."

I will not come between you and my host. Even though the superficial connection meant he was capable of targeting his answer to her alone, he responded carefully to both of them. Unlike the many mates Tianyi had taken over his years of reign, Isaac and his mate already shared a bond nearly as close as his own with his host. He'd been with enough females to know this was a rare treasure. *I wish for his well-being and happiness. You provide fulfillment and companionship that I cannot.*

"Like last night." Isaac snorted and Becca punched him playfully in the arm.

"Isaac said you saved his life." Becca traced the fading scar on her husband's chest. "Thank you."

Isaac saved me from worse. The men who hurt him would have taken me to a powerful man who wished to use me to become a war god. Belenos carefully kept his memories of Tianyi from her, pushing them back to Isaac instead. Isaac responded with gentle sympathy. *We would stop him before he finds another source of power.*

"Or uses one of the other weapons he's already stolen." Isaac reminded him aloud.

Becca looked at him sharply, then back at the rune. "Isaac says you two will be a superhero."

Yes. It hadn't been a question, really, but she seemed to want his confirmation.

She pushed free of her husband's arms and rounded to her side of the bed where the baby was beginning to stir. She scooped the baby into her arms, circled back, and placed the baby in Isaac's arms, then hugged the two of them while she placed her hand over the rune again.

"You may be some highly trained alien warrior prince, but Isaac is my husband and Aster's father. You can find another host, but he's the only one we have."

Belenos disagreed strongly. Losing another host would probably kill him. *Isaac is important to me as well. I can protect him.*

"Hmm. I want your word." Becca hugged Isaac closer as her fierce protective feelings rose above all the others. "Swear to me that you will bring him back to us safely."

By the grace of the Creator, I swear I will return him to you unharmed or be destroyed myself protecting him.

She looked up at Isaac without taking her hand off the rune. "Is he powerful enough to do that?"

"He healed a bullet wound to the chest and shielded me from a grenade without a scratch." Isaac chuckled. "I think he can do as he said."

Satisfied, Becca leaned in for a deep, lingering kiss. Once it ended, she rested her head on Isaac's shoulder and the small family cuddled together peacefully.

Almighty Creator, please help me to keep my word.

Chapter 11

Isaac arrived at work the next evening with a mixture of excitement and nervousness. He'd never been to a fancy art gala, hence the excitement; and he'd never had to pretend to be a bodyguard, hence the nervousness. *Dani is right, Bel, I'm just a high-tech janitor. If Mr. Koine suspects, I could be putting Dani and Steve in danger.*

You've done a pretty good job protecting Mr. McGuiness, even as a 'high-tech janitor.' Bel's distaste for the slight was clear in his tone. *Besides, my family and I have had plenty of bodyguards. I can guide you.*

Somewhat relieved, Isaac went to Steve's office where Steve and Dani were already waiting for him. His nerves jumped back to eleven when he saw Steve dressed in a full tuxedo, complete with cummerbund, bow tie, and diamond cufflinks shaped like the Starship Enterprise, and Dani dressed in a sparkling black sequined sheath dress complete with a slit that nearly reached her hip, black stiletto heels, and a wide network of diamonds around her neck.

An image filled his head of a creature standing in front of a mirror with a long snout and thick tail, small ears and arms, thick brown fur on its front and scales down its back dressed in a bright blue cape intricately embroidered with yellow stars and studded with diamonds, a yellow jacket with a fur collar, and black pants. A wreath of round gems and stars made of Bel's familiar russet metal was on his head and a large brooch shaped like an eight pointed elongated star with diamonds filling some of its arms was pinned over his heart. A servant was placing filigreed caps on his long, painted claws. *Formal occasions are not new to me. We can handle this together.*

That's what you looked like before? Isaac held the memory and focused. Bel looked regal, even in clothes that looked absolutely strange to Isaac. He'd never seen him without the armor he wore as Tianyi, and the impression of a giant pangolin held true. His tapered face was sober, and his manner to the servant was polite as the servant finished and bowed seven times.

It was many lifetimes ago, but I haven't forgotten. Adapting to your culture should be easy enough.

"Isaac?" Steve's voice interrupted and chased the memory away. He stood in front of Isaac offering him a garment bag. "As soon as you change, we're ready to go."

Isaasc blinked. He'd completely forgotten that the others were in the room. "Uh. Right." He ducked into Steve's private bathroom to change out of his jeans and polo into the suit, tie, and sunglasses that seemed obligatory for a bodyguard. He looked at himself in the mirror and curled his lip. *No one's ever going to believe I'm a bodyguard, Bel. I'm pretty sure even on your planet you hired the biggest, meanest looking... Vistkians you could find. Not some scrawny lightweight.*

True, but presence is everything. Bel infused a sense of defiance, arrogance, and some unidentifiable fierceness into their connection. *Stand up straight, square your shoulders, lift your head, and scowl just enough to make it clear no one should mess with you or Mr. McGuiness. Make every movement deliberate, and every glance look like you're both aware and unimpressed with everything going on around you. And if someone even smiles wrong at Mr. McGuiness or Ms. Apryl, take a step forward and glare at them silently. If we have to actually step in to protect them, I'll back you up.*

The sudden boost of testosterone was thrilling, but not quite what Isaac was looking for. *Can you, like, I don't know, armor my chest and right arm so I look like I'm a threat at least?* Isaac raised an arm and glared at his skinny wrist in the mirror. *I can bluster all I want, but I'd rather they knew I could follow through.*

As you wish. Amusement followed as Bel's armor filled out his too-loose suitcoat and covered his right arm.

Isaac flexed his armored hand in the mirror and smiled. This might not be so hard after all. He practiced Bel's advice by trying to look intimidating in the mirror until he was concerned Steve and Dani would think he chickened out. *Let's give this a try.*

He took a deep breath and stepped back into the office. Bel boosted his attitude again, and he adjusted his posture to match. Dani and Steve had been talking, but fell silent to stare at him. *It's not just a show, Belenos and I* are *the most powerful bodyguard on the planet.*

"Dang, Isaac, even I'm afraid to mess with you." Steve grinned widely and didn't look even remotely scared. Isaac was beginning to be convinced he saw this as nothing more than one of his sci-fi movies. "Don't forget, we're not supposed to be truly in any danger. Your primary job is investigating his highrise for the stolen alien artifacts. We're just your ticket inside."

"Neither of you are going to listen if I repeat, once again, that Isaac is a janitor, none of us are *actually* superheroes, these bad guys have killed already, and that alien technology could be reprogramming Isaac's brain as we speak, are you?" Dani crossed her arms over her chest and glared, pretty much her familiar stance at this point.

Steve looked from her to Isaac, let his gaze travel down Isaac's armored arm, and looked back at her. "Nope. I'm pretty sure they *are* superheroes."

"And the fact that those guys *have* already killed is why we're doing this." Isaac kept his voice low and controlled, channeling the"deadly bodyguard vibe" Belenos had given him. He clenched his armored fist in front of him and mentally prompted Belenos to add spikes for emphasis. "I'm done with you insulting Bel, and he's done with you insulting me. We saved your life, and may well have to do it again before we're done tonight. So maybe be a little more grateful and a lot less critical."

Dani flushed red, opened her mouth to retort, looked from Isaac's hand to the deadly expression in his eyes, and thought better of it. "Let's get this show on the road, then."

Isaac played the dual role of driver and bodyguard, getting Steve's limo to the red carpet entrance to Olympus Art Galleries – a fourteen story highrise in the heart of the city. Isaac put the limo into park and tried not to gawk at the shimmering blue mirrored building as he rounded the car and opened the door for Dani and Steve. Practicing the aloof awareness Bel had recommended, he stiffly took Dani's hand and helped her to the carpet. He then stepped back and held the door for Steve, handed the keys to the limo to the valet and dropped in step behind the other two.

Pretending to scan for threats, he let his eyes trail over the rich decor on the ground floor. The blueprints Steve had been able to get from the county clerk marked this floor as a huge foyer and the public gallery. Even so, it was more ornate than anything Isaac had seen in his life. Pink marble flooring stretched from art covered wall to art covered wall. Bizarre mobiles and statues stood behind burgundy velvet ropes. He caught a glimpse of the price tag on a statue made of reclaimed bourbon bottles. Twice his current salary, adjusted for Belenos. And that was just the public showroom. His consternation must have crossed his connection to Belenos, because the alien replied, *The wealthy are strange on my world as well.*

You have no idea. Isaac joined Dani and Steve in a huge glass and gold elevator manned by a man dressed in a more expensive suit than he was wearing. He stood in the back, hands clasped behind his back and feet spread slightly, at the ready. *How are we going to know where to look?*

I've begun a preliminary scan of the building looking for anomalies or excessive radiation, as well as interplanetary signals your scientists might miss. As soon as we're free to slip away, I should be able to give you a more pointed analysis.

Good enough for me. They reached the penthouse floor, and the elevator operator let them out into an immaculately landscaped greenhouse, with paintings and statues displayed in garden beds or groves. People dressed in clothes Isaac had only seen in news reports of the Oscars milled around, while others dressed like Isaac and carrying gold plated trays of hors d'oeuvres and champagne mingled unnoticed.

Isaac hung back from Steve and Dani a step, aloof and alert, as they were greeted by a tall, broad-shouldered man with stylishly long gray hair and an easy smile on his face. He offered a white gloved hand to Steve and beamed at them.

"Steve! You finally decided to take me up on my offer. All this time I thought you preferred starships to Stingel. Do you have money to blow," He raked his eyes over Dani appreciatively, "or a lady to impress?"

"Anders, meet Ms. Dani Apryl, the most beautiful and intelligent woman I have ever met." Steve shook their host's hand eagerly, then put arm across Dani's shoulders.

"You know how prone Steve is to exaggeration." Dani scoffed as she offered a graceful hand to Mr. Koine. "I'm sure a man of your experience can set him straight."

Mr. Koine took her hand gently, bowed, and kissed the back of it. "As a man who takes pride in being surrounded by true beauty, I can assure you Steve is not exaggerating at all." He flicked a quick glance at Isaac that lingered only on his armored hand. "I can also assure you the bodyguard isn't necessary, Steve."

"Forgive me a touch of paranoia, Anders." Steve's voice was tight and low, and his face grimmer than characteristic for him. "I was kidnapped from my own facility less than forty-eight hours ago. I wouldn't go to the Vatican without a bodyguard."

Mr. Koine gave Isaac another, longer look, shrugged, and took Dani by the arm. "Have you seen works by Brea'n Thompson? I think you'd find them quite interesting."

Isaac followed for a while, until he became just another invisible servant, then melted into the crowd.

Where to, Bel?

Floor thirteen is listed on the blueprints, but not on the elevator.

That's not actually odd. People think the number thirteen is unlucky, so just skip the number when numbering the floors. They probably just called it 'Fourteen' and kept going.

No. There is an unnumbered thirteenth floor. Ultrasound reveals that it's not only occupied, but heavily secured.

Huh. Okay, then, if we can't take the elevator, how do we get there?

There seems to be a dedicated elevator from Mr. Koine's private office suites. Bel pushed directions to him. *I copied the signal from Mr. Koine's passkey. We should have no trouble getting in anywhere we need to with that.*

When you said you were the most powerful being in the universe you weren't joking, were you? Isaac watched in muted awe as the door to Mr. Koine's private office suites slid open.

You are impressed by the strangest things. Belenos laughed.

Isaac kept his head up, confidently behaving as if he had every right to be in the restricted area. The offices were opulent, spacious, and fortunately empty. He could always have Bel zap anyone who confronted him, but he'd rather not go around zapping innocent secretaries and janitors. They made it safely to the secret elevator with a combination of hubris, luck, and Mr. Koine's copied tag.

There are two guards on the other side of the door. Belenos warned as the elevator neared the bottom. *If you allow me to armor us, we'll be better prepared to take them down without risk of injuring either ourselves or them.*

Yeah, I'm pretty sure I'm not convincing them I belong down here at this point anyway. Isaac shrugged out of the jacket and suitcoat, wondered briefly if Steve would charge him for losing them, folded them gently, and laid them in the corner of the elevator. As soon as the visor covered his face, he could see the heat signatures of two guards in the hall beyond.

The door opened silently, and the guards turned. The nearest wasn't even halfway around when Isaac clamped a clawed hand onto his shoulder and Bel silently drained enough energy from the thug to drop him before he could cry out. The second saw them, though, and reached for a button on his uniform to signal for back up. They jumped the distance between them and crushed the device in an armored fist before he got a word out, then sent him to join his partner.

That's new. Isaac frowned at the fallen thugs and decided it was probably better than electrocuting them all the time. *Is there any more security we should worry about, either human or electronic?*

Figures Isaac didn't understand scrolled down the side of their visor. *Bel...*

Sorry. The door is wired to send out a signal if it is opened. I can disrupt the signal long enough for us to get inside and close the door behind us. There are no more humans on this floor.

Do it.

The door slid open silently to reveal a different kind of art gallery. This one was carpeted with plush burgundy carpet, with cherry wainscoting, and rose paint. Deep frames on the walls and ornately carved pedestals filled the room.

What is this stuff? Isaac stared at the artifacts, arranged on pedestals like pieces of fine art. *I mean, I know some of it is Steve's alien gear, but what is it?*

Even I can't answer for all of it, but the vast majority of it seems to be harmless junk. Bel drew their attention to a rectangle container with strange symbols on it. *That's military rations from Alpha Prime, for example.*

Still priceless—

But not world endangering. Bel overlaid a series of small diagrams on their visor display. *Several items are still missing, though. The ones that seemed most likely to be a threat.*

But we can pin the thefts to Koine?

Is possessing stolen goods a crime?

Yes.

I have taken several photographs if that will help your—

What? Isaac froze. Intense shock, anger, and fear flooded their connection. *Bel, what is it?*

Something triggered a countdown. An x-ray of one of the podiums appeared on their display. A digital timer and a series of cylinders were tightly packed inside. *Every one of them contains this and is wired to the timer.*

A bomb? Isaac's own fear spiked. There were at least twenty podiums here. If they were bombs, the whole building would go. Surely Koine wouldn't bomb his own building. *Nerve gas?*

I cannot say unless we access the compartments.

Will it trigger... whatever if I just tear into them?

Bel was silent for a moment. *Not if we're careful.*

Patch me in to Steve. Either way, this place needs to be evacuated. Isaac stabbed the sharp claws at the ends of his armored fingertips into the top front edge of the podium and pulled down, crumpling the thin veneer and exposing the device.

"Isaac?" Steve's voice was soft as if trying to not be overheard.

"We've got a problem." Isaac read from Bel's rolling readout as they prodded the various components. "I have twenty bombs wired to go off in nine and a half minutes. They look like they're linked in such a way that if we don't disarm every single one, the whole group goes off anyway."

Steve took a sharp breath. "Can you disarm them?"

Bel?

Yes. But nine and a half minutes may not be enough time.

"We're going to try. Can you get everyone out?"

"Consider it done." A shrill squeal filled the building and echoed over the watch communicator. The lights began to flash in sync with the pulsing noise. "Good luck, guys."

If they blow in the middle of the city, it could take down more than just this building. Isaac looked away from the descending timer and at one of the cylinders. *Please tell me it's at least not nuclear.*

It is not.

Do, uh, Vistkian general princes generally need to disarm bombs?

This would not be my first time. Bel shared amusement, calm, and confidence. *I will walk you through it.*

You know, if Koine actually cared about these people, he could come down here and disarm these himself. Or send his security to deal with us first. Isaac disconnected the wire Bel indicated. *Covering his butt doesn't need to mean killing hundreds of people.*

There are four hundred thirty-six people in the building. Mr. Koine is not one of them.

Ha. Of course not. He was probably notified as soon as the timer triggered and bailed.

No. Bel's response was soft and grim. *It was not an automated trigger. He triggered it himself.*

Seriously? He planned to kill all these people? That was one disarmed, only nineteen to go. *Can you, I don't know, hack his wifi and figure out why he'd do something like that?*

I can if you allow me to access it through your phone.

Sure, can you do that and walk me through this? Isaac chewed his lip as he disconnected another set. He wanted to make sure that Koine went down for trying to kill an entire building full of people, but actually saving those people was far more important.

I can, yes.

Let's get it done then.

Bel's presence felt spread thin, but the instructions kept coming, so Isaac kept working. Each one seemed easier and quicker. Still, he was only half done with four minutes to spare.

Bel, we're running out of time. Sweat beaded on Isaac's forehead as he moved to the next platform. *Is there any way we can speed this up?*

153

I have the files downloading, so I can disarm one beside you. Bel suited action to thought and extended a tendril from their armor to the adjacent podium, deactivating his in half the time it took Isaac.

Isaac let out a slow breath. Maybe they could handle this after all. *Three minutes now and seven to go.*

Civil authorities are arriving now. Bel seemed tired as he stretched to deactivate two at a time.

Patch me in to Steve again. We need to make sure the first responders know what we're dealing with. Four left.

Belenos didn't respond and the tendrils he'd been using to deactivate the bombs were still.

Bel? There was no answer and only deafening silence in his mind. "Belenos!" Their armor was still intact, but their connection wasn't. He hadn't realized how dependent he'd become on Belenos's sensors. Losing them made him feel as if he'd suddenly gone blind. He could barely see through the visor and had no idea how to open it. Panic spiked his heart as he tried to deactivate the final bombs half blind and from memory. He fumbled once and caught his breath. He was nearly out of time, and there were still two left. All that work. Desperation over Bel's absence was drowned out by a crippling sense of failure. He reached for the last bomb with a clawed hand just as the timer hit zero.

SONG OF THE STARS

Chapter 12

Belenos wasn't exactly sure what happened. One minute they were standing there, the next he'd blacked out. He'd never done that before, and this time nearly cost him his host's life. It had taken him seven weary hours to heal Isaac enough to dare wake him. Even still, his legs and pelvis were crushed. The rubble from the collapsed building weighed heavily on them. It was nearly all Belenos could do to keep his armor strong enough to keep them from being crushed to a pulp and synthesize enough oxygen for Isaac to breathe, taking on Isaac's pain as his own was a distraction he could ill afford, and a choice that toed the borders of what he could do without unintentionally deepening their bond. Still, the damage to Isaac's body was extensive, and largely his own fault for failing to protect him in the collapse. He would ease that pain as much as possible.

Then he nearly blacked out again. No wonder his host had not regained consciousness. The pain feedback was incredible, in spite of the fact that Belenos suspected Isaac's spinal cord was severed. He fought for consciousness, desperately aware that if he lost it they were both dead. He'd shield Isaac from the pain as long as he could, but survival came first.

"kzzt – Sitrep, Isaac, report, do you copy? – tzzk" A mangled transmission came through the channel Steve used to communicate with them.

Belenos prodded Isaac psychically. Telepathy didn't work over radio waves, but they needed someone to know they survived if they wanted to be rescued.

"kzzt – Collapse – search and rescue – where are you?—tzzk"

If they were fully bonded, Belenos could answer through Isaac. Heck, if they were fully bonded, Isaac would be fully healed by now and able to answer for himself. He'd been a fool to think they could take on this kind of mission without complete symbiosis. Isaac was not his brother; fear that he would be could very well cost them both dearly.

Alive. Damaged. He managed to signal with the code Isaac had insisted he learn. The series of clicks was tedious, but effective.

"kzzt – Belenos? Full report.—tzzk"

In code? Belenos wasn't about to risk using his limited energy stores to communicate in that tedious code. *Thirteenth Floor. Energy reserves low.*

"kzzt – Copy. Give us time.—tzzk"

Time was something they didn't have much of.

✳ ✳ ✳ ✳ ✳

Isaac woke up to absolute darkness, even the comforting glow of Bel's visor display was missing. He was laying flat on his face, his body twisted into an awkward position. He tried to push himself up, but could only manage to squirm in place

Bel, what happened? Where are we? Isaac tried to regulate his mental tone, even though he knew Belenos already sensed his rising panic.

The building collapsed. Bel sounded thready and strained in his head.

Isaac's panic spiked. "We're buried alive?" he squeaked. "You can get us out right?"

My sensors were damaged in the collapse. I have no idea how deeply we are buried. I have managed to alert Steve that we survived, and am sending a local signal on the emergency bandwidth to alert any search and rescue teams.

How long have we been down here? Something was wrong, maybe very wrong. The courage and determined confidence that had accompanied Bel's presence in his mind since they had bonded seemed, not missing exactly, but hollow and forced. *Are we in an air pocket?* He moved his arm, or rather tried to. It only shifted a couple millimeters.

Seven hours, at my best guess. And no, we are not.

Isaac squirmed again desperately. Becca had to be worried by now. *Seven hours... Wait. If there is no air pocket, how am I breathing? Am I going to starve to death?*

I can sustain your life indefinitely. Bel sent him a feeling of tired assurance, that held a hint of his normal fierce determination. *You will not die today.*

Why can't I move? He tried to wiggle his body systematically. His arms and hands seemed fine, other than stuck in place by the rubble. But his legs...

"I can't feel my legs! Bel! Why can't I feel my legs?" He was screaming now. Not that there was anyone to hear him.

We have sustained significant damage. Bel made it sound like an apology. *The continued pressure of the rubble requires me to divert significant resources to survival. Our superficial connection makes intricate repairs difficult. Further repairs to either of us will have to wait until after we are rescued.*

"But we – I – can be repaired, right?" Isaac felt sick and wondered what would happen if he threw up down here, inside Bel's armor, buried in a hole, unable to move. He swallowed back the nausea and willed himself not to cry.

Bel chuckled weakly. *Yes. Human body structure is much simpler than Vistkian biology. With the proper supplies, we both can be repaired.*

Isaac took a deep breath, one he still wasn't sure how he was able to take, and clenched his fists. *Be straight with me, Bel, what's wrong with us – both of us. I need to know.*

I... Do not think that is wise. I cannot offer emotional support through our bond and absorb the pain from your injuries at the same time.

It was very bad, and Isaac was about to lose it. Even if he did see his family again, he'd never be the same. Becca would have to quit school to take care of him. If they ever found him. He could be buried too deeply, never to be found, sustained for eternity by a stubborn alien symbiote with no sense of time or space.

If... If they don't come for us, I don't want to live like this. You said you could sustain my life indefinitely. I don't want that. Trapped. Paralyzed. Life moving on for those I love. Isaac hiccupped back a sob. *Maybe you can sustain my life indefinitely, but I want you to promise me that you won't. That you'll... ease my passing when hope is gone.*

Bel was silent, but his response was still strong. Sadness, disappointment, and more than a little sympathy crossed their bond.

After my brother banished me, I spent many of your years trapped in that prison pod. Trapped, paralyzed, and hopeless. Worse, our bond had taken root deep into our subconscious, and having that torn away nearly drove me mad. Your scientists' probing was the final straw. I wanted nothing more than to end my existence, to cease from suffering, and to eliminate any risk that I could be used again to create the monster my brother had turned out to be.

But then I remembered how I got this way. The sheer hopelessness that drove me to sacrifice my body for this form, my life for the lives of my people. As long as the Creator allows life to continue, there will always be hope, no matter how small the spark.

A shudder rippled through Isaac's body, but its origin was Bel's consciousness. Isaac wondered briefly at the new sensation, but decided there were far more important questions on the table, like the one Bel seemed to be avoiding.

Yes, I could do as you ask, more easily than you probably care to know. However, I will not take your life under any circumstances. It is not mine to take, no matter how dark things are. I will, if you request it, place your body in a deep hibernation so that you are no longer aware of our surroundings, but I will preserve your life as long as it is in my power to do so.

Tears trickled down Isaac's face and he bit his lip. It wasn't the answer he'd wanted, but he did find it oddly comforting that, even though Bel could likely turn off his nervous system with the same ease as flicking off a light switch, the symbiote valued his life enough not to do it.

That assurance did little to comfort him now, however. He still couldn't feel his legs, Bel still wouldn't tell him how bad things were, and they were still buried under who knows how much highrise rubble. He'd seen the news before, it could be weeks before they were rescued. He caught a breath as his mind teetered on the choice between panic or despair. Instead he just wept.

Please, Isaac, I need you to trust me. I can fix this, but I need us both to survive. I need your help to make sure that happens.

He swallowed back his sobs. *What do you need me to do?*

* * * * *

I need to complete our bond. Belenos tried to shield Isaac from his own feelings of terror as well as he could, but Isaac's blood pressure spiked and he was acutely aware he'd failed. His host didn't need his stress on top of his own.

What does that mean? Isn't our connection enough? Isaac started to panic again, but Belenos didn't dare divert his dwindling energy from pain management and armor integrity to calm him. Words would have to do.

I am a symbiote, which means that I draw strength from you just as I grant strength to you. Specifically, I can borrow from your body energy to power my systems.

Yes, you explained that.

With a partial bond, I am limited in how much I can draw from you, without harming you, just as you saw with that guard. He pushed the memory of them incapacitating the thug by a draining touch to Isaac's memory. *Under normal circumstances, I can draw from the sun, or another energy source. There is nothing here I can draw from.* He had tried to reach the energy sources that had supplied the building before its collapse, but couldn't reach anything without thinning his armor too much and placing Isaac at risk.

Isaac was silent, but his thoughts were anything but silent. Belenos could sense a swirling fear battling hope, desire, and indecision – all with the toothed, black, tendril monster lurking in the background. If Bel had his own breath to hold, he would have held it. If Isaac still harbored a fear of him being that *thing* in the back of his mind, it might be better if they both died here.

If you reject our bond, I will not force it. Either way, I will do everything in my power to preserve your life until we have the power necessary to heal you fully. Bel tried to keep his own need from the connection even as he scrambled to make an alternate plan. He had enough energy resources to convert their armor into an airtight cocoon, place Isaac in stasis, and repair the damage to his spine. After that – well, he wasn't entirely sure what would happen if he diverted resources from sustaining his own lifeforce. If he crippled his own armor to save his host, there might not be enough energy on earth to bring him back. *I swear by the Creator that you will return to your family either way.* Tianyi's atrocities rose up in his memory unbidden, racing across their connection unfiltered by Bel's strained resources. *I am a monster.*

He hadn't meant to think that last, much less to share it with his host, but it was done. He retreated from Isaac's mind to hide from his response as far as he dared, and prepared to fuse the scales that made up their armor.

"Belenos, stop!" Isaac's fear spiked to terror as he shouted into their armor. Bel's own plan pushed back to him across their connection, laced with a nauseating blend of Isaac's pain, Belenos's rejection, and both their fear.

Belenos winced. He hadn't meant to share that either. *It is not right for you to be forced into this choice. I will heal you regardless of your decision.*

And it's not right for you to take the burden alone without telling me the cost to you. Was Isaac *angry* with him? *You are not Timir and we are not Tianyi.*

It is my burden to take. I created Tianyi. I am not what you fear, but I should be feared.

I. Don't. Fear. You. Isaac thought to him slowly and with emphasis. *I'd be lying if I said I wasn't afraid of what an eternity as a symbiotic superhero requires, but I don't fear you or us.*

Confidence and decision pushed over their connection and Isaac relaxed. *I trust you, Belenos. I choose bonding. Do what you need to do.*

Tianyi's abuses had nearly destroyed Belenos, much less his hope of finding a suitable host to replace him. Isaac was offering him life, he could ill afford to refuse him in spite of his own lingering fears.

We are not Tianyi. I choose to trust us. Creator help them, he was decided. *It's going to hurt. My energy is stretched too thin to minimize the pain.* Belenos wasn't sure that he could do it without diverting some of his energy from pain management altogether, but also he wasn't sure the bonding process would take if his host passed out from the compounding pain.

There is a ritual, a vow of sorts. You'll need to repeat after me. Faith, Honor, Justice, Protection, Peace, Family, Duty. Belenos intoned the words soberly, then repeated them in his native language. Perhaps this host would actually honor the words of the ritual.

"Faith, Honor, Justice, Protection, Peace, Family, Duty," Isaac echoed, then stumbled through the Vistkian pronunciations with Belenos's aid.

Belenos felt Isaac brace himself even as he himself tried to absorb as much of his host's pain as he could. Still, after healing much of the damage, and taking much of what was left, Belenos felt sick and distracted with pain. *Creator, allow our deeper bond to enable me to heal him fully.* He worked swiftly, his familiarity with his host's body guiding him as he threaded a thin tendril close to Isaac's brainstem. Isaac stiffened and whimpered a bit at the pain, but held his consciousness. The difference was instantaneous, but not as drastic as Belenos had expected. Their connection had grown so strong in the last few days, bridging the gap seemed minor. The oneness of mind and body was comforting, as well as urgent. The most crucial difference was that he could now sense Isaac's body – and all the injuries to it – like a map, down to the individual nerves severed in his spinal column. Thank the Creator, he could heal them now. His relief calmed the spike in Isaac's anxiety from the bonding process.

I can heal you now, but it will be slow, and likely painful. Especially since he could work faster if he could divert some of his waning energy away from pain management. *I would like to place you in hibernation until you are fully healed.*

Isaac's own relief grew. *But you* can *heal me?*

As if this had never happened. He might even be able to figure out a way to get them out after he didn't have to focus so much on his host's health.

I... heard that, Belenos. How bad is my health? Isaac asked without fear.

Belenos consciously ran a scan of his host's injuries and passed them to him, healing some of the more minor injuries as he did.

Isaac cringed as the scan reached his severed spinal cord. *Enough, Bel. Put me out. I trust you. Just take care of me.*

Good night, Isaac. Belenos triggered a deep sleep, started a playback of The Song of Polaris, a song of praise for the Creator's creation, and immediately went to work reconstructing his host's body.

✳ ✳ ✳ ✳ ✳

Isaac woke again gently, tired but no longer in pain. He could feel the difference in his and Belenos's bond, a closeness he couldn't feel before. They were tired, and given what Belenos had said about lack of energy resources he wasn't sure that was a good thing.

We can contact Steve, now. Belenos seemed pleased with himself anyway. *I have managed some repairs on our armor and believe we can make a radio call, then sustain a homing signal for the foreseeable future.*

How long was I out? The answer flashed back with a thought. The repairs had been intricate and time consuming. Eighteen more hours had passed. Becca was going to flip.

They flexed their toes just to confirm the repairs had worked. Their relief was profoundly encouraging. If they could come back from that, they could do anything. *Let's make that call.*

"Belenos?" Steve's voice rang clear in their helmet.

"Steve? It's Isaac."

"Thank God, Isaac." His voice called out away from the speaker, "It's Isaac! He's alive!" Muffled cheers sounded in the speaker. "We were worried sick. Your wife has called every hour since the building collapsed. I think she's somewhere outside the perimeter the rescue crew set up." Steve sobered. "It's been nearly two days. The crews were getting ready to call it a recovery effort instead of rescue."

"How many are dead?" Anger flared in Isaac's chest at the thought that Koine had tried to sacrifice his own employees to protect himself.

"Far fewer than would have been, thanks to you and Belenos." Muffled talking interrupted them for a moment. "Isaac, your wife wants you."

"Isaac!" Becca's voice caught with a sob. "When Steve couldn't get ahold of you and Belenos, I came right down. I was so scared."

"We're fine, we made all the necessary repairs and we'll be safe until Steve's crew can get us out." They were running out of energy quickly and needed to cut this short. "I love you, Bec. I just need to get some details straightened out with Steve."

"How are you really?" Steve's voice was low as if trying to keep from being overheard. "When I, er, spoke with Belenos, he said you were 'damaged' and low on energy. He could barely maintain a signal long enough to message that to me and now..."

"It's a long story, and even though Belenos tells me he can maintain us forever, I get the distinct impression it gets pretty miserable for us both after a couple hours." Isaac felt Belenos protest. *Sorry, you can't hide things from me anymore. How long do we have before things get uncomfortable?*

Four hours until I have to start prioritizing resources. Ten at the most before I have to place us both in hibernation.

"How long?" Steve asked grimly.

"Ten hours, max. We can give you a signal for you to track until then." Isaac didn't relish the idea of being placed in hibernation again, but he found that it didn't spark anxiety any more. Whether that was Belenos' influence in his mind, or simply the fact that he had no doubt that if Belenos could repair his broken body, he could certainly sustain it, didn't matter. He was more calm than he'd been since the explosion.

"What happens after that?" Steve's voice was low and worried.

Bel?

Between four and ten hours, sunlight and food will be enough. After that, we'll need a stronger source of power.

Isaac repeated that back for Steve, then yawned. "And Steve, we were in the thirteenth floor, east corner, when the building came down, in case our signal dies. Make sure they do what they can for any other missing people first."

There was a pause while Steve passed that information on to someone in the background.

"You guys are under the worst of the rubble and our scans didn't show an air pocket in that area." Steve grunted. "I'm not sure how you've survived this long, but you two better not die on me now."

"Not planning on it." Isaac yawned again as they cut off the signal. *I'm tired, Bel.* His stomach growled. *Tired and hungry.*

I know. Sleeping will help conserve energy, but I can't do anything about your hunger. Belenos was apologetic and exhausted.

Wake me if the crew gets here. Isaac felt himself nodding off and knew simultaneously that he wasn't waking up on his own and that he trusted Belenos explicitly to wake him when it was safe.

Chapter 13

Isaac woke with a gasp. He sat up sharply and scanned the room wildly as he tried to get his bearings. They were at SentryTech, on a medical table in one of the labs. One of Dani's techs was gathering electrodes, while another was attaching different ones to his bare chest and scalp. He touched the rune in the center of their stasis necklace and sought Belenos's presence, part of him fearing the symbiote had sacrificed himself to save him after all. Bel was there, but different now. He'd been too tired to recognize it immediately after the bonding, but it was as if Bel's presence had blurred with his, barely separate and only distinguishable from his own thoughts when he focused. *We made it.*

We did. Praise the Creator. Relief, gratitude, and strength filled them, so different to their feelings in the rubble only hours before.

How long has it been?

"Thank God, Isaac!" Steve lay a hand on his shoulder and squeezed. "I'd nearly started calling in your insurance policy. When we pulled you out of there, you were unresponsive, not even the EMS defibrillators did the trick. You drained their power packs without reacting. Dani suggested we bring you here to revive you, but getting the authorities to agree to that was a red tape nightmare. Even then we nearly brought down the city's power grid and Dani was starting to research what it would take to tear you out of the armor by force."

Isaac remembered Bel's backup plan and shuddered. "What day is it? When can I see Becca?" He swung his legs over the edge of the table and nearly cried to feel them move easily. Bel's presence steadied him, but Isaac wondered at his silence. They were awake, but not out of danger. The electricity they'd absorbed crackled through them as Bel silently repaired lingering damage to both Isaac's body and their armor systems.

"It's been four days since the gala. Becca and Aster have been sleeping in my office since we brought you here." Steve lowered his voice. "Dani's techs didn't find any vital signs when we brought you in, which understandably frightened her, so Dani recounted the last time Belenos killed you to comfort her. I think it worked? She agreed to try to get some rest after that anyway."

"I did not kill him, not then, not now." Belenos's words came from Isaac's mouth, his voice Isaac's own, but his inflection and accent unfamiliar.

Isaac and Steve both froze and looked at each other in shock.

Sorry. Belenos sighed audibly in his head. *This will take some adjusting to.*

No kidding. Isaac snorted a laugh. *Saves on translating, though.*

"That was... new." Steve looked at Isaac with wide eyes. "What just... Was that Belenos?"

"Yes." Isaac drew the word out slowly. "You know how Bel and I agreed to a temporary superficial connection? The explosion took us off guard and we were both pretty injured. In order for Belenos to heal me, we had to complete the total symbiotic bonding ritual."

"Fine. Great. And in English?"

"Uhh, we are Gemini?" Isaac sighed. If he couldn't explain this to his alien tech savvy boss, how was Becca going to take this? "It's no longer as simple as me wearing Bel. The armor – and Belenos's consciousness – are part of me. If we separate now, it could kill both of us."

"Wow. This is a game changer." Steve was firing off texts and only casting sparing wide-eyed glances at them. "Dani is going to have to run some tests, obviously. How does this affect your skill set? Wait..." Steve's eyes narrowed. "Belenos healed you when you were shot in the chest without a total symbiotic bond. What kind of injuries are we talking about?"

"A lot, Steve." Isaac rubbed the bridge of his nose wearily. "Is there any way I can see my wife first? Then I promise that we'll answer all your questions and submit to whatever tests you and Dani like."

"Right. Sorry." Steve blushed and looked up from the phone. "I'll get her myself. Take all the time you need."

Why did it take so much to wake us? Isaac asked as Steve closed the door.

It took them fifteen more hours to find us after I put you in hibernation. I kept my systems operational until there was no more risk of the weight of the building affecting armor integrity. It was a costly calculation, but we were able to absorb all we need to complete repairs and to maintain both biological and armor function until Mr. McGuiness and Ms. Apryl get tired of using us as test subjects.

We're not going home tonight, are we? Isaac sighed.

Perhaps not for several nights. I get the impression that 'sapient suit of armor' was easier for them to accept than 'biomechanical symbiosis with psychic synergy.'

When you put it that way, I barely understand it, and I agreed to it. Maybe I'll just have you answer all their questions, since that's actually an option now. He picked off the electrodes that the techs had left. He'd probably have to get used to them over the next few days, but for now he just wanted to hold his wife without them in the way.

The door opened slowly and Becca stepped tentatively into the room. She was alone, and Isaac was both relieved and disappointed. As much as he wanted to see his daughter, this conversation would be way easier if his focus wasn't divided.

"Isaac!" As soon as she saw him sitting up and alert, she slammed the door behind her, dashed across the room, and threw her arms around his neck. He lifted her up onto the medical exam table so she was sitting halfway in his lap.

He held her closely as she sobbed into his shoulder, raking his fingers through her braids and enjoying the familiar smell of her shampoo. There'd been a serious moment where he hadn't been sure he'd ever be able to do this again. *Thank you, Bel. You saved my life.*

Bonding literally saved mine, so we are quite even.

"I thought I'd lost you." Becca stopped weeping and rested her head on his shoulder, but didn't let go. "Mr. McGuiness never doubted, even when the fire chief told him it was impossible you survived. He just told them his bodyguard was wearing a highly experimental suit of armor and to keep looking. When they pulled you out, the armor was so battered and deformed, and neither you nor Bel responded. Even all of SentryTech's high tech equipment couldn't find your heartbeat. All I could think about was how I wasn't ready to be alone, and how much I hated Belenos for taking you from me."

Isaac opened his mouth to defend Bel, but Becca laid her hand on his lips and kept going. "Then Dani – Ms. Apryl – told me all the stories about how Belenos had saved your life when it looked grim. How by all the science she knew, you should have been dead twice already. And how, if Belenos could bring you back from those he could bring you back from anything."

"Huh." Isaac frowned slightly. He'd thought Dani disliked both him and Bel.

"Thank You, Belenos, for keeping your word and bringing my husband back to me." Becca laid her hand on the rune as she'd done before when she spoke to Belenos.

Isaac gasped as everything about her flooded their connection at her touch, from her feelings of gratitude and fear, down to a flood of biological data like heart rate and blood pressure.

Sorry. I normally just pushed the relevant data across our connection. Belenos hurried to mute the overwhelming sensory data.

"Wait." Isaac took Becca's hand and held it to the rune again. *Show me again, slower. I... I thought I saw something important.*

"Isaac? What's going on?" Fear spiked in Becca's voice and through their connection as her heart rate and blood pressure rose.

What do those numbers mean, Bel?

Bel's amusement confirmed his suspicions just as if he'd spoken. *Congratulations.*

Isaac grabbed his wife by the shoulders and pressed his lips to hers enthusiastically. She murmured a confused protest at first, then relaxed into his arms and deepened the kiss.

"Mmm. I'm glad to see you, too." She pulled back and toyed with his top button. "But maybe this should wait until you get home." Her coy smile turned into a frown. "You *are* coming home, aren't you?"

Isaac blew a slow breath through pursed lips. "Not tonight." He shifted to set her on the exam table beside him and took both her hands in his. "We need to talk about a few things. The last mission didn't go exactly as planned."

"Really? Because I thought you and Belenos planned to cave an entire high rise in on yourselves." Becca gave him a wilting look, then a critical gaze. "You're really okay, though, not just trying to keep me from worrying?"

His deeper bond with Belenos gave him an almost surreal awareness of his own body and lingering injuries. "We'll be completely healed in a few hours. Belenos kept his promise, Becca." He looked away. "I was injured in the explosion, Bel was damaged, and we couldn't reach any resources to recharge. He... was willing to sacrifice himself for me." He fingered the pulsing rune on their stasis necklace. Loyalty and fierce devotion filled him, blending both his and Bel's aura. "I didn't let him, but it cost me something." He caught his lip in his teeth and felt Bel raise a prayer that Becca would accept their bond.

Becca took a deep breath and tightened her grip on his hands, but didn't interrupt.

"He's part of me now. I don't know how to explain it, other than that the borders between him and me in my head are blurred. We're... Us now. Before, the armor was Bel and I was me. I could take it off, but, well, you saw what happened. Now the armor and Bel are part of me, and the consequences of taking off the armor are far worse."

"What does 'far worse' mean?" Becca's voice was small and tremulous, and her grip tight enough it would have hurt if they hadn't been actively moderating the pain.

"Bel's last host was a dictator that would have made Stalin proud. When Belenos was forced to sever their bond to keep him from killing more people, his host was crippled and driven mad. Humans are more vulnerable than Vistkians." Isaac took a deep breath, thankful for Bel's subtle help explaining the mechanics of their bond, but hyper aware of the need to make sure the words were his. Becca needed to see that Bel wasn't controlling him. "I'm only a janitor, Bec, not an alien warlord. It would probably just kill me."

She pulled her hands free and turned away, hugging her arms to her chest. Her back rose and fell with rapid breaths, but she made no other sound or movement.

"One of us would have died otherwise." Isaac laid a hand on her back. "I'm not saying it isn't weird, because it is. I get it. I'm still me, that hasn't changed."

"Can I speak to him?" She shook off his hand and turned to him with a fierce expression. "Like before. I want to talk to him."

"Well, I mean, you could just ask him a question and he could answer through me..." Isaac trailed off as Bel sent him a clear sense of warning.

"Stop it, Isaac, I'm barely holding it together as it is." Becca's voice rose a note. "I want to talk to him just like I did last time."

"Right." Isaac cleared his throat and held his hands open at his sides.

Becca pushed her hand against the rune roughly enough to knock him off balance. He caught himself with his hands behind him on the exam table.

Belenos? You promised you could protect him. She closed her eyes and her lips didn't move, but Isaac could hear her as clearly as if she was speaking out loud. *You failed and he nearly died. Now... Is he even the same man I married? Or is he just you in his body?*

Isaac opened his mouth to protest indignantly, but Bel stopped him with a firmer warning. *If you don't let me handle this, she will never have the answers she needs.*

Your husband's personality and will are his own. Bel directed his answer to her. *We did not anticipate Koine destroying his own building or wielding a weapon that could disrupt my powers.* He pushed the memory of the two options they faced to her. *I would have healed him either way. This was the decision he made.*

You could control him, though, couldn't you? Like a walking puppet, or... or... being possessed. Tears streamed down Becca's cheeks from her closed eyes. *How can I ever be sure he's him?*

I have kept my word to you. I would have sacrificed my life to protect Isaac. Bel's tone was gentle and soothing, even though he struggled with her use of the term "possessed." *You love and respect him. As do I. Too much to subvert his will or destroy his personality. I chose him for who he is, and I swear by my hope of an eternal heaven I will not change who he is.*

She nodded slowly. *On a more personal note, when we're... you know... can you take a nap or something? Anything to give us some space?*

I will do my best to make my presence as subtle as possible. Belenos agreed solemnly, but kicked amusement back to Isaac. *Stars, you two are different from my brother. He always insisted on rubbing his lovemaking in my face.*

Your brother was a disgusting person.

Yes. Thank the Creator, I am far better off with you.

Becca let her hand slide down until it rested on Isaac's bare chest and cuddled against his shoulder with a sigh. "When will you be home? Aster misses you and I'm not sure how much longer I can keep your secret from Mom and Dad."

"We don't know. Steve and Dani are going to want to run tests to see what the effects of our new bond are, and we have to stop Koine before he hurts anyone else." Isaac slipped his arm around her waist and held her closer. "We can try to convince them that we need to come home for dinner most evenings if we want to keep up our cover, but we're going to have to tell Frank and Alice something sooner rather than later. Even if it's just the basics of 'I'm helping test a new super suit for SentryTech.'"

"Mom and Dad won't be thrilled, obviously, but I think they already suspect that something else is going on than just a promotion." Becca shrugged. "It was hard enough explaining why Mr. McGuiness would take you to the gala."

"Eventually, I'd like for them to more or less know everything, but let's take it slow." Isaac moved his hand to her belly. "Also, uh, hey. Now that Bel and I are bonded, I can read anyone who touches the necklace. You might want to take a pregnancy test."

"Seriously?" Becca sat up and looked at him wide-eyed. "Aster's not even a year old yet! How are we going to manage another child with me finishing school and you being a superhero?"

Isaac lifted her chin and gently kissed her again. "We've got this, Bec. Between Bel and your parents, we've got the best support system in the universe."

"I know, and I am happy. At least, I will be. It's just a lot all at once." Becca sighed, pulled away, and stood. "Come home as soon as you can. We'll figure it out together."

That went better than I expected. Isaac watched her leave with a sense of relief. He stood up and stretched. *Dani and Steve will be here soon to run tests. Is there anything else I should tell them? What else can we do now?*

Everything we did before, just without the delay of needing to communicate with each other. If you want to activate the armor, for example, you just do it. It's as much a part of you as your own hand.

"Huh. That's cool." Isaac played with activating the armor and forming it into different shapes at a whim.

We can also locate Koine and the rest of the alien artifacts.

Wait, really? Isaac deactivated the armor as he remembered the downloads Bel was working on as they were disarming the bombs. A stream of data scrolled over his field of vision. *Uh, Bel, I'm not wearing the visor. How am I seeing this?*

Our bond gives me direct access to your sensory processing. He drew Isaac's attention to a shipping manifest. *The artifacts were sent here.* The image changed to a map location and a satellite image. *It appears to be one of six homes Koine owns.*

The door opened and Dani entered with a team of techs.

I guess we'll get to that after the testing is over.

Chapter 14

After sitting for nearly twelve hours of testing, that only served to confirm scientifically what Isaac and Bel were already telling Dani and Steve, they managed to convince their friends that they were ready to follow up on the information Bel had downloaded from Koine's computers. Steve gave Dani an additional twelve hours to sift through the data Belenos had collected before he'd gotten disconnected, then he was turning everything over to the cops, including Bel's video and audio logs leading up to the explosion.

That meant Isaac and Bel had twelve hours to locate and secure the stolen alien artifacts before the police got involved and all that potentially dangerous tech got hustled to some less than secure facility for the next super criminal to find. Four hours to airdrop from one of Steve's private jets left them with eight hours to locate the artifacts, secure them, and secure Koine and his staff if necessary.

A quick phone call on the way to the airfield was all the explanation Becca got, along with a profuse apology for the short notice and the promise to make it up to everyone eventually. The jet ride was quick and uneventful, air dropping from the plane was awesome, and Koine's compound was easy to find. At least to this point things were going their way. Koine's sprawling mid-century ranch wasn't huge, but the iconic architecture and detailed stone work hinted at a cost far more than its size suggested.

I hope he doesn't blow this one up, too. Isaac stepped pensively into the recessed porch and checked the running readout on their visor. Belenos seemed distracted. *What is it?*

The list of artifacts still missing flashed across his field of vision. *Many artifacts are still missing.* Belenos was uncharacteristically anxious. *We take unnecessary risks if we don't know what we're up against.*

Is there an alien weapon we can't stand against? Isaac was mostly teasing, still, maybe it was best they did a little more recon. This style of house was known for its excessive number of plate glass windows.

Belenos sighed, his blackout at the high rise at the forefront of his mind.

We don't know that was a super weapon, Isaac reasoned. Goodness, he hoped that wasn't a super weapon. Something that could just turn Belenos off like that could kill them in a heartbeat. *We had a fourteen story building dropped on us. You can be excused for a little malfunction.*

I do not malfunction. Belenos wasn't indignant, offended or boastful. If anything the statement conveyed even more worry.

Recon it is then. How many guards?

The visor viewscreen faded to infrared, revealing three forms on the other side of the breeze blocks. *If we can get to them without being seen, we can take them out easily.*

Isaac pointed at the flood light illuminating the backyard and fired a small projectile into the bulb. A couple of voices cried out. Guards probably. Their sensors indicated there were only half a dozen people on the grounds, including the three in the yard, but they had to assume they were all armed, possibly with weapons like the microwave gun Koine's thug had tried to use on Dani.

They're wearing armor as well. None of it matches, but I do recognize a mix of Centaurian infantry armor and Corellian insurrection suppression gear. Neither conducts electricity.

So you're telling me the gear has to come off before we can knock them out?

Just enough to allow our armor to contact their skin.

We really need another trick, Bel. They vaulted the ten-foot breeze block wall easily and landed on the other side with a dull thud behind two of the men. Bel's familiarity with the armor allowed them to slash the coupling that held the man's arm guards in place, slice through the American made synthetic bodysuit underneath, and grab them each by the forearm. A carefully controlled burst of electricity sent them both to the grass. *Knock-out darts, or sleep gas, or something.*

If Dani helps supply the needed ingredients, we can do anything you request. Memories of Tianyi wielding weapons with destructive capabilities Isaac had never imagined flashed into their mind and were swept away quickly with a shudder that actually shook their body. *I would welcome the chance to create a non-lethal offensive arsenal.*

The ground rumbled as if a train was approaching.

Nova. A very large figure stomped into the field of their infrared sensors.

Is that a mech? Isaac froze in awe. The robot was at least twenty feet tall, made of bright, polished blue metal, and roughly built like a professional wrestler. Its hands were shaped more like pincers and it had a cannon of some kind on each shoulder. *Steve will be so jealous.*

Let's try to survive long enough to tell him. Bel subtly shifted the composition of their armor to allow greater protection as they took a defensive stance. *There is a person inside the chest, and the CPU seems to be housed in the stomach.*

Interplanetary or terran? Isaac snorted at his familiar use of a term he wouldn't have even known a week ago. *If that thing was made on earth, we should be able to take it easily.*

Interplanetary, by my best guess. Possibly Andromedan. They flexed a clawed right hand, sharpened to an atomic cutting edge. *There's only one way to tell if we can take it.*

Right. It's not like we're keeping this fight secret anyway. They leaped at the mech, aiming their claws for the belly.

The mech swiped at them with a spinning pincer, sending them flying into a tree trunk so hard the tree snapped in half where they struck.

They landed at the base of the tree on their knees and elbows, gasping for breath. Even with their armor, the impact still knocked the wind out of them. *That wasn't supposed to hurt, Bel.*

We have sustained some minimal damage. Bel synthesized extra oxygen to help them breathe easier. *The positive side is that we now know the mech's composition.*

Isaac looked at the readout on their visor and sighed as he pushed himself to his feet and braced for the next attack. Their bond meant he understood it, it didn't make him like what it said. Their claws were only going to scratch the metal – some alien composite not even Belenos had heard of – and channeling all their remaining energy into an electrical charge would be about as effective as zapping a tractor tire. *Can we use heat energy to burn out the pilot? Find a gap in the access panel?*

The mech's twin shoulder mounted cannons glowed a blinding white as Isaac braced for the impact. *Is there a limit to how much we can take before we cook ourselves?*

As long as we are fully functional, I can redirect anything less than the heat of an actual star. Both blasts hit them with enough force to drive them back against the broken tree trunk, but they remained upright and aimed a short burst at each cannon. Both cannons exploded and the mech staggered back. The rest of the blast they aimed at the control panel in the stomach, but the mech lumbered aside enough that the blast just tore a deep scar into the sapphire side.

Well, it's not indestructible, anyway. Isaac rolled away as the mech stabbed its closed pincer into the ground where he had been standing. *What next?*

If we find a source of power, we can superheat our sword to cut through the metal.

As you wish. Isaac jumped toward the overhead power lines, intending to use them to supercharge their armor for the fight. With a whir, the mecha spun around at the waist and clamped a pincer around their chest. Their hand closed over the power line and they hung suspended between the power line and the mech by one hand. Quickly, they formed a sword in their other hand, slashed through the line, and held the exposed line to their armor just as the mech yanked them away. Superheating the sword blade with the energy they absorbed from the power line, Isaac twisted his body to take a swipe at the mech's head.

The mech caught their sword arm mid-swing, twisted and pulled, tearing both their armor and arm off at the shoulder, and throwing it aside. Isaac and Bell both screamed as pain and terror flooded over them. Bel recovered first, and automatically went to work sealing both the armor and the wound and shutting down Isaac's pain response. His grim determination took the edge off Isaac's fear, but the arm was still gone. Broken was different than gone.

I...How did this happen? Isaac whimpered. He tried to flex the fingers of the missing hand, but was greeted only by empty space. Panic bubbled up in spite of Bel's steady personality. *You can fix it, right? Please tell me you can fix this.*

I can. But we have to survive this battle and retrieve the severed limb quickly. Red numbers flashed across their visor readout. The mech was tightening its pincers around their chest. Bel's voice lowered to a prayer. *Creator help us, we must end this now. I do not believe I can reattach a severed torso.*

Isaac took a shaky breath, called the sword up with his remaining hand, and brought it down on the mech's arm in one super-fast motion. They fell to the ground in a crouch at the mecha's feet and channeled all the energy they could spare into superheating the sword as they thrust it upward into the belly of the mech. The sword burned a watermelon-sized hole into the control center of the mech, freezing it in its tracks. Isaac stood and took a step back, sword still raised warily as he watched to make sure the mech was no longer a threat. When it didn't move, and the human pilot made no effort to exit the mech and attack, they recalled their sword.

I'm going after the arm, Bel. Cover us if the pilot decides to be a threat. Isaac felt weak and sick to his stomach. They'd nearly expended all the energy they'd absorbed from the power line, and shock was starting to set in. They grabbed the loose hanging wire again and held the bare end for a long minute, then sprinted after the arm that lay at the border of the property, a solid twenty yards away. *Spiteful jerk.*

The 'spiteful jerk' just abandoned the mech and ran off as soon as our back was turned. Bel made a sound that reminded Isaac of a dog growling. *Not nearly as brave without his mech.*

Don't fault him, Bel. I'm not nearly so brave without you. Isaac scooped up the arm and breathed a sigh of relief, while simultaneously avoiding looking too hard at the bloodied stump. They sat down against the breeze block wall and laid the arm in their lap. *What now?*

This would be easier if I dared put you in hibernation like before, but the risk of a secondary attack is too great. The scales of their armor folded around the arm. *This is a very intricate surgery and will take several hours. Perhaps it is best if we call Mr. McGuiness for an extraction?*

We don't have time for an extraction. There's less than seven hours before we have to be clear of the property. Would you trust Vistkian civil authorities with this stuff? Isaac leaned his head back and closed his eyes. This was going to be fun to explain when he got home. *Bel... You said that you didn't think you could reattach a severed torso. What happens to you if I die?*

Bel was silent for a long moment as the bump in the armor that was their arm shifted into position. *I would most likely die, also. This is not something I have experienced or have any desire to experience.*

You were damaged this time. I felt it. It was more than just our shared pain, our armor being torn hurt you. Isaac trailed off, not certain if he wanted to finish his next question. He'd thought Belenos was invincible. Sure, he'd said something about damage and stuff when they were buried in the explosion, but it hadn't really seemed to affect him that Isaac had noticed. They weren't invincible, and Isaac felt like the Grim Reaper had slapped him across the face. *How much damage can you take before you... die?* Whatever dying meant to an alien soul housed in a suit of armor.

Pain burned across the stump of their severed shoulder. Isaac sucked a sharp breath between his teeth, and subconsciously willed the nerves to stop firing. They did, and the level of control Bel gave them over his body both amazed and frightened him.

I... do not know. Bel sighed. *I can repair nearly any damage given the proper resources. My consciousness is housed in the center panel of the stasis necklace. If that were destroyed, I presume I would cease to exist.*

Isaac fingered the pulsing rune in their chest. *Would I also cease to exist?*

The pain in their healing arm increased, and Isaac realized his questions were distracting Bel from his efforts. Bel's consciousness seemed distressed and one of his star songs started to hum in the background of their mind. Isaac didn't want to push him to answer, but Bel's growing anxiety affected him greater than he had anticipated. He swallowed back his terror and prodded. *Since we're fully bonded, our fates are bound aren't they?*

I swore by the Creator that I would preserve your life even at the expense of my own. By His aid, I will keep that vow. The pain dulled and the sense of distress calmed. *I served as Tianyi for nearly a century and through twelve interplanetary wars without losing my host. There is no reason to fear that would be different now.*

That's not an answer, Bel.

I'm afraid it's the only one I have. I've never died before, either. The alien's amusement seemed forced.

What... what do you think happens after death? Isaac was almost embarrassed to ask, but if Bel was inside his head, he already knew how screwed up his relationship with God was.

Our scientists tell us there is an essential part of us that transcends our bodies. My existence is evidence of that. Our prophets tell us that the faithful will join the Creator in the highest heavens. My hope for that is all that kept me through the dark times where I served Tianyi, and the darker times where I was separated from him. Curiosity brushed over Isaac's mind. *Surely your prophets and scientists teach the same?*

Some of them, but more teach us that this life is all we have.

If that is the case, how do you find hope when life is less than you desired? Bel's pity was palpable.

Many do not. Isaac recalled his debates with his professor, and the day hope died inside him. That was when he'd dropped out. Becca had never condemned him, but they'd really never discussed his loss of faith, either.

I am sorry. If I could share my faith with you, I would. There was no condemnation in Bel's tone either. *Every man must choose to follow the Savior promised in the stars on his own. It is not something I can choose for you.*

I still don't quite understand how you learned about Christ from the stars. Isaac shook his head in amusement and amazement. *Or how you continued to trust Him after all you went through with your brother.*

And I cannot understand the gracious hand of the Creator that allowed me to be banished to the world He was born to. Bel's tone was amazed, but much less amused. *Or how your whole planet does not follow the Savior you call Christ.*

The shoulder reconstruction froze and their attention was suddenly directed back to the house. Three more men rounded the corner of the building, walking toward them cautiously with bizarre looking weapons drawn, two of which Bel identified as coming from Steve's collection. Which they hadn't even flagged as weapons at all, much less identified what kind of weapon they were.

How's the shoulder coming? Isaac tensed, but didn't move. If those were regular guns, they could take them with one hand. They clearly weren't regular guns.

Slowly. I suggest we surrender.

Chapter 15

What? Isaac started and the three armed guards froze and aimed their weapons at them.

Koine clearly wants me. We have a considerably higher chance of survival if we follow along until I can rebuild our shoulder. We may also be able to locate the rest of the artifacts. A shudder of fear threaded through them. *Please, Isaac. It is hard enough for me to divide my focus to heal you while you're conscious. We cannot afford another battle at this time.*

Fine. Isaac raised his good arm above his head and shouted to the approaching men, "We surrender." He lowered his helmet. "We defeated your mech guard, but sustained serious injuries. Besides, we're here to see Koine. Tell him Steve McGuiness's bodyguard is here. I might know something about the artifact he's looking for."

The men paused, guns still trained on them, as one spoke into his watch. He nodded to his partner and gestured for Isaac to stand. "Koine's been looking for the artifact for a long time. Remove the armor, and follow us."

Isaac recalled the armor to cover only his chest and right arm. "The armor is repairing my injuries. This is the best I can do. Your mech ripped my arm off."

The guard gave him a look that was a combination of skeptical and impressed. "Whatever. We have uranium hand cannons. Try anything and you're dead."

"That... sounds horrible." Isaac awkwardly pushed himself to his feet, struggling to get off the ground with only one arm. He finally managed and fell in step between the two men.

"Oh. It is." The guard behind them chuckled. "You'd better hope it kills you outright. The radiation burns are terrible."

Bel's disgust was palpable. *I can separate the hydrogen and oxygen from the water in their bloodstreams and burn them from the inside out. I promise that whatever terrible weapon they invented, Tianyi had them beat.*

Let's stick to electricity, okay. Isaac's stomach turned as they entered the house. He'd told Dani and Steve that he believed Bel's power to be far greater than they had tapped yet. He really hadn't stopped to think about what that would mean for an alien soldier used as a weapon of mass destruction for over a century. Bel's memories opened up to him at the thought, horrible memories of battles won by wiping whole armies off the battlefield, tens of thousands of strange alien creatures left mutilated beyond recognition, and conflicted feelings of victory, pride, shame, and disgust that seeped into Isaac's own soul. "Dang, Bel," Isaac muttered under his breath as he shook off the thought and took a shaky breath. *That's horrible.*

We never lost a battle, a hint of fear that Isaac would despise him as he learned the depth of the atrocities committed by Tianyi colored his thoughts, *but we lost ourselves in the process.*

Isaac clenched his good fist. Taking Bel's lifetime of guilt and painful memories on himself was going to definitely take some adjusting to, but maybe they could be the hero Tianyi never was. A force for good to redeem the evil in Belenos's previous life. Besides, Bel had already willingly taken Isaac's own human weaknesses on himself more than once.Together, they could handle this.

Appreciation kicked back at him from Bel's consciousness. *We're inside.*

Snapping out of his musings with a start, Isaac looked around the room. It looked very similar to the private display room they'd blown up, only with a retro mod sixties vibe. Bright colors swirled the walls and the pedestals the artifacts stood on had a space age look. Some of the artifacts were the ones taken from SentryTech, the rest were unfamiliar, but just as ominous looking. Some of the pedestals were empty, awaiting new additions to the collection. A worn, pockmarked, rocket-shaped object about the size of a small car sat on a lighted platform in the center of the room.

Run a scan, Bel. I want to know what the immediate threats are as soon as possible. He rolled his injured shoulder. *And what's the time frame on the arm repair? I'd feel a lot better about this if I knew we were up to facing whatever he throws at us.*

We'll be operational in seventeen minutes and optimal in forty-three.

Let's settle for operational, then.

Koine walked into the room, dressed as immaculately as he had been at the gala, a tablet in hand. He looked up from the tablet to stare at Isaac critically.

Isaac responded by channeling the testosterone-fueled posture he took at the gala and met Koine's assessing gaze defiantly.

"What is McGuiness's bulldog doing in my yard?" Koine's gaze rested on the pulsing rune on their chest and lit with desire. "My guards tell me you know about the artifact I seek. Perhaps you possess it yourself and are willing to negotiate a trade?"

Obviously, Isaac was not in the least interested in a trade, but he needed to delay for the fifteen odd minutes Bel needed to get their arm and armor back online. He traced the rune with his finger. "Before we talk about mine, we need to discuss this." He gestured to the collection surrounding them. "I've been tasked with retrieving all the artifacts you've taken from SentryTech, or destroying them if that's not possible. Tell me why I shouldn't just blow us all up here like you did your high rise?"

Koine's eyes darted to his, as if trying to check if he was serious. Isaac tried to look very serious, even though getting blown up was pretty high on the list of things he never wanted to do again.

"No one who works for Steve McGuiness would have enough ice in their blood to blow up themselves and five other people just to destroy some space junk." Koine's nervous chuckle indicated he wasn't quite as sure as his words implied. "Besides, there's no reason to be that drastic.

It's all harmless. What serious collector doesn't have a few things in his collection acquired outside normal channels?"

"I know what the artifact you seek is capable of, and it is certainly not harmless. I'm willing to bet some of these items are similarly powerful." Isaac accessed the results of Bel's scan and crossed to an odd staff lying on one of the pedestals. "This is the Ceremonial Staff of the High Priest of the Bagmar people of Sirius Twelve." The stone at the top of the staff started to glow. "Do you even know what this does?"

How do we know what this is, much less what it does? Isaac looked at the twinkling blue crystal in puzzlement. *Would I rather not know?*

Probably. Bel apologized. *It's enough that you know that it's capable of mass mind control.*

Isaac fumbled the staff, and gripped it tighter when he regained control.

"No one does. That's the beauty of all these artifacts." Koine took a step toward them as he gestured widely at the room. "The mystery. The discovery."

"We know enough to know some of this stuff should never have existed in the first place." Isaac was having trouble keeping his eyes off the brightening glow of the staff. *Umm... Bel, are we going to activate this thing on accident?*

More than likely, Bel replied dryly. *Tianyi didn't really get an opportunity to figure out how it worked. We were more concerned about stopping it from ever working again.*

How much longer until we can burn this whole place down? Isaac set the staff back on the pedestal gingerly. *I'm not sure I even trust Dani and Steve with this staff.*

Nine and a half minutes.

Isaac swore. None of this stuff was going back to SentryTech, obviously, but they kinda needed to survive long enough to make sure it was all destroyed.

"Why did you blow up your own building?" Isaac shifted the conversation, both to buy time and because he seriously wanted to know why he'd spent more than two days buried under a skyscraper.

"Bah. It was supposed to be a tragic accident that took my life and brought awareness to the dangers of alien technology." Koine rested his hand on the pedestal nearest him and scoffed. "McGuiness and SentryTech were supposed to take the heat, because even though I procured them through less than legal means, SentryTech has been hiding them for decades. And I was supposed to be free to formulate my transition to world leader in peace. Steve's *never* accepted my invitations before. You weren't even supposed to *be* there."

"You killed people!" Isaac's brain scrambled to understand how someone could so cavalierly kill people even as he tried to analyze the threat of the object on the pedestal Koine was touching. It was an open case the size of a shoe box that might hold Aster's shoes, made of a highly polished black chrome and lined with a shimmery fabric. Five small spiked balls sat inside, about the size and appearance of a seed pod from a sweetgum tree. An empty divot indicated there had originally been six of the spiked balls. He grimaced. The natural tree pods hurt bad enough, a weapon based on them couldn't possibly be good.

"It wouldn't have been believable if I had been the only one to die." Koine shrugged and moved his hand to rest on the open lid of the box. "These weapons were supposed to give me incontestable power. The artifact you possess was to be the payment for that power. I owe a very powerful man a debt. One you're going to have to pay."

Bel... Isaac braced for whatever those balls did.

Four minutes.

We don't have four minutes. They activated their armor just as Koine grabbed the shiny box and flung its contents at them. Bel's focus on rewiring the nerves in their arm slowed the armor coverage time a fraction, allowing one of the spiked balls to catch Isaac in the arm as their armor closed over it.

"Ow!" Isaac flinched and went to grab his good arm with his bad, which didn't move because Bel hadn't finished connecting the nerves. Ice seemed to spread from the spike ball now embedded in his arm, leaving a rapidly growing wave of numbness in its path.

Nova, Bel swore. Their armor quickly expelled the poisoned spike ball, which bounced off the cement floor with a ping.

"You see, I need that symbiote. I do not need you." Koine circled closer to them. "I'm willing to bet that aliens are no more virtuous than us. When that poison ravages your body, it will abandon you rather than risk suffering the same fate."

The icy feeling raced up their arm. Once it hit their neck, Isaac felt his whole body drop from under him. Only their armor kept him standing upright. His heart stuttered and his lungs refused to take another breath. Panic grabbed his mind as his consciousness faded.

I'm still here. I won't let you die. Bel's determined confidence soothed his terror as the symbiote took over Isaac's autonomic functions from his failing body. *I will not abandon you.*

Chapter 16

Isaac's heartbeat steadied under Bel's control and he took a deep breath. He still couldn't feel his body, and even his senses had faded to only what the armor's sensors supplied. It was horrifying, being so disconnected from his own body that even his stark terror had no impact on it. Was this what Bel had endured during the time he was trapped in his prison orb?

"My man's heart stopped seven seconds after he touched the ball. I saw the horror freeze on his face as he realized he was dying. Nothing we did could revive him." Koine edged closer to them and reached out a hand to touch their armor, frozen in place like a museum display. "Symbiote, your host is dead. You belong to me now."

Anger, protectiveness, and a harsh jolt of electricity met Koine's touch. The entrepreneur jumped back and swore.

"Hateful thing. I'll let them decide what to do with you." He tapped the tablet in his hand a few times. He snapped his fingers at one of his guards. "Get the other mech in here. We'll use it to put this thing in stasis until they come for it."

Fire burned in Isaac's fingers and toes, signaling a return of sensory input that would have made him cry if he had the ability. Bel didn't mute the pain, which spread even from his reattached left arm. Tears streamed down his face, both from the pain and the relief.

I apologize. The pain input is necessary for me to make sure everything is working correctly.

And I apologize for being a worthless host. The entire point of you taking me as a host to begin with was to keep you from this very situation.

We are not done yet. Bel calmed him. *I took you as a host because I need a host to function. You apparently need a symbiote to survive. This is what is meant by 'symbiosis.' Apparently humans struggle with this concept.* His tone was both dry and teasing. *Humans are defenseless, yes, but I did not want a warrior for a host. You were not designed to take on these kinds of weapons alone. I was not designed to be a weapon of destruction. The Creator in his wisdom brought us together.*

We've been nearly killed twice in the last hour, and you want to talk to me about the designs of a Providential Creator? Isaac hiccuped a sob and realized Bel was no longer controlling his breathing.

Are you ready to take these guys down? Bel didn't comment on Isaac's agnostic opinion, but his own opinion was clear across their bond that their lives being preserved to this point was all the proof of a Providential God he needed.

Isaac flexed the fingers of his reattached arm. *What if they have more weapons?*

They obviously do. When our armor is fully functioning, we are nearly invulnerable. We are functioning at eighty-nine percent. The odds are in our favor.

Hmmm. Isaac wasn't impressed with "eighty-nine percent," or the amount of energy they used up in healing or repairs. The mission was supposed to be to secure the artifacts and call in Steve for pick up. They weren't equipped to destroy this stuff. They took a step toward something that looked like a B-movie ray gun. *What of these things can we use to destroy the rest of them?*

I'm pretty sure Koine will help us figure that out, Bel wryly drew their attention to Koine screaming instructions at his men as he noticed they were moving again.

"That poison should have killed you!" he yelled, approaching a pedestal on the fringe of the massive collection while staying well out of Gemini's reach. "You should be nothing more than a powerless casket."

Isaac retracted their helmet in spite of Bel's strong protest, noting that the symbiote complained but didn't stop him. "I'm not dead, you monster. I told you the alien artifact you seek is far too powerful for someone like you to control."

Koine actually looked confused for a moment, then his face flamed red with anger. He grabbed the artifact off the nearest pedestal – a pair of pancake-sized disks that popped out five spikes around the edges. Electricity arced around the points of the throwing stars as he threw them at Gemini.

You said we needed more energy. Isaac reengaged their helmet, but didn't move to dodge the sparking stars. They caught the stars in each hand, drained the electricity from them, and dropped them to the floor with a clatter. The batteries had been unexpectedly high capacity, and while they didn't give them the same boost as palming a live power line, it made enough of a dent in their energy deficit Isaac felt Bel relax significantly.

"What good are these things if I can't even defend against one armored alien?" Koine cursed as he scrambled to the B-movie ray gun and squeezed off a sustained blast of heat.

Remind me how much of this we can absorb? Isaac marveled at the fact that the temperature inside their armor didn't rise a single degree, even though the readout on their visor indicated the temperature on the surface of their armor was over one thousand degrees. Koine's men ducked far out of their reach and even Koine was backing away from the extreme heat his weapon was creating.

We can manage triple that for a brief period, but we are going to have to get rid of this energy eventually.

I guess Koine showed us how to get rid of these artifacts after all. Isaac smiled as he imagined all the artifacts melting on their pedestals.

"You know what, we're going to give you a choice." They advanced toward Koine. "You see, we need these artifacts. We do not need you. We, however, are significantly more virtuous than you. We'd rather not kill you and your men. We're going to give you one chance to get out of here before we melt this whole compound into a sheet of alien metal."

They took another step toward Koine, but their sustained closeness to the nearest podium combined with their extreme surface temperature caused it to burst into flames. The overhead sprinkler system activated, dousing them in a stream of water that vaporized into a cloud of steam on contact with their super-heated surface.

Isaac swore as they activated their infrared sensors to track Koine, who immediately dropped the heat ray gun and darted to the opposite side of the room.

Infrared isn't nearly as effective as actual sight, Isaac grumbled. *I can't tell what he's doing.*

Probably grabbing another weapon. Bel prompted them into a defensive position. *If he gets close enough, we can convert some of this heat energy into electricity and take him out.*

Here he comes. They flexed their fingers as Koine made his way through the clearing steam toward them. *Just don't toast him, alright. We took a lot of energy. we can't funnel all that back into him.*

It's harder to regulate when we've absorbed so much, but I will do my best.

Now, Bel! They grabbed Koine by the wrist and pulled him close enough to place their other hand against his chest.

He responded by touching whatever was in his hand to their chest, right against the blue pulsing rune in the center of their armor. It was the glowing orb at the end of the Bagmar mind control stick.

Bel's consciousness inside their head gave a strangled cry and they pulled away quickly, their own attack on Koine forgotten.

"Yield, alien." Koine's voice was in their head now, too, foreign, intrusive, parasitic. Where Bel's consciousness brought calm and confidence, Koine's felt like a black mold that corrupted everything it touched. "Reject your host and retreat to your natural form."

I cannot... Bel's voice sounded forced, as if even responding was a struggle. He pulled away from Isaac as far as he dared in an attempt to keep Koine's control from spreading to Isaac, an act that brought a pounding migraine that didn't fade. *If I do, we will both die.*

"Disarm him, then, and I will deal with him myself," Koine commanded. "Your new owner can figure out how to separate you."

Isaac's migraine throbbed with blinding intensity as Bel made a sound between a sob and a gasp, then retracted their armor to stasis. The light in their rune corrupted to a brackish black and the symbol that meant "protector" contorted into the logo of Olympus Art Galleries. Isaac felt his companion's presence submit to Koine's, a stubborn, unwilling submission laced with fear and hatred. Those feelings crossed their bond in spite of the distance Bel was trying to enforce, tainted with hints of Koine's command to fealty. Bel was still fighting, and his battle was all that was keeping Isaac's own mind from falling to Koine's influence.

"Are you serious?" Isaac shouted at Koine. His own voice made his migraine worse. He swore under his breath. This was nearly as bad as when he had taken the necklace off that night after they first met.

"I don't even have to use the staff on you, do I?" Koine grinned maliciously. "The alien controls you entirely, even down to the cellular level. That's how you survived the poison, isn't it?"

Isaac took a deep breath and drew himself up to full height. As long as Koine controlled Bel, life would be very difficult for him. He needed to watch for an opening to seize the staff and free Bel from Koine's influence.

"Alien, hurt him." Koine's voice echoed in their head as the orb at the top of the staff glowed brighter.

Bel's distress spiked, then faded into malicious compliance as Isaac's left big toe throbbed in pain.

"Ow, hey!" Isaac tried not to laugh at Bel's spiteful adherence to the letter of Koine's command. The staff seemed to only give Koine control over Bel's actions, but hadn't affected his will yet.

"Nice try." Koine's grin widened. "I can get more imaginative if I need to." He gestured at them with the staff. "Alien, stop his heart."

Their heart rate sped as Bel fought the command. Rage, impotence, hate, and fear hit Isaac full force as he blacked out like a switch had been flipped.

He woke up on the floor, Koine's chuckle echoing in his ears. Belenos's rage and humiliation were stronger in his consciousness, but so was their sense of Koine's presence. Bel had had to breach his own barriers to keep Isaac alive, allowing Koine's power to take a foothold in Isaac's own mind.

I... I am sorry. Bel's turgid emotions mirrored those Isaac had felt right before Bel had threatened to brick his own armor to save Isaac after the building fell – desperate, determined, and reckless.

Don't do anything stupid, Bel. Isaac rolled over and pushed himself to his feet. *Just keep him out of my head and I'll handle this.*

"The alien's consciousness is woven with yours. When he wearies of fighting the power of the staff, your mind will fall to me as well." Koine looked at them with clear disappointment on his face. "I almost regret having notified my benefactor that I found the symbiote he sought. I could use a soldier like you in my employ."

"Heh. I'm not a soldier, I'm a janitor. And the alien is an intergalactic protector, not your footsoldier." Isaac sobered and rested a hand on the corrupted rune over his breastbone. "We will never stop fighting you, and I'm afraid Bel would kill us both before we fell completely under your control. So if your benefactor wants us alive, you might want to back off."

Koine hesitated, and Isaac felt the pull of Koine's consciousness in his head draw back a little. "No. I don't think he would. He clearly resists a simple command to hurt you, he wouldn't kill you. He's told me as much."

"To keep us from becoming another WMD? Yeah, I wouldn't test that theory." Isaac crossed his arms over his chest and tried to look nonchalant, even though his heart was pounding. He desperately wanted to go home to Becca and Aster, but being dead was better than being some supervillain's winged monkey for eternity. Bel's presence was weakening, and if they didn't get free soon, the decision would be made for them.

"Hmmm. I will simply have to remove that ability from him." Koine gestured at them with the staff and a beam of inky smoke traveled from the orb to Bel's rune. "I'm done fighting. The alien is mine."

SONG OF THE STARS

Come on, Bel, keep fighting. Isaac could feel Bel struggle against Koine's control, but more weakly, like a lost memory at the back of his mind. Bel was losing, and if the staff took Bel, Isaac didn't stand a chance.

You're mine. You will give me your allegiance. Bel's voice came across their bond with Koine's words and a strong compunction to obedience. Isaac felt the pull of the staff coming from Bel's consciousness. Tendrils of black smoke seemed to swirl Isaac's consciousness, dragging him down as well. *Kneel and acknowledge your new master.*

Isaac gritted his teeth and locked his knees. "Go die in a hole." He swore silently as Bel's consciousness tried to make him kneel. He'd defied Bel's will when he'd lowered his helmet to show Koine he was still alive, but doing it long term wasn't an option. Having a symbiote meant working together, not fighting each other constantly like Tianyi. Besides, he couldn't fight both Koine and Bel. He needed Bel back on his side. He closed his eyes and focused on one of Bel's star songs, the Song of Polaris Bel had sung when he had healed him after the building exploded on them. It was a song of praise to the Creator. Isaac's relationship with God might be a bit undefined, but Bel's was as steady as a rock. Maybe they could tap into the strength of his faith to break the hold Koine had on them.

The black, corrupting smoke pulled back from Isaac's mind, and while Koine's hold on Bel's consciousness didn't lift, Issac could sense Bel singing along in the background, like an intergalactic earworm, helping him through the unfamiliar lines.

Back me up. Gemini will be no man's slave. Isaac moved, activating their armor and augmenting his speed himself while Bel turned up the mental volume of their song to drown out Koine.

"Alien –!" Koine cut off with a scream as he got a mouthful of spiked gauntlet with enough force to snap his head back and send him sprawling ten feet away. The staff and Koine's tablet clattered to the floor where he had stood.

Isaac stomped the orb at the head of the staff with an armored boot, grinding the crystal into the concrete with his heel. Black smoke spiraled from the crushed weapon and their own rune as Koine's presence was abruptly cut from their mind.

Thank the Creator. Bel's presence returned clear and strong and their rune returned to the shape they'd chosen to represent themselves, glowing brilliant blue in time to Isaac's heart once again. A feeling of appreciation, concern, and indignation washed over them as Bel ran a diagnostic scan to make sure the last hint of Koine's violation of their bond was healed. *Thank you, my very not worthless host.*

Isaac snorted in laughter. *We're not even close to even here, but yeah. I'm just glad the star song helped. If I had lost you, I don't know what I would have done. How did you and Timir survive a century of conflict like that?*

It wasn't that bad until near the end. Bel's bitter memories of his last days with Timir returned. *And we didn't. Our bond is strengthened when our minds are in synergy.*

If that means we're stronger together, I'll agree with that. Isaac looked over all the artifacts in the room. Koine's flunkies had run off sometime during the mind control battle – not that Isaac blamed them for wanting to be as far from that thing as possible – which left them alone to dispose of the artifacts however they saw fit. *Do we have enough energy left to melt all this, or did we burn through too much of it fighting Koine?*

We don't need to destroy it all if we can determine what is truly dangerous. Bel directed their attention to the fallen villain and his dropped belongings. *Koine is stirring. If he will not help, perhaps his tablet has the information we need to finish our task.*

Isaac gestured to the billionaire and wrapped him with a tentacle and focused a blast of heat with his other hand to incinerate the remains of the staff. Once the staff was nothing more than a black smear on the concrete floor, they scooped up Koine's tablet, which had survived the fall without a scratch. *Uhhh, Bel?* Isaac turned the tablet over in his hand. It was made of the same unusual reddish metal their armor was, with a darker, fluid surface etched with runes like the ones on Belenos's artifact.

It's a Vistkian translator tablet. Not too unlike your ereaders. Belenos's voice was low and grim. *He sees it in your language, just as you would if we were to lower our visor.*

Being bonded to Belenos meant they didn't have to. They could read Vistkian runes just like the alphabet. It gave the locations for each of Sentry Tech's labs, and a list of weapons housed in each lab. If they tapped the name of the weapon, a picture and description popped up. Most of them were ones Koine had stolen, but the last was sickeningly familiar.

The title "Prison Orb" accompanied a photo of both Belenos's artifact and the housing it had been contained in. The description was "This isohedral orb houses a traitorous symbiote who nearly assassinated our emperor. Handle with extreme care. Any objects you locate with this tablet are yours to do with as you please. As payment, the Prison Orb must be returned to Vistke."

"How were you to return the Prison Orb for payment?" Isaac turned the tablet to Koine and pointed to the diagram. "Did you have a way to contact your benefactor?"

"You're holding it." Koine shrugged as well as he could while bound by their tentacles. "I was supposed to tap the title and check the found box. My client would come and pick it up personally."

Come personally? Isaac looked back at the tablet and the bright yellow box marked "Found."

It means my brother lives. Belenos seemed mildly relieved he hadn't killed Timir when he'd broken their bond, but quite less than relieved that Timir knew where they were. *And it's just a matter of time before he finds us.*

Chapter 17

In the end, Gemini only had to destroy about a third of the artifacts. Steve complained a little when he arrived, but silenced quickly when they recounted their encounter with the mind control staff. They watched without comment as Sentry Tech's team collaborated with an FBI unit to clean up the artifacts, Koine, and the thugs Gemini left unconscious.

"You're sure you're alright?" Steve looked them over as if scanning for after effects of their fight with Koine. Isaac was aware he looked like garbage. With their armor in stasis, it was easy to see the blood that stained his pants and crusted his side as well as the fresh red scar where Bel had reattached their arm. Steve's gaze rested on the scar and an eyebrow tilted toward the ceiling. "I'm beginning to suspect you're looking for ways to cash in that insurance policy."

"We're fine. At least... we will be." Isaac rolled his shoulder. It was still stiff and sore, but Bel was too drained to continue healing. "We need a break. The injuries we sustained here so soon after the explosion are more than even Bel can keep up with. We need to sleep for a week."

"Done. The holidays are around the corner and you've completed your first real assignment anyway." Steve took their hand and shook it warmly. "Meet with Dani to debrief thoroughly, then we'll discuss your ongoing responsibilities after the first of the year. That should give you a quiet few weeks with your family."

"Yeah, about that." Isaac held Steve's hand a moment longer than necessary and met his eyes grimly. "Bel's brother is coming for Bel. Koine sent for him. Bel says it could take time before he gets here, but he'll be here eventually and we need to be ready."

Steve took a sharp breath and swore softly. "He's nothing without Bel, though, right? The two of you can easily take him, can't you?"

"We don't know what technology he may have developed to defeat Bel. Bel has weaknesses, and his former host is definitely going to know what they are." Isaac sighed. Bel hadn't been real forthright about what those weaknesses were. Isaac wasn't even sure if he knew, but if anyone could figure them out, it would be his sadistic brother. Isaac lowered his voice so the agents buzzing around the room couldn't overhear. "We're afraid he'll try to kill me to take back Bel and force Bel to help him conquer earth out of spite."

Steve's eyes and mouth made wide O shapes. He wetted his lips and tried again. "That changes things. Take two weeks. I'll send some guys to keep an eye on your house in the meantime. We'll discuss permanent arrangements the Monday after Thanksgiving." He gave them an uncharacteristically sober look. "Ask Bel if we have two weeks."

"Even if my brother is in your star system waiting for Koine's signal, we must rest and heal before we can face him," Bel answered through Isaac, his voice weak and quiet. "We are only functioning at sixty-five percent, have sustained multiple critical injuries, and have had our bond violated. Your guards cannot hope to stop my brother if he arrives before we are repaired, but knowing that they are there to protect Isaac's family from my brother's vengeance will allow us to heal in peace."

"That... Will never not be weird." Steve shook his head. "But that settles it. I'll send a team of my best men to watch your house. You can figure out however you want to explain it to your family. Just let me know when you're up to full power again and we'll make a better plan of action."

"At this point, I think it's time they knew everything." Isaac sighed. Alice and Frank might not be nearly as understanding as Becca had been. "Yay me."

Getting home took way longer than Isaac had hoped, and by the time he pulled into his driveway, he was being kept awake by the sheer force of Belenos's will.

We need a hot meal and to sleep for a week. Isaac whimpered as he stumbled up the stairs.

Another bolt of electricity can give us enough time to warn your family. Bel stretched a tendril to the outlet beside the door. *Then, yes, food and rest will allow us to heal properly.*

Bel... Isaac felt more awake, even if the boost didn't do much to take the edge off the stiffness and ache in his bones. He entered their hallway and closed the door behind them. *What if your brother gets here while we're recuperating?*

Ms. Apryl called in a favor and your NASA doesn't detect any threat within your star system. Vistkian starships are fast, but not that fast.

"Issac!" Becca ran and threw her arms around Isaac's neck. She kissed him deeply then pulled back to look at him. Worry filled her eyes as she stared at the blood stains and scar. "You're okay? For real?"

"We'll be fine. I could really use some of your mom's pot roast and several good night's sleep." He kissed her again. "Maybe a little alone time with my wife. But first, it's time to have a talk with your parents. They need to know about Belenos."

"Oh. Mom is just finishing up dinner and Dad's arguing with someone online." Becca's mood sobered. "You're sure though? I'm not sure how they'll take it."

Isaac sighed and ran a hand through his hair. "I'm sure. Let me change and shower and we'll just get it over with."

Once he was certain the blood was gone and he put on new clothes, Isaac rejoined his wife. *If you have a line to God, Bel, you might want to use it. I wasn't looking forward to this conversation already, but having it feeling like this and following up with the worst news possible isn't going to make it easier.*

I will do my best to mitigate the effects of the battle for the duration of your conversation, Bel assured him. *And I will pray.*

Becca took his hand as soon as he reached her and led him up to the kitchen. "Dad, Mom, Isaac's home."

"I hope you're hungry, this pot roast is nearly finished." Alice smiled at him. "I know it's your favorite."

"I'm looking forward to it." Isaac forced an uneasy smile and gestured to the table. "Do you mind taking a seat for a minute? I need to talk to you all about my new job."

Alice's smile wavered as she glanced at Frank and sat at the table beside him. Becca sat across from her and gave Isaac an encouraging nod.

"So, you all know about the attack at SentryTech a few weeks ago. Well, um. I kinda nearly died. But an alien symbiote saved me and helped me rescue my boss and he gave me a promotion and..." Isaac trailed off. Alice and Frank were looking at him with a mixture of panic and confusion. *Ugh, maybe I* should *have slept first.*

Try again, slow down, and try not to use the word 'symbiote.' Bel reminded him of the hideous movie symbiote that had haunted their connection for a while. *Humans do not react well to that word.*

"Let me try again." Isaac took a deep breath and began unbuttoning his shirt. "I was cleaning like always when the attack happened. The mercenaries were looking for alien tech that could be used as weapons. They were especially searching for a sapient suit of armor that SentryTech didn't even know they had. I found it first, and they shot me to get to it." He opened his shirt and touched the fading scar in his chest.

Alice covered her mouth with her hands and gasped, while Frank just hummed and nodded grimly.

"The armor healed me, and helped me stop the bad guys and rescue Mr. McGuiness." He shrugged out of his shirt and laid it over the back of a chair. "Belenos – the alien soul that powers the armor – refused to work with anyone but me. Mr. McGuiness promoted me to basically SentryTech's resident superhero and science experiment." He activated the armor and stood in the middle of their kitchen fully armed. "Belenos has saved my life more than once since then, and we managed to stop the guy who blew up Olympus Art Galleries and attacked SentryTech in the process."

"Is Belenos safe?" Alice demanded. Her tone and body language were hostile.

"Ha. No. Not remotely. We'd be a pretty lame superhero if he was safe." Isaac retracted their helmet and met her gaze firmly. "He is good, though. Maybe more good than I am."

"I think what Alice is asking is whether he's a threat to the family." Frank slipped an arm around his wife's shoulders.

"He is not, but his brother might be." Isaac sighed and retracted their whole armor to stasis. "Bel was once the power behind an evil intergalactic warlord. He escaped and his brother wants him back. Koine alerted Bel's brother to his location. We think it might be best if you all go into hiding for a while."

"Alien warlords? Putting your life at risk when you know how many people depend on you?" Alice's face grew red and she stood from her chair. "Did you even think about others before you put the whole family in danger?"

Isaac flinched and looked away as he felt Bel's indignation rise. He clamped his teeth closed as he felt Bel's protest rise to his lips. *That's definitely not a good idea here, Bel.*

Someone needs to defend you, if you will not defend yourself. Bel backed off, but only because of his promise not to violate Isaac's will. His displeasure at being told to stand down was abundantly clear.

"That's not fair, mom!" Becca stood and put her hands on her hips as she scowled at her mom. "Isaac and Bel *have* been looking out for all of us. This is way bigger than just our family."

I knew I liked her.

A smile twitched at the corner of Isaac's mouth at Bel's comment in spite of the tension in the room.

Frank stood as well, his hand steady on Alice's back. "What kind of threat are we looking at exactly?"

"We don't know. We don't believe they have the technology to recreate another Belenos, but even without him, their technology is far more advanced than ours. Imagine if a modern general could take his whole unit to capture Joan of Arc." Isaac carefully dictated Bel's answer rather than allowing him to speak through him, in hopes that it'd be less disturbing for his family. The cold facts were disturbing enough as it was. "Timir is ruthless and more than capable of killing any one who stands in his way. We're afraid that he'll threaten the family to manipulate us." Isaac took both Becca's hands in his. "Steve found a place you all can stay for a while until the confrontation is over. It'll be safe and comfortable until –"

"No," Frank interrupted firmly. "I have enough shotguns to go around, and you know Becca can shoot better than I can. This family stays together."

"Frank, shotguns aren't going to be a match for him." Isaac let go of Becca's hands and gestured to the bright scar where Bel had reattached his arm. "I just finished a battle with a mech that ripped my arm off, armor and all. We barely survived the collection of alien tech Koine had, and he didn't even know what half of it did."

"Then tell your boss we need some of that alien tech, but either way, we're not running like scared children." Frank placed his hands on the edge of the table and leaned toward him angrily. "That's not how this family works, and you ought to be ashamed that you'd think we'd just abandon you at the first sign of danger."

Isaac stopped and his mind scrambled to process this new turn. He'd kinda expected his mother in law's reaction, mostly because he felt a little guilty for having to have this entire conversation to begin with. He was totally unprepared for Frank's response, and had no idea how to respond. Even Bel reacted with a mixture of confusion, awe, and admiration.

"Dad's right, Isaac." Becca hugged his arm and rested her head on his shoulder. "You're a superhero now, do you expect us to run and hide every time you make an enemy?"

"I guess that *was* kinda what I was thinking." Isaac rubbed the back of his neck awkwardly.

She punched him lightly on the shoulder. "Don't be ridiculous. We're family; we're in this together. You and Bel are just going to have to figure out another way to keep us safe."

Isaac nodded. "We have time. Timir isn't even in our star system yet. Bel and I need to recover from the damage we've sustained over the last week. Then we can brainstorm together to have a plan for when Timir gets here. Steve and Dani will help, and possibly a rep from the US Space Force.

Timir used Bel to subjugate an entire star system. We're literally looking at defending our planet from that guy."

"And, Alice, I did think of others before I took on Belenos." Isaac tapped into Bel's indignation and gave in to his continued insistence that he defend himself. "I didn't like the idea of Aster growing up in a world like the one Bel's brother created. So here we are, protecting the world – and my family – from an intergalactic threat. There was no one else, and I'm not the least bit sorry it had to be me." He nodded to the stunned group. "If you'll pardon us, I think we're going to sleep for a week."

Chapter 18

Alice and Becca had really out done themselves. The ground floor of the house looked like a magazine interior. A tree decorated in a different theme sat in each room, lights and garland framed all the windows and stair rails, low instrumental Christmas carols played over the MP3 player, and the smells of hot cocoa, coffee, and hot mulled cider mingled in the air.

Isaac stood in the foyer, greeting relatives as they came in. A heavy sweater knitted with the image of a pair of kissing reindeer, one with a red nose that lit up, hid the stasis necklace from prying questions.

Too many questions anyway.

"So Isaac, Alice was telling me you got a raise." Uncle Buck shook his hand more firmly than was strictly necessary. "What do you do again?"

"I work for SentryTech as a..."

Problem solver, Bel prompted. It had been nearly two weeks since their battle at Koine's compound, and Bel had them back to one hundred percent in time for their annual Christmas party. And two weeks of family, Christmas decorations, and peace did much to repair the strain all their relationships had suffered from the fallout of that battle.

Worry over Timir's unknown yet imminent arrival was little more than a nagging concern, and did nothing to dampen the festive mood.

"... problem solver for Steve McGuiness." Isaac flashed his wife a grateful grin as she passed him a mug of hot cider. She wrapped her arm around his as she sipped her own hot cocoa silently. The constant opening and closing of the front door was making him cold. No sooner did he think it, than he realized he wasn't cold any more. Being fully bonded to Belenos was weirder in more than just the obvious ways.

"How does a janitor become a 'problem solver' for Steve McGuiness himself?" Isaac's cousin Trey scoffed. "Unclog his toilet?"

"Something like that." Isaac smiled sweetly back at him. They didn't need to prove anything to jealous family members. "How's your job at Goodyear going?"

"I got another promotion and my own office." Trey smiled back not so sweetly. His eyes drifted to Becca, a bit too obviously enjoying the way her gold satin wrap dress highlighted her post-baby curves. "Do you ever wish Isaac was something more than chief toilet plunger for the second richest man in the country?"

Becca smiled at him again, tightly. "I'll have you know, Trey, Isaac's job is very important." She slid one arm around Isaac's back and tucked her hand in the back pocket of his jeans. "He works hard to make sure that our bills are paid and I can go to school. Besides, I doubt your office job saves lives."

"Babe," Isaac wrapped his own arm around her waist and pulled her close. He kissed her nose lightly and tried to give her a look of warning. "I'm sure Trey doesn't want to hear about my job."

Becca opened her mouth to protest, then closed it into a tight line. "Trey, can you excuse us?"

"Don't be gone too long." Trey smirked at her retreating form as she dragged Isaac down the half-flight of stairs to the laundry room.

How much trouble would I get in if I punched him in the nose? Isaac asked Bel as he trailed after her. Trey had always been insufferable, but after Becca chose Isaac over him, he never seemed to pass up an opportunity to show up Isaac, or openly ogle his wife.

We could teach him a lesson without leaving any lasting damage.

Hold that thought. Becca had closed the laundry room door and set her drink on the dryer. The muffled noises of partygoers continued upstairs, but the grim look on her face didn't seem very festive.

"Isaac, you're a hero." She clenched her fists at her sides and scowled at him. "Trey has always been jealous of you. I just want them to know the truth."

Taking both hands in his, Isaac laughed softly. "Trey's only jealous because I managed to snag the most beautiful girl at school." She blushed as he swept his eyes over her himself. Nursing had been very generous with her, and it was hard not to notice with the cut of her dress. Isaac pulled her in closer, resting his hands on her hips. "I can't say I blame him."

"This isn't about me, silly." She pushed him away half heartedly. "If you just told him what you actually did... I can't believe he had the guts to call you 'Chief Toilet plunger!'"

He leaned down and kissed her mouth, a bit longer than he had her nose. He pulled back just a little to whisper. "We talked about this. It has to be a secret. Do you know what kind of circus our lives would become if people found out about Belenos?"

"I guess." She sighed deeply and rested her head on his chest. "Do you know how hard it is to know your husband is a superhero and not be able to say anything?"

"Do you know how hard it is to see the way he looks at you and not be able to do anything?" Isaac's voice hardened.

"I never knew it bothered you so much." Becca laughed and slipped her hands under the hem of his sweater. She nibbled his ear and whispered, "Guess which one of you gets me in the laundry room?"

"Bec, everything that's happened..." Isaac pulled her close, struggling to put his thoughts into words. They'd had precious little time alone since the night he'd met Bel, and most of their conversations had been about the monumental life changes that night brought about. "I love you. More than anything. More than *anyone*. You know that, right? After everything that's happened the last few weeks, I just need you to know that I would never do anything to hurt you or our family."

"I know that. And I love you too." She kissed his cheek. "I just don't want to lose you. That's a fear that won't go away anytime soon. I just keep reminding myself that God has you, and He has given you the best possible backup team you could have." She stood up on her tiptoes, pressed her body to his, and whispered in his ear, "And it's kind of hot being married to the only superhero I know."

With a laugh, Isaac pressed his lips to hers, forgetting Trey and the guests, Bel, and everything but the very beautiful woman in front of him and the fact that no one was going to be worried about doing laundry in the middle of a party. He lifted her up onto the top of the washer and fumbled with the zipper at the back of her dress as he traced her collarbone and the curve of her neckline with his lips. Her breathing was heavy as she pulled his sweater over his head and placed her hands on his bare chest. Although Belenos was conspicuously silent, Isaac was aware that his senses were heightened by his bond. Her beauty, her touch, even her smell, thrilled him in a deeper way than before.

They finished with a sigh and another lingering kiss, their foreheads touching as they tried to catch their breath and steady their legs. Isaac's phone rang in the pile of clothes at his feet, but he ignored it completely. Whoever it was could give him a minute. He sought Becca's mouth with his, considering a second round.

Timir's squadron has entered your star system.

Isaac pulled back with a jolt. *How far away is he?*

His space dilation tunnel opened near Saturn. At sub-light speeds, they'll be to earth in days. Bel's tone was quiet and well controlled, but fear and toxic memories roiled in the back of their mind, completely changing Isaac's mood.

"Isaac? What's wrong?" Alarm etched Becca's face.

"Timir – Belenos's evil brother – just passed Saturn." He pulled on his pants and fished his phone out of his pocket.

The missed call had been from Steve. The screen lit up as he tried to call again. Isaac tapped to answer and held the phone to his ear. "Hey, Bel told me. Do you need me at the office now?"

"Dani and I are heading there now. Sorry to leave early." The sound of Steve starting his car crossed the phone. "I'll coordinate with NASA, you finish your party and meet me there. You don't think there's any chance you can convince your family to go to that safehouse now, do you?"

Isaac looked at his wife as she adjusted her dress and stepped into her shoes. "Unlikely. They're pretty stubborn."

Becca stuck her tongue out at him as she smoothed down her hair. "We're not leaving, Isaac. How long do we have?"

"A week, tops." Isaac turned the phone from his mouth to answer her.

"We'll be ready." She smiled, kissed him on the cheek, and slipped out the door.

"Give me a couple hours, Steve. Bel and I will do what we can to help." Isaac hung up and pulled his sweater back on. They'd rehearsed this already, and were as prepared as they could be. *Start praying, Bel. We need all the help we can get.*

I have been, trust me.

I do trust you and I'm certain we can face your brother in single combat. It's the squadron I'm worried about.

We will face him in single combat. He will have it no other way. The squadron is a show of force to make sure your space force doesn't get in his way.

We don't have a space force. Isaac mounted the stairs to join the festivities at least halfheartedly.

He doesn't know that. Bel returned wryly. *You need a space force.*

Take that up with Steve. I'm just the janitor. Isaac gave Trey a sour smile and turned away to get another cup of punch. *Until I met you, I thought aliens were a myth. You don't build an army to fight a myth.*

The last guest left two hours later, and Isaac was nearly beside himself trying to plaster a fake smile on and pretend life was normal while trying to figure out how to stop a real life alien invasion.

The family stood on the front porch grinning and waving until the last guest was out of sight, then Frank turned to face Isaac with a sober look. "Becca told me. Before you go, I need you to see something."

Isaac followed him down to the storm shelter they had built under the middle level of the split-level home. Frank flipped on the light switch to reveal food, guns, and other supplies lining the concrete walls.

"We've got enough here for a month, and enough ammunition to stop the National Guard." Frank patted an AR-15 hanging on the wall beside the entrance. "You say the word, and we can all bunk down here for safety."

"Hopefully it won't come to that, but I'm glad we have a plan." Isaac looked at a pile of board games on one of the shelves. "I'm going to meet with NASA and the US Space Force rep to see if there's any chance we can keep him from making landfall."

Frank clapped a hand on his shoulder and pulled him in for a side hug. "Look, Isaac, I know Alice's been a bit testy about this, but we're both really proud of you – worried –

but proud. If there's anything we can do, let us know. Saving the world is hard enough without us throwing family issues on top of it."

"I have an insurance policy, Frank, more than enough to support the family until Becca finishes if I don't make it." Isaac fingered the rune under his shirt nervously. "Bel... isn't sure how we can defeat his brother. One to one, there's no chance he can defeat us, but a whole squadron?" He looked his father in law in the eye grimly. "I saw the things Timir made Bel do to his own people, I can't let that happen here. No matter what. Can you help Becca understand?"

"I can, if I have to, but I'd rather not have to." Frank took a step back so he could look at Isaac's face better. "Promise me you're not going to do anything foolish?"

"Heh, Bel won't let me. I'm pretty sure he's more worried about protecting me and making his brother leave us alone than he is saving the planet."

I do not wish the abuses of Tianyi on any planet, but there are very few outcomes where we succeed in stopping him if you do not survive. Bel was quietly indignant.

I've seen one in your mind, a power you're too scared to admit you even have. Isaac set his jaw and clenched his fist. *We can stop him. We will.*

We would both die. That is not a power, that is ultimate destruction.

If there is no other choice? You'd just let Timir use you again?

I will seek any other option before that one. Bel seemed to sigh. *I refuse to think that is the only way.*

"Uh, yeah..." Frank coughed intentionally. "That's another thing. I don't even begin to understand your relationship with 'Bel', but how's your relationship with God? I never asked about your leaving school. I didn't think it was my place, especially not when the job that kept you from church with the family was the only income we had. But if you're questioning your chances of survival, you might need to pay a bit more attention to your relationship with Him as well."

Bel agreed with a sense of approval and the low hum of a star song.

"It's complicated." Isaac shrugged them both off. "I don't have the faith I used to – the faith you and Bel seem to find so easy. If God's out there, why are there so many questions? If He's not there, why is there so much beauty? I... just can't seem to be able to get past all the doubts."

"Maybe we're not supposed to." Frank closed the door of the shelter and started back up the stairs. "Maybe that's where faith comes in. I'd bet your Bel had a time in his life where he had to choose God in spite of the doubts. That's faith, and it's something we all have to face in our relationship with God at one time or another. It's not easy, but then no relationship is."

Isaac stood at the bottom of the stairs for a moment as Frank carefully made his way to the top. He knew Bel's story. He knew the pain the alien had had to push past to cling to his faith. Was it really as easy as choosing God in spite of the doubts? Bel's quiet presence in the back of his mind assured him it was, but Professor Price's voice in his memories was nearly as loud. He shook his head to clear the conflicting thoughts. *We have time, Bel. I'll think about what Frank said.*

I pray you find your way soon. I fear we have less time than you think.

Chapter 19

"How many ships again?" Isaac leaned forward in his seat in the posh executive meeting room at SentryTech and stared at the huge screen on the wall. The satellite imagery wasn't nearly as clear as it looked on the internet.

"Five, as far as we can tell." An older man wearing khakis and a polo with the NASA logo embroidered on it gestured with a pointer at an irregular blob on the screen. "Four small combat vessels and a larger, er, mothership."

Timir will be in the flagship. He will likely take position in a distant orbit and send the fighters to initiate negotiations.

"Mr. Smythe, has NASA received any communication from the alien ships?" Steve wrinkled his face at the screen as if he couldn't make it out either. "Bel has indicated the aliens use radio waves for communication."

"Nothing, yet." The older man shook his head. "We can try sending a message. Hitting on the right frequency would be nearly impossible, and even if we succeeded, there's no chance they'd understand us."

"Given the right equipment, we can contact them," Bel answered through Isaac. His host was much less resistant to him communicating through him in a work setting than in a family setting, and the shortcut made communication easier for both of them. "We speak the language fluently and are familiar with the radio channels the Vistkian military uses."

"Remind me again *how* a janitor knows so much about an alien race?" General Donaldson, the Space Force representative, folded his arms over his chest and glared. He gestured at the screen. "And how do we know those lights are aliens in the first place? This could all be the fever dream of a mentally ill cosplayer."

"He's for real, General," Dani assured him. "You're more than welcome to take a look at all the data we've collected from our testing."

If he can understand it. Isaac scoffed.

How is the man in charge of your Space Force not prepared to defend against an alien invasion? Bel was both confused and irritated. He expected competency from his generals.

He probably thought he'd be defending us from the Russians or Chinese or something. Isaac shrugged. *Nobody really believes in aliens.*

Wonderful.

"Assuming I decide to believe you, what kind of military capability are we looking at here?" General Donaldson gave them a challenging look. "Or is the alien just a janitor as well?"

"Before I took habitation in this armor, I was Warrior Prince Belenos Arkadia, Heir to the twelve thrones of Vistke and commander of the unified armies of the Vistkian stars System." Bel infused Issac's posture with confidence and emphasized his own voice and accent. "I have led my armies to more victories in my century of service than you've even fought. You would do well not to insult a royal ally on the eve of a battle, human."

General Donaldson paled, then reddened with anger as Steve and Dani smirked and Mr. Smythe stared with wide-eyed horror.

Bel armored their right arm and sent a tendril to the USB port of the computer linked to the screen. Experimenting with Isaac's phone had given him a fair idea of how to interface with terran technology. He brought up a schematic of an asteroid hopper from the data he retained as commander of the Vistkian forces, the light jump pod Timir most likely brought for backup. "This is likely what the smaller ships are, though this is an older model. I have to believe they've made at least some improvements in the years since I was banished."

"Huh." General Donaldson grunted as he looked at the schematics. "Mind giving me a copy of those so we can get a better idea of what we're up against?"

Bel questioned the wisdom of handing Vistkian technology over to any government power, especially one as backward as Terran governments seemed to be.

Not nice, Bel, Isaac scolded. *At least we're the good guys.*

Governments only seek to serve themselves. You may be 'American', but I am not. As we agreed, I will not be involved in petty Terran politics.

"I will give the relevant information to Ms. Apryl and you may consult with her technicians." Bel changed the slide before the Space Force General could object. "This was our flagship when we ruled the Vistkian stars System as Tianyi. Toward the end of our joint reign, it was converted to more of a luxury ship, but there's no guarantee my brother didn't have it retrofitted to its original battle specifications to hunt me down–"

"So this is really all about you?" General Donaldson interrupted again. "Like that superhero movie, you made enemies, took refuge on our planet, and now *your* enemies are threatening to wreak havoc on *our* planet to get you back."

Bel didn't get that reference, or appreciate the implication Timir's pending attack was his fault. *What is he talking about?*

I've seen this one. Let me handle it.

"With all due respect, sir, it's exactly like that movie." Isaac leaned forward and met the general's gaze firmly. "The superhero willingly submitted to the government's cowardly demand that he surrender to save his adopted planet, but the aliens decided to destroy the planet anyway. In the end the superhero was all that stopped the aliens from trouncing the US Army and destroying the planet. We'd like to save everyone the trouble and skip straight to the part where we work together to whip alien butt."

Steve barked a loud laugh and slapped his hand down on the table. "Yes! I'm totally on board with whipping alien butt – no offense to Bel – and SentryTech is more than willing to share our resources." He pushed away from the table. "In fact, I'm pretty tired of the talking. Isaac... Uhh Bel... Gemini, send those specs to Dani. She and General Donaldson can collab on our defensive measures. Then I can show you and Mr. Smythe the space radio equipment. If there's any chance this guy can be negotiated with, or even bluffed away, I'd like to try that first. I think we'd all like to keep potential collateral damage to a minimum here."

Memories of the destruction Tianyi wreaked in battle filled their mind and Gemini shuddered. "Timir is not easily deterred, but, yes, we will try diplomacy first. We would not wish the destruction we have seen on any other people."

"This way, General." Ms. Apryl pushed her chair back and stood to lead the general to the lab.

General Donaldson gave a tightlipped nod, but his eyes never left Isaac's face. Bel had seen that look before, in the eyes of many opponents just before negotiations went south.

I do not trust him.

Me neither. He's totally going to steal your tech and toss us to your brother.

They quickly activated their armor enough to cover their right arm and caught Ms. Apryl by the wrist. *He is not our ally. Give him only what you must to appease him until we can formulate another plan.*

Ms. Apryl gave a curt nod, pulled her hand free, and gave General Donaldson a smooth smile. "Like Isaac said, let's go kick some alien butt."

As Ms. Apryl hustled the Space Force general from the conference room, Mr. McGuiness turned to the NASA scientist. "Are you ready to call the mothership?"

"Do you have any idea how historic this is?" Mr. Smythe scrambled after him as they headed down the hall toward the space radio.

"Believe me, I feel like I've been living in a sci-fi movie for the last three months." Steve clapped his hand on Isaac's back and chuckled. "These guys have given us so much information, and I get to manage a real life superhero. They can take this goon, and I can't believe we get to watch!"

'Thanks for your vote of confidence, Steve," Isaac answered softly. "We'd rather not fight him at all if we can help it, so let's hope the radio contact works." *What are we hoping for here, Bel?*

Best case, we can convince him to go home and leave us alone. Worst case, he will respond with threats and ultimatums. Either way, confirmation that it is indeed Timir and that his intention really is to reclaim me as his own.

They entered a large sterile room filled with banks of computers that connected to the giant space radio dish on the roof. A couple of white-coated techs bustled around the room under the watchful eye of Dr. Judah.

While Mr. McGuiness explained why they were there, Gemini walked over to the control panel and looked it over. It was basically similar to the ones Bel had used on Vistke, other than being in English, which was no longer a barrier. Tuning it to the frequency the Vistkian military used for communication was simple, and quickly resulted in a signal.

The room hushed at the otherworldly, barking voice coming over the speakers – clearly speech, but also clearly no tongue spoken on earth.

"People of Sol 3, you are harboring a fugitive from Vistke," Gemini translated. "My representative will be in your orbit in five solar days. If you surrender the fugitive, you will be left in peace. If you protect him, we will raze your most populous cities one by one until you do surrender him. You are defenseless before our superior might."

"He can't possibly know that." Steve scoffed and folded his arms over his chest.

"He can't *not* know that," Bel returned gravely. "You have no military outposts, no deep system sensor arrays, no asteroid mining colonies, and made no attempt at first contact. There are no signs of any people traversing this system, much less any prepared for space warfare." They shook their head and clamped their lips closed as the message continued. *He continues with a personal message to us. 'Belenos, you must know that this backward race cannot protect you from me, and you are incapable of protecting them all from my wrath. As always, you have no choice but to surrender your will to me. The blood of these people will be on your claws.*

He's a monster. We'll find another way, Isaac assured him.

We have five days. Bel wasn't sure the mocked plan to surrender them for the sake of the collective people of earth was as terrible as Isaac felt it was. At least a forced battle on the Vistkian flagship would limit Terran casualties.

"The message repeats itself." Gemini turned to the awestruck scientists and smirking tech billionaire. "Do we answer with a challenge of our own, or allow my brother to remain uncertain if his message was received?" Bel had his own opinion as a military commander, but Terran strength seemed focused on informational technology and nuclear intimidation, perhaps not the right combination of skills to confidently face an intergalactic force with technology generations beyond their own.

"Is there any chance we can turn him away before his vanguard gets to earth's orbit?" Mr. Smythe asked as he continued to stare at the radio broadcasting the looping message. "Do you understand the level of panic we'll have once amateur astronomers get sight of a real UFO?"

"Just handle it the way you guys have for years." Steve scoffed. "Tell them it was a military drone experiment and move on."

Mr. Smythe tore his gaze from the radio and gave him a withering glare.

"Do you have the technology to turn him away? Because mere words will not be enough." Bel knew the answer, at least he suspected he did. Isaac's knowledge of terran space warfare technology was a mess of sci-fi movie tech and internet rumors, and very little help at all.

"That would be a better question for General Donaldson, but..." Mr. Smythe shifted his feet nervously.

"But it is unlikely." By the stars, they *were* these people's only hope. "We suggest you allow us to return his challenge and instead focus on managing the circumstances of our inevitable confrontation. You have cities you wish to preserve, and we have family we wish to keep from Timir's vengeful hand."

"I... Yes. That may be best." Mr. Smythe nodded. "We'll have to clear it with General Donaldson first."

I doubt he'll care. He acted like he'd rather sacrifice us anyway.

Agreed. At least this way we control the battle, and perhaps increase our likelihood of winning.

And keep your brother as far from Becca and Aster as possible. I'd rather he didn't even know they exist.

That in itself will greatly increase our likelihood of winning. They had enough weaknesses without bringing friends and family into Timir's sights. *Creator grant we face him alone, and have grace to defeat him.*

Amen to that.

Chapter 20

By the time Timir's squadron passed Mars, SentryTech and the US Government had set Gemini up in a shack deep in the wilderness of Area 51. The tiny house was part of a mock street for alien invasion drills and had clearly seen better days. Bullet holes and odd scorch marks marred the dusty aluminum siding and the building next door was nothing more than a pile of rubble with a brick facade facing the empty street.

"Well, if it does come down to a full on battle, at least we don't have to worry about collateral damage." Isaac fingered the peeling paint on a seven foot tall wooden cutout of an alien with three heads and a ray gun in each of his six tentacles.

"I wonder if they actually fought real aliens here?" Steve led them into the narrow two story home. Inside was spotless and furnished with bare essentials for a short term stay. Steve looked over the worn, but clean furniture. "Or gave refuge to one."

"Both, now that we're here." Isaac smiled. Being halfway across the country from his family and miles from civilization made him feel much more optimistic about their face off with Belenos's brother. "Did Dani get the radio set up?"

"She's working on it in the kitchen. You and Bel can answer his brother's challenge from here." Steve rested a hand on Isaac's shoulder. "I set up a team of bodyguards to watch your house. A crack commando unit. Tricky to track down, but they're the best there is. If Bel's brother somehow figures out where your family is, they'll protect them."

"Thanks, Steve. You have no idea how much that means to us." Not that he didn't trust Becca's shooting or Frank's survivalist stash, but if guns were worthless against him and Bel, they didn't have much confidence in their ability to protect their family against the same people who had created Bel.

"Ready to go." Dani stood from the kitchen table to let them take over the radio. "They're still broadcasting the same message on a loop. A couple other government agencies have attempted to answer, but have gotten no response."

Timir will only answer to me, or to someone replying in my name. Bel's confidence and military experience was a steadying influence in the back of their mind. Alone, neither of them stood a chance against Timir and his invaders. Together, they were everything Tianyi should have been.

"Great. We can handle this from here. You two should probably be in Vegas before they get here." Isaac sat in the chair Dani had vacated and started tuning the radio signal.

"We've got time. I want to hear Belenos tell that guy off." Steve took another chair, spun it around and straddled it. He rested his arms across the back and looked at them expectantly.

Dani rolled her eyes while Isaac smiled and shook his head. He turned back to the radio and took a deep breath. *You're up, Bel. Is there any chance he gets cold feet and goes home?*

No chance in the galaxy. Bel was sober, but still confident. *We will fight, and by the grace of the Creator, we will defeat him.*

"You guys realize we'll be answering back in Vistkian, right?" Isaac finished tuning and didn't turn around.

"But you can translate for us right? It's going to take time for the signal to get to him and for him to respond." Steve wiggled a little like he was making himself comfortable, then gestured to the radio to signal he was waiting for Isaac to get on with it.

Dani and Steve watched in rapt fascination as they dictated the message in the same barking language that the original transmission had arrived. Bel carefully infused their voice with all the proud confidence of their station, as well as with a stern rebuke as of an older brother to a foolish younger sibling.

"I... wow... I didn't realize a human could make those sounds," Steve commented as soon as the transmission ended.

"Bel had to practice." Isaac chuckled as he turned to face them. "Apparently 'human vocal cords aren't optimized for Vistkian speech,' according to him." He shrugged. "Timir can't possibly misunderstand the nuance, and it's not like anyone else on this planet can speak Vistkian."

"What did you tell Timir?" Dani interrupted.

"Warrior Prince Belenos Arkadia, Heir to the twelve thrones of Vistke, commander of the unified armies of the Vistkian Stars System, slayer of Tianyi the Great, and now protector of earth, known to Prince Timir as Sol 3, demands the immediate removal of the Vistkian forces from the Sol star system. Any attempt to make planetfall will be interpreted as a declaration of war and will be met with the full power of Gemini, synergistic protector and dual guardian of the Terran people." Bel's voice repeated their message in English. "We also added a more personal note to my brother, as he did to us. 'Timir, we are well aware this people cannot protect us, which is why we will stand against you with our full power. Any Terran blood you shed will be required of you by our hand. There is no victory for you here. Take heed and return home.'"

"Nice. Is it going to work?" Steve frowned.

"Ha. No. We basically insulted him, reminded him of what Bel did to defeat him before, and told him Bel's full allegiance lies with earth." Isaac shook his head. "He's coming fast, he's going to be furious, and hopefully he's going to make a mistake." It was a calculated gamble to insure Timir went after them immediately, before realizing where their weaknesses lay. "In the meantime, you guys really should get out of here. Bel estimates Timir's herald could be here sooner than we anticipated if his brother shows the same chronic lack of concern for his men that he showed as Tianyi."

"Do you need anything specific? There's food and supplies here for a week." Dani opened the well stocked fridge to demonstrate. "Cell phone and TV reception are terrible here, but you can reach us by radio if you need to."

"We'll be monitoring the squadron's approach and update you as needed." Steve stood and spun the chair back into its normal position. He cleared his throat and looked grim. "You should also know that General Smythe has a full sized nuke pointed at this house. If you lose, Timir becomes a smear of toxic waste."

"That should be enough. We're hoping it doesn't come down to tha–" A shrill sound and piercing pain stabbed his brain and a scream echoed in his head. He pressed his hands to the sides of his head and dropped his elbows to the table with a moan. *Belenos!* Something was wrong with his companion.

"Isaac!" Steve jumped to his side and laid his hand on their back. "What's wrong?" He offered him a fistful of napkins. "Your nose and ears are bleeding!"

"Something attacked Belenos." He sobbed, the pain was fading to migraine level and he still couldn't hear Bel. "He's– he's hurting and it feels like someone's tearing my brain out of my head." They sat back in the chair and closed their eyes as they held the napkins to their nose. *Come on, Bel, what's going on?* Tears streamed down their face. If Belenos could take his pain, was the reverse true? Was he taking Belenos's pain?

I'm still here. Belenos sounded thready and unsteady. *Some kind of supersonic attack. I'm doing what I can to keep us from sustaining significant damage, but pain management is somewhat out of my control at the moment.*

"We're running out of time." Isaac groaned. Steve and Dani were going to be caught in the crossfire if they didn't leave now. "You have to go."

We need to suit up. Belenos started the process slowly, as if he was struggling to focus as well. *I can calibrate our helmet to block the frequency.*

Please. Isaac's own feeling of urgency seemed to push Belenos faster. The relief was almost immediate once the helmet closed over their head. Isaac breathed out a sigh of relief as the headache dropped to a dull throb, then faded further as Belenos healed the damage to his eardrums.

Isaac? He's here. Belenos's anxiety spiked in a way Isaac had never felt before, and frankly scared him. Even without asking who "he" was, he heard Belenos's terror clearly.

Your brother is nothing without you. Isaac tried to scoff confidently, but Belenos's terror was taking over their bond. *He's only here because he knows it.*

He knows it, and I fear he will kill you to take me again. Belenos's usual confidence seemed to shatter. *The technology that created me is generations beyond anything in your star system. He may have the power to do exactly that.*

The memory of the blackout at the explosion and the pain from the sonic attack was proof enough that all their power didn't make them invincible to someone that was intimately familiar with them.

He led Dani and Steve out to the street, hoping that they could still get to the car and get out before Timir's herald made planetfall. The alien starship already floated above them, a massive version of Belenos's artifact, multiple reddish metal sides with three near the top appearing to be reddish windows. Three rings like the electrons on a model of an atom circled it at zero, forty-five, and ninety degrees, each ring a track for some smaller satellite Isaac somehow knew were docking bays for single manned starships. A bright pinkish light shone from the bottom segment into the backyard, giving the ground a Dr. Seussish look.

Was everything on your planet red? Isaac looked down at their own armor critically.

On my planet, no. When our planet was consumed by one of our stars slowly going nova, we moved to build colonies on a series of red asteroids. The metal was good for construction and endured the stress of space travel well, so we complained little about the color. Isaac couldn't really tell if Belenos was amused or irritated, since his feeling of fear overpowered everything.

Isaac took a deep breath and tried to remember one of the Psalms he'd memorized as a child, since Scripture seemed to calm Belenos. '*The LORD is my light and my salvation, whom shall I fear, the LORD is the strength of my life, of whom shall I be afraid?*' *I need you to pull it together, Bel. I'm scared enough as it is, and our bond is just multiplying our fear.*

Bel didn't answer directly, but the soft tune of one of his star songs played in their memory and their fear eased.

A small hovering platform lowered from the spacecraft in the circle of light to the street. Standing in the middle of the platform manipulating a control board at the top of a narrow pillar located at the front of the platform, stood a bizarre looking being like those from Belenos's memories. Unlike the shades of brown most of the aliens in Bel's memories seemed to be, this one was nearly as white as the sand he landed in. He wore a colorful tabard of midnight blue with a unique star pattern in the middle, belted in the middle with a yellow sash. Heavy metal scaled boots protected his feet, and a razor ridge of linked metal ran from his forehead to his tail. One earring hung from his left ear, a rune in the same style of the ones that ornamented Bel's artifact.

Your brother?

His herald, probably. The earring marks him as servant to Tianyi and the Vistkian flag on his tabard marks him as a representative of state.

The herald gestured to them and spoke in a high pitched, barking language, which was translated by the control panel and broadcast after a slight delay.

"Earthworms, your god, Tianyi the Powerful, has tracked a sacred artifact to your world. Surrender the artifact and the one who has bound himself to it, and Tianyi will be merciful with you."

Isaac just glanced at Steve standing beside him. A fight here at full strength would kill both Steve and Dani, if Timir didn't just do it out of spite.

"Isaac, don't worry about us." Steve didn't even look at him. "If that messenger is from Tianyi, he'll kill you to get to Belenos. If he doesn't just want to kill both of you and eliminate the competition."

"I've seen Belenos's memories of his brother. If I don't, he'll kill others to get to me. It's how he controlled Belenos. You guys are in more danger than we are." *Bel? You were once a great general, right?* Isaac blew out a short breath through his nose as he gathered his strength to meet Belenos's brother.

Irritation and shame were Bel's only response.

We can face him, together. But only if you can get past your memories of your bond with him and look at him as any other enemy you faced. Forget he's your brother. Forget what he did while you were bonded. Today he's just another despot threatening to hurt innocents. We can take him. We have no choice.

They stepped between their friends and the herald. "We would speak to Tianyi, herald, he has insulted this planet with his presence and must give an account for his actions."

"The great Tianyi does not give account to anyone." The herald gestured to the spacecraft as another platform lowered toward them, carrying another alien.

This one was covered head to tail in spiked armor. He looked almost like a metal model of a Stegosaurus up on his hindlegs, except his eyes glowed red and the symbol that the herald wore on his ear glowed in his breastplate.

Tianyi. Isaac didn't even need to ask Belenos to recognize the alien. His armor was in much the same style as what he'd worn Belenos's memories of when he and his brother were bonded – terrible and excessive. Had Timir found another symbiote, or just modeled his replacement armor off Belanos? They desperately hoped it was the former. They weren't sure they could face a more powerful version of themselves.

"Timir!" Gemini stepped forward, speaking directly in the alien's language. "Your quarrel is not with them. Release them and speak with us."

251

"Tianyi, brother. Timir has not existed for over a century." Tianyi turned his glowing eyes on them. "You of all creatures should know that." He paused as he looked them over. "You should be pleased to return to Tianyi, this species is weak and soft."

"My new host is more noble and just than Tianyi ever was." It was weird enough to allow Belenos to speak through him, and even more so to hear his own voice speak the alien language, but hearing Bel's compliments from his own lips was just awkward.

"I still heard 'weak' and 'soft.'" Tianyi scoffed. "Abandon your pet human and return to me, and if he can survive you breaking your bond I will let him live." He raised his voice to the growing crowd. "I will graciously allow them all to live. Defy me and I will bring the entire force of my fleet down on the earthworm cities."

"The risk of separation is too great, greater even than with you." They answered softly as Belenos impressed an apology on Isaac's mind. "If he survives, he will be crippled or worse."

"Weak. Worthless," Tanyi mocked as he shuffled closer to them.

"Compatible," they returned without giving ground. "Our bond is deeper after mere months than Tianyi's was after one hundred years because we did not have to fight over every decision we made. If you promise to leave the humans alone, I will return with you, Tianyi, but I cannot return *to* you." Fighting here was out of the question. Not with Steve and Dani standing by. Not when Timir could order a strike on the terran cities as they fought. They had to get Timir out of orbit and away from earth.

"That is satisfactory. This star system is not a threat to us." Tianyi steered his hover platform back up toward the ship. "We have developed methods to make you cooperative. Orion, have the guards collect my brother, his host, and his companions. I await them on the ship."

"Tianyi, you faithless dust maggot!" Gemini cried as a swarm of armored Vistkians hovered down from the ship and surrounded the three of them. "You agreed to leave the humans alone."

"And I have spared eight billion of them as agreed. These two are insurance." Tianyi disappeared into the base of the spacecraft.

Steve whispered a mild expletive. Dani's was not so soft or mild. Gemini looked at them both and sighed. They'd hoped to shoulder all the risk alone and not involve anyone else in this. Of course Tianyi would have other plans.

The swarm of soldiers separated them and swept them up into the star ship, each sharing a hover platform with an armed guard.

What happens next? Isaac couldn't help but feel a little relieved they escaped so easily, in spite of the risk to Dani and Steve. Belenos's memories of razed cities and public executions were still burned into his own mind. *Can we protect them?*

As long as we do exactly what Tianyi demands. Anxiety seeped across their bond and tainted Isaac's relief. *But, Isaac, that will only work for a short time. Eventually he will demand your life, and theirs will be forfeit. We must find a way to take his ship before that happens.*

You know your way around this ship, help me watch for an opportunity and tell me what to do. Isaac looked back down at his home and remembered who he was doing all of this for. *We're all going home. There's no other choice.*

Chapter 21

The deep regret Belenos felt was hard to keep back from his host. He regretted the choices that led him to create a permanent bond with another host, not because he regretted the host – which he feared Isaac would think if he felt his regret – but because there were not enough scenarios where this ended well for Isaac. Even if they managed to free their friends, a fight with Tianyi would be hard to win. If they couldn't free their friends, a deal with Tianyi to spare Steve and Dani would be little better than suicide.

Stop it, Bel. It wasn't your fault. None of this is. Isaac's eyes trailed sharply over the area as they split off from the others and glided down the hall. *I chose to bond with you. I chose to go with Tianyi. Not because it was the only choice, but because it was the right choice. Someone had to stop your brother and people like him. We're the ones who can. I don't know if God's really paying attention to us – He and I haven't been on good terms for a while – but if anyone can get His attention, it's you. At the very least, you seem to grow stronger when you remember those star songs. Either way, we need all the help we can get.*

Belenos called to remembrance the Song of Sirius, a song of thanksgiving. Isaac was a host worth fighting for. *Creator, allow me grace to bring him home.*

Isaac pretended not to hear any of that, though Belenos could feel his awkward appreciation. They switched their focus to the guard sharing their hover platform. He was dressed very similarly to the herald, but with less elaborate spikes on his back. A short dagger hung from his waist sash and Isaac briefly wondered if they could take the dagger to use as a weapon. Which was just silly since their armor could form any weapon they needed. *What was Tianyi thinking to bring us here? He knows he can't beat us.*

We have developed methods to make you cooperative. They remembered Tianyi's words before they left the ground.

He meant Steve and Dani, didn't he?

Among other things. Memories Belenos was trying to suppress rose up forcefully. He shuddered and refocused. *I fear what technology and weapons they may have devised in the years since I was banished.*

I guess we're going to find out. They stopped at a pair of ornately painted double doors that slid open silently at their approach, revealing an even more elaborate throne room. The walls and floor were gilded, an immense expense on its own since gold was nearly unheard of in the Vistkian colonies, and a runner of thick, plush carpet led to a dias with a diamond inlaid backless throne. Tianyi sat on the throne, still in full armor, not that they expected anything else. Without Belenos, his power was built on intimidation and ruthlessness. The armor definitely was intimidating.

The hover platform stopped half a dozen feet from the foot of the throne and the guard shoved them toward the edge of the platform. At his touch, they absorbed enough of his energy to send the guard tumbling off himself.

"We join you by choice, brother." Gemini stepped off the platform and stood at the foot of the throne. "Your men will do well to remember."

"Your friends had slightly less choice, you would do well to remember." Tianyi grunted. "What name do you go by now? Have you taken a human name to become closer to his people?"

"We are Gemini to those we protect. Our friends know us by our names." Something was wrong with Tianyi. His claws dug deeply into the arms of the throne and he had barely moved since they had entered the throne room. His voice was stiff and strained, and the absence of females was conspicuous.

"I wish to see your host." Bitterness dripped from Tianyi's voice and his head tipped downward ever so slightly so he could look them over better.

"I wish to protect my host." Yes, they could reengage their armor at a thought, but the sonic attack at the house was just too fresh.

"I will not harm your pet earthworm, yet. I simply wish to see what you have chosen over me." Tianyi pushed himself to stand with effort and stepped down off the dias.

It's fine, Bel, just be ready to suit up if he tries something.

It wasn't, really, but it also wasn't worth harm coming to Steve or Dani over it either, so they pulled the armor back to the stasis necklace.

Isaac stood tall and still as Tianyi circled him slowly, examining him like a stock horse or circus novelty.

"What does my brother call you?" Tianyi switched to English to address them, much to both their surprise.

"My name is Isaac." Isaac held his breath as Tianyi's examination took him behind them and out of sight.

I've got it. Belenos assured him. *My sensors can cover the loss of sight.*

"Where are your scales?" Tianyi ran the side of one claw up Isaac's bare back, taking care not to touch the necklace. "And your tail?" He tugged at Isaac's waistband as if looking for it.

Belenos was offended for his host's sake, even though Isaac didn't flinch. *We are not a slave at market for your examination.* He tried to protest, but Isaac clamped his jaw shut.

Not worth it, Bel. I'm fine. As long as he isn't hurting me or the others, it's fine.

Tianyi was beside them now, and hooked a claw around one finger. "And your claws are too short. By the stars, no wonder my brother chose you, you would die in your first battle without him."

"Your brother chose me to stop an evil man that wished to use power to conquer our world." Isaac kept his voice steady and chose his words carefully so as not to give any reason for Tianyi to get angry. Not that Tianyi needed a reason.

"*Your* world." Tianyi was directly in front of him again, and his nearness made Belenos nervous. If he decided to kill Isaac, would he be fast enough to stop him? He hadn't been fast enough to stop him from killing General Mars. "Belenos belongs to Vistke. He took an oath to protect our star system and I intend to keep him to that oath." He pointed to the glowing rune in the center of the necklace. "'Protector.' Did you choose that, or did he?"

"Belenos agreed to work with me only on the condition that we were protectors, not... rulers." Belenos caught Isaac's quick reinterpretation of his original 'war god.' *Nice recovery.*

"My brother never did agree with my methods." Tianyi limped back to the throne, and lowered himself into it gingerly. He gestured for a drink a servant was quick to provide. "But we have had peace for well over a century now, no thanks to him."

Belenos scoffed, but Isaac was wise enough to keep it to himself.

"Why do you want him then?" Isaac framed his question slowly. "If you're doing fine without him, why bring us here?"

"Did my brother tell you what he did to me?" Tianyi's red eyes flashed as he sat up straighter on the throne, splashing the reddish brown liquid on his arm.

Only one color, Bel. Isaac was trying not to laugh. Belenos steadied him and assessed his health. Too little food and sleep and too much adrenaline was taking a toll on them. Belenos rerouted some of the energy from their armor to Isaac's body.

"I'm sure he told you the risks of bonding, or more specifically, the consequences of severing that bond." Tianyi continued without seeming to realize Isaac hadn't answered the first question. "Would you have bound yourself to him if you knew he had, suddenly and without warning, severed our bond?"

This time he waited for a response.

"I knew." Isaac answered softly. It didn't help anyone for them to argue with Tianyi over the justification for Belenos's extreme action.

"Do you know what the consequences were?" Tianyi stood again. "Did he tell you it left me a cripple? Did he tell you I couldn't leave my quarters for more than a few hours at a time for nearly a decade because of the dangerous hallucinations I suffered?" With each question his voice rose and shook. "Did he tell you that I was forced to replace him with this cheap imitation of his armor, that can only support my life, not heal me?"

A tentacle shot from his hand and wrapped around Isaac's waist, but they reacted in time to engage the armor before it could touch Isaac's bare skin. Belenos tried to probe his brother's mind, then to siphon energy from his brother's armor, but it didn't seem to work without a biological connection.

"Did he tell you that being bound to him keeps you from aging?" Tianyi's helmet folded back to uncover a narrow, graying face remarkably like their father's. "When we bonded, Timir was in his prime. As Tianyi, I didn't age a day. Weapons of war couldn't hurt me, and any injuries I happened to sustain were healed instantly. I was a god. Without him, I'm nothing more than an aging, crippled emperor. The hallucinations are gone, but nightmares plague my sleep, and times of dark depression threaten my will to live." He snapped the helmet back up. "My scientists were able to recreate the armor that houses my brother, but lacked the time, skill, and suitable volunteer to create another symbiote. I may be the most powerful being in the galaxy, but without Belenos, I am still dying. Only he can reverse the damage he has done."

"I will ask him to try to heal you if you agree to let our friends go." *If we can feel his pain when we touch him, perhaps we can take some of it as well. You know his body well enough to try to restore the damage.*

Maybe. Or contact with his nervous system may confuse our bond. Or disrupt it. Belenos felt the call of the bond he used to share with his brother. It was weak, the needs it had fulfilled now satisfied by his bond with Isaac, and easily denied, especially when coupled with his revulsion at the things Tianyi did. They couldn't guarantee that would hold true if they initiated deeper contact.

"You don't understand, earthworm." Tianyi crossed to a large column on the other end of the dias and tapped a few buttons with his claws. "I don't want to be healed. I want to live forever."

A feeling of cold numbness spread over them, along with a sense of hearing something just outside the range of audible sound. Belenos recognized the feeling and panicked. It was the same feeling he'd felt before he'd blacked out when the building collapsed on them and nearly killed his host.

Creator!

✳ ✳ ✳ ✳ ✳

Belenos's terror nearly undid Isaac, but the abrupt cut off of his presence was far worse. He dropped to his knees in grief as nausea gripped his stomach and expelled what little he had eaten before Tianyi had arrived. In the back of his mind, he could sense Belenos wasn't gone, but it was as if they had been separated from each other. The armor folded back to stasis, leaving him exposed to Tianyi, but he struggled to bring himself to care. *Belenos!* A deep feeling of loneliness seeped into his soul and all he wanted to do was curl up in the plush runner and weep.

"It's not pleasant, is it?" Tianyi's voice drew closer and reminded him why he had to hold it together. "Now imagine that plus crippling physical pain." His claw pricked the back of Isaac's neck near the base of his skull and Isaac flinched. "Did he tell you that he's actually in your brain? My physician told me that when he severed the bond, he damaged the brainstem and medulla." Tianyi pushed hard enough to force Isaac's head down. "It was like someone had pierced my skull with a long thin blade."

"What did you do to Belenos?" Isaac tensed himself to fight, but didn't fool himself about the outcome. Belenos could have killed their opponents any one of a million ways, but had no desire for needless bloodshed. Tianyi's track record was decidedly in the other direction.

"When my scientists scoured Zosma's notes from when he built my brother's armor, they discovered our father had required a fail safe trigger in case we became too powerful and tried to overthrow him." Tianyi scratched him all the way down his neck until his claw stopped at the top of the necklace, then went back to the throne in apparent exhaustion. "They may not have been able to replace my treacherous brother, but they did give me the tool to bring him back to me."

Isaac rubbed his hand over the scratch on the back of his neck and looked at the line of blood on his hand with a frown. Bel was still silent, the rune in the center of his broad collar necklace dull and lifeless. Isaac wasn't sure what the alien warlord had done to him, but the emptiness was nearly crippling. He felt like part of him had been ripped away.

He wants Bel back as his slave, he wouldn't kill him. Isaac tried to reassure himself. The silence in his head was less than convincing and his aching body served as a reminder that killing him would guarantee Bel fell to the alien.

Trapped, without backup, in an alien space ship that made the labs at Sentry Tech look like a kid's chemistry kit, wasn't exactly a good combination for survival. He was a janitor, not an astronaut.

"Perhaps now, without the influence of my brother, you will be more willing to negotiate." Tianyi steepled his claws and looked at him shrewdly. The doors behind them slid open and four guards led Steve and Dani inside. Isaac turned and was relieved to see they were unharmed.

"I'm listening." Isaac turned back to face Tianyi, his mind racing for a solution. There were six armed aliens – one with super armor and a grudge – and the three of them, unarmed. *Not good odds. Belenos, I need you. We're not leaving this room alive otherwise, and you'll be waking up with Tianyi as your master again.* His friend didn't answer.

"You surrender my brother of your own free will. My chief scientist will walk you through the steps. Perhaps if you are the one initiating and we take it slowly we can minimize the damage." Tianyi shrugged. "Either way, your friends would be free to take you home to recover in the expert care of your own doctors."

"Isaac, you can't leave Belenos with this monster," Steve shouted. The nearest guard jabbed him hard between the shoulders with the hilt of his dagger to shut him up.

"My scientists have found ways to take him from you by force, though the damage to your body systems would be irreparable." Tianyi looked at Steve and Dani. "I would prefer to make you cooperate willingly."

Chapter 22

Bel? Panic rose up in Isaac's chest as he looked at his friends. If he could contact Belenos, they could at least fight for their lives. Without Bel, the right thing wasn't readily obvious. If Belenos was going back to his brother no matter what he did, shouldn't he at least save Steve and Dani's lives?

"You see, even though we were never able to replicate the technology that turned my brother into a symbiotic superweapon, we were able to repurpose some of the components of his armor." A Vistkian in white robes shuffled forward carrying a small device that looked like one of the scales from Bel's armor. She nodded to the guards flanking Steve, who responded by taking him tightly by both arms and shoving him to his knees by the back of his head. The Vistkian scientist placed the device at the nape of Steve's neck and took a quick step back. "We could not obtain synergy, but we did find a way to override a subject's nervous system to allow control over his body."

"Release the male earthworm." Timir gestured at the guards. He pressed another button on the console near his throne. "Earthworm, take the weapon from the guard nearest you."

Fear lit Steve's face as he instantly turned to take the staff offered to him by the guard to his left.

"Twist the control ring and execute the Terran who has stolen my brother's loyalty," Timir ordered with pleasure in his voice.

With a sharp movement, Steve twisted the ring set in the middle of the staff, creating a bright, double-edged arc ax at the top.

"Steve, come on, it's me, Isaac." He couldn't fight his friend, even if the alien warlord had somehow taken possession of him. *Bel, I really need you here.* Nothing.

Steve's terrified eyes stared past him as he advanced with the glowing arc ax. He was close enough now that Isaac could smell the ozone from the electric arc and hear it crackling across the electrodes.

"Surrender Belenos and we will simply wipe your memories and return you home." Steve's voice sounded strangled and harsh and his movements jerked awkwardly like a robot from one of his classic sci-fi flicks. "Refuse and we will separate it from your lifeless corpse."

"Steve. You can fight this." Isaac backed into a metal bulkhead. He'd just run out of room. "You can't let this monster make you into a murderer." He remembered the nightmares he'd had when he'd first bonded with Bel. The alien warlord had turned his own brother – a nearly unconquerable soldier before he'd been turned into a nearly invincible weapon – into a murderer. Steve didn't stand a chance.

Which meant he didn't either. He slid his hand to the rune on his chest and tapped it sharply with his fingernail.

SONG OF THE STARS

I'm a janitor, not a martial artist, Bel. I can't take him down barehanded. Fear that whatever the alien had done to Bel was permanent seeped into the void left in Isaac's brain, wrapping his consciousness with panic and paralyzing depression. His knees buckled and he leaned harder against the bulkhead, his hands pressed against it to keep from slipping to the floor.

"You do well to fear me, earthworm." Not-quite-Steve spun the ax in a choppy circle, swiping the electric blade close enough to Isaac's bare chest that he could feel the heat. "You soft, scaleless creatures offered my brother little advantage as a host to begin with, but the fool had to choose a menial slave among your worthless kind. At least the slug I have chosen as my champion has power and training." The ax swung again more smoothly and Steve's voice sounded more natural even as a tear traced down his cheek from one wide, terrified eye. He was losing to the alien and whatever resistance Steve was giving to killing Isaac outright was wearing down.

At least if he kills me, the pain of losing Bel will end as well. The thought came startling and unbidden, followed by dark fingers of conviction that squeezed his heart and told him it was true. Bel had warned him of the consequences of a severed bond. Even more than that, he'd felt the effects of it in Bel's own broken consciousness. But now that he felt it himself, it was as if that was *all* he could feel. Consuming, black, overpowering grief, overwhelming even the looming threat of immediate death.

God help me! He closed his eyes and dropped his head back against the bulkhead. He had to fight both the pain and Steve, if only for Becca and Aster's sake. *Forgive me for leaving you. I was a fool. Bel trusted you in spite of all the horrors he suffered. Give me a portion of his faith.* If Bel were there, he could just ask him to share, to bolster his nearly nonexistent faith with his own deeper, stronger one. But it still wouldn't truly be his. *Whatever happens here, accept my life as bound to you first.*

"I surrender!" Isaac looked to Tianyi and Steve checked his advance. "Just, promise me that you'll let us return to our homes safely and that you'll leave our solar system for good." *I'm sorry, Bel, the chance of survival is better for all of us if I surrender. Maybe if I initiate the severing of our bond carefully, it won't kill us. Allowing your brother to rip us apart certainly will.* He wasn't sure if Belenos could hear him. Perhaps it was better if he didn't. It was definitely better that he couldn't share the skepticism Isaac felt. He'd separated willingly the night he'd told Becca about Bel, and had been miserably ill by morning, and they hadn't even been fully bonded yet. *It's going to be bad, isn't it?*

"Easily. What use do I have for scaleless earthworms?" Tianyi's aquiline face became grave as he gestured for his scientists to free Steve from the mind control device. "There is still considerable risk in breaking your bond with my brother. I cannot swear to your condition when the process is over. It might be best for you to share your goodbyes with your friends now."

That was when Isaac realized that Tianyi intended to kill him once he had Belenos. Still, it was better if it was just him rather than all four of them. Besides, if Timir bonded with Bel again, maybe Bel would have better luck stopping him than Isaac had to this point. He set his jaw and nodded, then crossed the throne room to where the others stood. The guards took a step back to give them space, but watched warily for any trouble.

"You can't do this!" Steve took him by the shoulders and whispered urgently. You know he's not going to let the competition for his brother's loyalty walk away." He laid his hand on the dull rune. "Tell him, Belenos..." His eyes went wide. "Isaac?"

"He shut down Belenos. I– I can't feel him anymore." Isaac fought to keep his voice steady. "He's going to kill all of us, Steve. At least this way there's a chance you guys survive."

"And Belenos." Dani rolled her eyes. "The alien wannabe isn't going to harm Belenos any more than strictly necessary to bring him back to himself."

"Unless he'd rather see his 'traitorous' brother dead than bonded with a new host." Steve squinted his eyes suspiciously at Tianyi. "Total supervillain move."

"Stop it, Steve." Isaac's blood ran cold. He didn't really put it past Tianyi either. *Lord, there is no good choice. We're toast either way.*

"Just saying."

Dani elbowed him hard.

"Look guys, either way we all know I'm cashing in on that insurance policy." Isaac avoided Steve's eyes. "Make sure Becca and Aster are taken care of, okay?"

Steve nodded and clasped Isaac's hand in a rough handshake that turned into a hearty hug.

"And, Dani, we both know you don't really like us –" Isaac was interrupted by Dani throwing her arms around his neck in an uncharacteristically impetuous hug.

"How's he controlling Belenos?" She whispered into his neck. "The same way he controlled Steve?" Her fingers felt the back of his neck for the device that had controlled Steve.

"No, I think it's some sonic signal from that control panel next to his throne." Isaac returned her hug uncomfortably, even though he knew it was more about plotting than seduction. "But there's no way to get to it, and even if there was –"

"Have we sufficiently dismissed your friends, earthworm, or must we wait while you make love to that female?" Tianyi tapped the arm of his throne with an impatient claw.

"She's not, I mean, I'm not..." Isaac flushed deep red and stepped away from Dani quickly. Part of him knew that it was better for Tianyi to think they were lovers than to suspect the truth, that they were plotting against him. A larger part of him rebelled against the mere suggestion that he might be unfaithful to Becca. He blew out a slow breath to compose himself. "I'm ready."

"Good!" Tianyi sat up straighter and motioned for a scientist to come closer. "Cassopia will guide you through the steps to separate you from my brother."

The white clad Vistkian shuffled forward with a vial of shimmering brownish liquid. She offered it to Isaac with a series of barking sounds that Tianyi had to translate for him. "This will ease your pain and relax your neural synapses to make the removal of the symbiote less likely to cause permanent damage."

Isaac had already felt like throwing up, but the smell of the concoction coupled with the clinical description of what he was about to do made his stomach turn. He took the vial in both hands and swallowed back the bile that rose up in his throat. *Forgive me, Belenos.* Holding his breath, he knocked back the drink before his taste buds could refuse. It tasted like a mixture of urine and paint remover, and burned all the way down to his stomach. For a brief moment, he remembered Steve's prediction that Tianyi wouldn't let him live to compete for Belenos's loyalty and wondered if he'd just willingly drank poison.

"You will start to feel numb in both mind and body." The alien scientist pointed to the carpet. "You may be more comfortable if you sit down."

He did, somewhat abruptly, as the liquid burned through his veins and faded to a quiet numbness. It wasn't that he couldn't feel, but it was the exact opposite of his bonding with Belenos. If Belenos enhanced his senses, this drink muted them, to the point where he felt sleepy and disconnected from his body.

"Lay your hand on the rune in the armor's necklace and repeat what I say exactly." Tianyi stood and shuffled to the control column and tapped a few buttons with his claws. "I, Isaac Anderson, renounce you, Belenos, and reject you as my symbiote."

"I, Isaac Anderson, renounce you, Belenos." Isaac choked on the statement just as the flood of Belenos's presence filled him again.

Isaac! What have you done? Even Belenos's horror felt distant against the power of whatever he'd just drank.

I'm sorry, Bel. Forgive me. All his reasons and grief clashed with Belenos's own. He placed his face in his hands and pushed on. "And reject you as my symbiote."

Belenos didn't answer, but his grief-stricken presence forced a tremulous feeling of understanding and forgiveness as the dullness of the medicine pushed its way into the space Belenos occupied.

"Faith, Honor, Justice, Protection, Peace, Family, Duty." Tianyi intoned the series of words in English, then again in his own language. "Say it!"

"Faith, Honor, Justice, Protection, Peace, Family, Duty." Isaac could barely force the words out in English, Vistkian wasn't happening. Belenos compassionately spoke the words through him, his final act as his companion. With a crack and a stabbing pain between his shoulders where the necklace had joined, the necklace fell off Isaac's neck.

In spite of the alien concoction, Isaac screamed. It was worse than anything he had anticipated. It felt as if someone had reached in and ripped his spine from his skull, then stabbed him in the chest at the same time. The emptiness he'd felt after a night without Belenos before they were fully bonded was nothing compared to the bleak darkness that flooded his mind now. He clutched his hands to his head and wept deeply.

✳ ✳ ✳ ✳ ✳

Belenos had snapped awake disoriented, which only worsened when he realized that Vistkian sedatives flooded Isaac's body. The medicine was widely used in surgery and medical procedures on Vistke, but served here as an odd buffer between him and his host.

Isaac! What have you done? He knew what he'd done – or at least agreed to do – and the horror of his host's decision cut through him like a knife.

I'm sorry, Bel. Forgive me. Isaac's reasoning and grief seeped through their muddled bond, his desperation clear most of all.

"And reject you as my symbiote."

In that split second, Belenos was faced with the choice to fight. To purge Isaac's body of the medication that his brother had given him, to stop his host before he could complete the ritual – and to subvert Isaac's free will. Creator help him, Isaac's reasoning was sound, and exactly what he would have done in Isaac's place. Perhaps if he were returned to his brother, he could spare the lives of Isaac and his friends in a way he never could as Tianyi before. He tried to mask his own terror and grief with forgiveness and understanding, but was very aware that every emotion he felt crossed their bond as Isaac finished the ritual.

"Faith, Honor, Justice, Protection, Peace, Family, Duty." Tianyi intoned the series of words in English, then again in Vistkian"Say it!"

Isaac couldn't form the Vistkian words, not without Belenos's help. *Creator, protect him, allow him to return to his family in peace.* As Isaac choked out the final words of the Vistkian pledge of honor, Belenos echoed them in Vistkian. If there was any way that he could increase the odds that his host survived the ritual, he would do it, no matter what it cost him.

Once the final word rasped past Isaac's lips, Tianyi leaped off the dias with energy he hadn't shown to this point, catching the artifact in his hands before it even hit Isaac's lap. His armor folded away and a servant was quick to remove it to prepare for the rite to restore his bond with Belenos.

Belenos barely noticed. Isaac's scream was amplified in his own mind by his own cry of agony. Part of him worried about what the severance of their bond was doing to Isaac, the larger part was simply trying not to drown in the colliding memories of past and present. His brother's tyranny, the pain of their sudden separation, followed by decades of dark misery, tortured visions, and bleak loneliness.

He couldn't go through it again. *Creator, give me strength to bear this or allow my brother to kill us both.* He was telegraphing his fear and panic to his brother in spite of his best efforts to mask it. His brother, on the other hand, was making no effort to hide his enjoyment of Bel's misery.

I have no intention to kill you, brother. I need you and you need me. His brother caressed the runes on the outside of the artifact that housed him. *That earthworm had nothing to offer you. With my charisma and your power we could rule his entire worthless galaxy.*

We are this system's protector, not its war god. Bel chose his words carefully. His brother's use of the past tense to refer to Isaac terrified him more. If there was any chance Isaac lived, making him out to be a threat to the Vistkian war god would only result in his brother tearing out Isaac's heart. He scanned the room for Isaac's vitals. His former host's heart rate was dangerously elevated and he still lay crumpled on the floor between his friends, weeping brokenly. He hadn't moved, and Belenos prayed to the Creator it wasn't because he couldn't.

Bah. Because your host was impotent. His brother traced the first rune in his bonding sequence longingly. His lust for

Bel's power was strong, and the longer they were in contact, the stronger the pull of their former bond grew. *We were power. We were worshiped. We were feared. Our people were protected from every evil when we ruled together.*

Every evil except ourselves. Bel angrily pushed through their connection the memories of every murder his brother had committed with his power. All of them – their names, families, and petty crimes – had been etched in Bel's memory for years. The montage ended with the baker's daughter, who had dared refuse the amorous advances of the Vistkian war god. *I will not be used by you again.*

You like it brother, you know you do. Tianyi clutched the artifact tighter in his claws. *I showed you a life you never could have hoped to have before. We conquered every enemy of Vistke. I felt your pride and hubris when the final enemies fell. I shared your sense of accomplishment when Vistke reaped our first bountiful harvests and we declared a day of thanksgiving.*

Until you declared that thanksgiving was to be to us. Belenos felt overwhelmed with the memories, guilt, and shame, both from his time as Tianyi, and from his ill-fated bonding with Isaac. He was barely hanging on to his sanity, and Isaac's muffled sobs just seemed to nudge him closer to the edge. *Creator, grant me grace. I cannot save him if I lose my mind.*

"Oh, great, all-wise Tianyi." Cassopia shuffled over hesitantly, bowing seven times as she came. "I think perhaps it might be wise to wait to bond with the symbiote until we assess the damage separating him from his host may have caused. In your current state, we can't afford for you to bond with a damaged symbiote."

Belenos stifled a mad laugh. He wasn't sure what was worse, a power-mad war god, or a grief-crazed war god. His laugh wavered on the edge of hysterics and Tianyi hesitated.

Did you grieve like this when you betrayed me? Tianyi's claws tightened on the artifact as the accusation crossed their connection.

Belenos's laugh stuttered and silenced. *It was different,* he answered carefully. *The circumstances of our separation made it worse in some ways.* And far better in others, he managed to keep to himself.

Then you will recover quicker this time. Tianyi's answer was careless, but his eyes were narrowed on the three humans as Steve and Dani helped Isaac to his feet.

Send them on their way, as you promised. Belenos tried to keep his tone firm, but he no longer had any control over his emotional presentation and sounded plaintive instead. It was getting to the point he just needed his human friends to leave so he could stop fighting his descent into madness. He was losing anyway. Isaac looked so weak, so broken. If Tianyi didn't let them go... Belenos started weeping and couldn't keep the sobs from crossing their connection. *You don't need them, you have me already.*

Do I, though?

Belenos's fear spiked to terror as Tianyi stepped within arm's reach of Isaac. *No, Tianyi, please. I beg you to spare him. For our sake. I cannot bear the loss.*

Spare him? So that you can continue to pine over your precious earthworm? Bitterness edged Tianyi's words as his red eyes fixed on Isaac's pale face and hectic cheeks. *Even without completing the bonding ritual, I can sense within you more love for him than we ever shared.*

Steve and Dani interpreted Tianyi's intentions as well. Dani pulled Isaac away into her arms as Steve stepped between him and Tianyi.

"Spare him? So that for the rest of our eternity, I will have to fear whether you will betray me for a chance to be with him again?" Tianyi was bellowing with rage now.

Without the completed bonding ritual, or at least unless Tianyi chose to activate the armor, there was nothing Belenos could do to stop him. He tried to push a feeling of calm and peace across their connection, but he didn't have any left of his own to share. If he shared his terror and grief, Tianyi might kill all of them in his madness. *Creator...* What? The Creator seemed so far away and all he could hear was his own terror mingling with the evil his brother intended. How could there be any light when all he was surrounded by was darkness? *My God, My God why hast thou forsaken me?* The Song of Centauri threaded through his memory, its somber tune in sync with the darkness in his soul.

You left me for dead and at the edge of madness, brother. Do not lie and tell me you grieved for me like you do this slug. You would do all in your power to save him the misery you put me through. Tianyi cupped his metal tipped claws in front of him and looked at them in satisfaction. *I mean to oblige.*

He tossed Belenos's artifact aside as he swiped Steve away from Isaac and plunged his long claws into Isaac's chest with a soft, wet sound. Dani screamed a vulgarity at him as Isaac crumpled into her arms. She lay him on the floor beside her and began pressing her hands rhythmically to his chest, alternating it with pressing her mouth to his lips in some unfamiliar ritual as she wept.

"No, no, no, no!" Steve breathed from where he'd fallen beside Belenos.

Tianyi surveyed them dispassionately. "Now Belenos will owe me alone his loyalty. He cannot return to a corpse."

Chapter 23

Isaac was dead. Bel could sense the last beat of his damaged heart even from a distance. Something died inside him as well, a cancerous, spreading death that consumed not only where Isaac had been, but also Bel's own consciousness, leaving only barren emptiness inside him. His brother had taken everything from him. He would not be his brother's pawn, but he could be his brother's end. He would allow him to bond with him one last time, then he would destroy both his brother and himself. They were neither a war god or a protector. They were a plague that needed to be eradicated before it infected the universe. He had the power to end that plague. Perhaps in the end it was the only thing his power was good for.

"You're a monster!" Steve yelled as he broke free of the guards and knelt beside Dani as she continued the repetitive death ritual.

"Take the earthworms to my scientists." His brother gestured to his guards. "The living male and female may prove interesting as breeding stock for slaves. They can do as they wish with the body. Dissection may prove quite informative."

"Give us a moment, you overgrown anteaters." Steve angrily slapped away the hand of the guard that reached for him and swore. "He was our friend. The least you can do is give us space to grieve for him properly."

At a nod from Tianyi, the guards stepped back, watching Dani warily as if concerned her ritual would revive Isaac.

"He needs Bel," Dani whispered tremulously to Steve as she continued her futile ritual. "I– His injuries are too great. CPR can't restart a heart as badly damaged as his."

Steve nodded grimly and kissed her on the top of the head. The Vistkian war god would kill him as well, if he even made it past the guards.

Bel cursed the choice that bound him inside his artifact with no way to warn Isaac's friend – his friend – not to sacrifice his life foolishly. He'd never raised the dead. Only the Creator had that power. And the Creator had clearly abandoned them.

"You hateful monster!" Steve growled as he extended his arms and made a dash for Tianyi.

Tianyi raised his claws and waved off the guards. "Face me, then, earthworm, and suffer the fate of your friend."

Inches from Tianyi's claws, Steve veered, dove for Belenos's artifact, and scooped it up against his chest.

"Isaac needs you," he whispered into his chest as he popped back to his feet and pivoted toward their fallen friend.

Isaac is... Belenos muted a scream. *There's nothing I can do.*

Steve didn't respond, the guards were almost on him as Tianyi screamed for them to kill him before he could activate the armor for himself. It wasn't a terrible idea, if the symbiote within the armor hadn't been leaning over the edge of madness. *Don't, Steve. It's not safe.*

I don't plan on it. Steve grunted as a blast from a hand cannon hit his leg and he went down halfway to his goal. *You need Isaac as badly as he needs you.* He hit the runes he'd watched Isaac use before and tossed the artifact underhand between the descending guards.

Tianyi screamed and clutched at the artifact in midair, his claws grazing the metal as it passed. The artifact tumbled a bit, but landed on Isaac's still warm body.

The moment the artifact hit Isaac's bare chest, Belenos activated. If there was any spark of life in his host, he might be able to coax it out. He spread across Isaac's body urgently, engulfing him in a cocoon of metal.

Isaac was truly dead, his heart pierced in five places by Tianyi's claws. Grief slammed Belenos with an unimaginable force. *Creator, why?* He screamed into the emptiness that had been his host's consciousness.

You can fix him, right, Belenos? Dani's touch brought a desperate plea and a shaky confidence. She wanted to believe in him – she needed to believe in him – but just wasn't sure if she could.

Am I the Creator of life? Belenos snapped back angrily. He wanted to believe in himself as well, but that power was out of his reach. *Continue your burial ritual and allow me to take care of my brother.* The rage in his tone was scaring her, it was scaring him, frankly. If it wasn't for Dani and Steve, he would release all the power remaining to him in a blast that would destroy everything in this infernal starship.

Please, just try. You can rebuild his heart and close the wounds right? Start with that. She was barely holding it together, not unlike him. *If you can't heal him, we're all dead.*

I can try. Denial wasn't going to help either of them, but perhaps if he tried it would give them both something else to think about. Other than replaying every murder committed by his brother, with his brother in place of the victim. That wasn't going to help either, as satisfying as it might seem right now.

I'll try to distract the alien – no offense – he seems like the kind that might need a female touch.

Belenos couldn't possibly see what interest his brother would have in a female of another species, but he wouldn't put it past him to be arrogant enough to be flattered into trying.

The last thing he felt from Dani before she stood and broke the connection was a sense of revulsion as she pondered the same question.

He focused feverishly on the superficial wounds, healing cuts and bruising that hadn't been there before he'd blacked out. Restoring their bond was critical, but every fiber of Belenos's being revolted against the idea. It was nearly impossible to fool himself about the severity of the damage with the connection he had, bonding with a corpse would remove any illusions he had left about his chances of success. *Creator, give me strength.* He stopped repairs for a moment to still his trembling. He played the Song of Orion begging the creator for rescue and healing as he steeled himself to restore his bond with his lifeless host. Bonding was easy, but only increased the feeling of emptiness he sensed from Isaac's body. Even contact with his brain stem felt lifeless and cold. Feeding some of his energy to Isaac's nervous system allowed him the control and access he needed to make the deeper repairs, but Isaac was still gone. A deep sob gripped him. What was the point? Without life, he could use his host like an automaton, possibly even defeat his brother, but then what? It seemed sacrilegious, like a violation of Isaac's body and will.

The sound of a body hitting the floor behind him distracted him just as he was about to begin his own Vistkian burial ritual. Steve moaned and stirred at Tianyi's feet, wounded but alive. Tianyi's attention was on Dani, who sat on the edge of the table with her legs crossed and her chest thrust forward.

"I tried to get Isaac's attention, but he only had eyes for his own wife." She looked down demurely and toyed with the hem of her skirt. "I'm a very intelligent woman, and the men on my world find that intimidating. I'd hoped someone of his power could see the advantages I could bring him."

"My brother's host was a fool." Timir took a step toward her, his beady eyes sweeping over her curiously. "As Tianyi, I took as many females as I desired. I was a god. He could have been a god."

"I would love to be with a god." She stood slowly from the table and touched Timir's arm, trailing her fingers up it as she drew closer. She pressed her body to his and laid her other hand on his chest.

"Ugh, Dani, seriously?" Steve coughed and wiped his mouth on his sleeve, glared at the blood smeared there, then at her. His heart rate fluttered dangerously. "I thought you and I...."

"What's going to happen to Belenos now that Isaac is dead?" She stroked Tianyi's fur and pointedly ignored Steve. Her biological signs were more consistent with terror than arousal. She was staking everything on distracting Tianyi long enough for Belenos to heal Isaac.

Creator, guide my healing skills. If there is any way for me to revive Isaac and save our friends and this star system, show me.

The repairs to Isaac's body were nearly finished, and Belenos was aware both that he could use his energy to restart his host's heart and that he would probably not handle it well if he were to do so only to have a functioning, empty shell. *Creator–* He didn't have any words, didn't know what to pray. He felt as if he were coming apart inside, his soul as shredded as Isaac's heart.

Steve's heavy presence leaned against him. *How's it coming?* His biological signs teetered on the verge of shock. Tianyi's blow had missed his heart, but pierced his lung.

I have repaired all of the physiological damage. Belenos tried to steady his tone, but came off sounding monotonously lifeless.

But he's not waking up. Steve rubbed at his wound and coughed again. *You know your brother best. What happens to Dani if we don't do something fast?*

Belenos barked a mirthless laugh. *Exactly what she's pretending she wants. Her continued survival will then depend on her ability to keep him entertained until he decides he's ready to bond with me again.*

Then what happens? Steve's thinking was becoming sluggish. The small mercy would be that he would likely not be conscious to see the alien warlord seduce his girlfriend.

Then I tear him apart from the inside while flooding his mind with all the horrors he has committed over the past century.

Steve blinked slowly and recoiled, his horror palpable even without the connection. *Heaven help us all.*

Indeed. Heaven help them, he had to try to revive Isaac. He was losing it without him, slipping not-so-slowly into madness. Failure might push him over the edge, but he was heading over as it was, may as well make one last attempt to save all of them.

Modulating his electrical charge carefully, he mimicked the natural charge of Isaac's heart. It started gently, and he prodded his lungs to breathe next. Belenos scanned Isaac's brain function down to the cellular level and found no damage, but no consciousness either. *Creator of life, I can rebuild what you created but I cannot return Isaac's soul to his body. For the sake of the many people in this star system who serve you, please, return the spark of life to his body.*

Something changed. Belenos almost missed it at first, as minor as it was. A warmth of Isaac's presence where only ice had been.

Come on, Isaac, wake up.

Revulsion shot through him where Steve had laid his head on their armored chest. Tianyi had backed Dani against the control panel on the dias, held her in a close embrace and was stroking her ear and cheek with his long tongue. Dani was doing an impressive job of pretending she was enjoying herself, which probably made Steve feel worse. *I just need her to keep it up a little longer.*

Steve caught his breath and tensed, but remained silent.

Belenos pushed more energy toward Isaac's presence, trying to coax the spark into a flame.

Bel... What happened? I was having the most wonderful dream... Isaac felt tired and disoriented, but otherwise fine. Belenos just wanted to break down and weep.

I'm sorry– How much should he say at the moment? Belenos decided to stick to the critical information. *Steve is injured, Dani is pretending to seduce my brother to buy us time, and they all think you're dead. If we want to make a move to stop my brother, that move is now.*

Why do they think I'm dead? Isaac looked around the room carefully to assess the situation before moving. He responded with the same disgust Steve had at the human and Vistkian making out on the other side of the throne room. *How am I not dead? Why are you not with him again?*

Long story, one we don't have time for. Belenos passed Steve a warning they were going to move. *Steve needs medical attention soon, and I think Dani might appreciate a rescue.*

Steve gave a relieved sigh and rolled to the side. His vital signs were weak, but steady. Dani was bent over backwards over the control panel while Tianyi's paws strayed over her body. Gemini stood to their feet, eliciting a cry of alarm from the guards and an irritated glare from Tianyi, who didn't even bother to release Dani.

"Foolish brother, reanimating a corpse is beneath you and will not sustain you like a living host." Tianyi sneered derisively and pulled Dani close to his side.

Belenos shuddered. Reanimating Isaac's corpse would have been both a horrible violation of their bond, and an act of desperation he wouldn't quite have put past his desperate, grief maddened self as an alternative to returning to Tianyi.

Isaac sensed his horror and shame and sent him a calming reassurance. *I'm here, and not a zombie. We're good.* He willed the helmet visor to peel open and answered in his own voice. "It's pretty bad when your own brother would still rather bond with a corpse than with you."

"I felt your heart rupture in my claws." Rage contorted Tianyi's face and he dropped Dani as he stepped off the dias toward them. "There should have been no way for my brother to revive you."

Dani fixed her clothes and hair and made an obscene gesture behind Tianyi's back.

"Yeah, I don't get it either, but as you can see I'm not dead." Isaac's face twitched as he tried to suppress a laugh at Dani's behavior. "And since you've proved not to be an honorable dictator, I'm going to demand that you release my friends and us and get your spaceship out of my solar system."

Chapter 24

"You forget so soon that I can disable your armor. This time I will rip your limbs from your body so my traitorous brother can't possibly put you back together again." Tianyi snarled and lunged for the control panel.

Dani picked up the low throne and smashed it into the control panel with a loud, "Ooops." She spun out of the way of Tianyi's claws and scrambled to Steve's side where she rapidly began applying pressure to his wounds.

Tianyi roared in such rage that even his own guards took a step back. He snatched his armor out of the hands of the startled servant and activated it. "I am the better being. I can defeat you both myself."

Gemini quickly formed an electric sword in one hand and a gun in the other. *What are we going to shoot?*

Whatever we can get our hands on. Vistkian metal is the only thing that can penetrate his armor.

We're going to have to kill him. Isaac's nervous thought echoed Belenos's own.

I know. It was the only way to keep Tianyi from killing Steve and Dani, and hunting them down again and placing Becca and Aster in danger.

Tianyi formed a solid metal sword of his own and charged them with a cry. Their swords crossed with an arc of electricity, but no damage to either of them. Tianyi pushed them back weakly. The Vistkian may have been stronger in his youth, but age was telling on him and he was now a much more even match for Isaac. They drove him back with an energy blast from the gun.

We'll need an energy source if we wish to keep that up. Belenos drew their attention to the sparking, mangled control panel.

"I can absorb energy, too, brother. We're at a standoff. Equals locked in an eternal fight for supremacy." Tianyi returned a larger blast of energy as if to emphasize his point.

Gemini ducked and rolled out of the way, but the energy blast tore a hole in the bulkhead, sucking one of the guards through the hole. Dani screamed as the vacuum sucked her and Steve toward the opening. Gemini turned their boots into cleats that gripped the floor, and scooped Steve and Dani both into their arms as the second guard desperately opened the door to the hallway and crawled through. Steve was unconscious and heavy in their arms, but Dani seemed fine other than being terrified. Fighting the suction of the hole in the bulkhead was slow work, but Gemini finally managed to get them into the hallway.

"The guard dropped his spear, it should be enough to protect you and Steve while we take care of–" They broke off with a cry as another blast hit them from behind, knocking them to their knees.

A third, larger blast sent flames curling around them, licking toward Dani and Steve and forcing Dani to hunch over the injured man to protect him from the blast. They needed to get the door closed to separate Tianyi and the vacuum from their friends.

The room can be sealed to prevent an atmosphere leak. Belenos passed him the sequence of buttons to hit on the panel beside the door and they quickly pulled back inside and locked the hatch. They turned to face Tianyi. Fighting him and a hull breach was going to be incredibly difficult. *There's an emergency patch kit on the wall beside the door.*

They dodged another blast, tore the kit free, activated it, then let the rushing air take it toward the gap. The kit expanded, covering the whole breach and sealing the leak. They were free to take on Tianyi.

"You traitorous parasite!" Tianyi's next blast knocked them into the wall. "How could you abandon your own brother and the power of Tianyi in favor of this earthworm? What does he give you that I cannot?"

Gemini transformed their left arm into an arc ax and their right arm into a nanoblade sword and advanced on Tianyi. "Everything. We have attained a level of synergy that Tianyi never could. Life with you was a constant fight for our ethics, values, reputation, and even our souls. No amount of blood or power could make up for that."

They deflected Tianyi's next blast with the nanoblade sword and Tianyi traded his blaster for a sword of his own. They clashed, and Gemini pressed the weakening dictator back to the crumbled throne. "I will not return to you, Timir. There is no victory for you here. Yield, and we will allow you to return to Vistke in peace."

"I will not yield, faithless leech. I hope you are satisfied with your soul, because your betrayal will cost you and your pet slug your lives." Tianyi formed the breastplate of his armor into a quickly growing metal spike.

Gemini realized almost too late that the spike was aimed at their rune. They jerked back, enough to avoid an immediately fatal direct blow, but still caught the spike through the chest below and to the right of the rune. Pain ripped through them as the spike lifted them off the ground. Their scream echoed through the throne room. System alerts flashed across their visor. Stabilizing their injuries was taking nearly all their resources and armor integrity was obviously compromised, leaving them vulnerable. Tianyi could easily peel them apart and destroy them both. Isaac's consciousness flickered. The tentacle had missed his newly repaired heart, but had done critical damage to his lung and liver. Nothing Belenos couldn't heal under normal circumstances, but not when their armor was damaged or while the tentacle still impaled them.

Can we cut it off and assimilate it for repairs? Isaac groaned and sagged against the tapered metal limb. Blood bubbled from the wound with every beat of his heart. Belenos quickly sealed the armor around the tentacle and filtered his host's blood back into him. Belenos knew well that he was the only reason Isaac was still conscious, was still in pain, but the only way they were getting out of this alive was together. Belenos needed Isaac.

Not without risking further damage to both of us. Belenos remembered trying to bond with Isaac's lifeless body and nearly panicked. Stars, if his host died again he'd rather go with him.

Isaac shuddered as Belenos's shared memory, but pushed back against the panic. *Worse than what Tianyi is going to do anyway?*

"Good bye, Belenos." Tianyi bared a paw and laid it on their bloody rune. "I want to hear your screams at the end, brother, as well as the cries of your worthless pet. I hope an eternity of omnipotence was worth sacrificing for a few hours of synergy."

Gemini screamed again as Timir began expanding the width of the spike in their chest, then in a move of duel desperation triggered Bel's ultimate sacrifice play. Expending all the energy they could afford, they exploded their armor into a hail of shrapnel scales. Tianyi's scream joined theirs as the majority of the razor sharp scales sliced through his armor and into his body. He staggered back, retracting the spike from their chest and letting them fall to the floor as he sat down hard against the broken throne.

Isaac, please, stay with me. Bel spread what was left of their armor over the wound, but only had enough material left to manipulate their stasis necklace to seal the wound on either side. His friend's consciousness was fading and his heart rate flickered dangerously. That move had never been designed to allow them to survive, but they had done their best to pull back enough to allow them to heal enough to walk away – at least that had been the plan. Isaac's fading life signs made Bel fear they had failed that gamble as well. *Creator, intervene. Earth is not yet safe, and our friends are forfeit if we fail now.*

"Isaac? Bel?" Dani's pensive voice came from the cracked door. When she didn't get immediately sucked into the void or blasted by a vengeful alien dictator, she stepped in more boldly. "I heard screaming, then silence..." She broke off with a gasp and ran to their side. Steve's blood stained her dress and hands. "Isaac!" She placed a hand on the stuttering light of the rune. "Bel, what happened."

We defeated Timir, but may have sacrificed ourselves to do so. The toll of their gamble weighed heavy on him. It had been their choice, made together in a split second of mutual desperation, but he would be the only one that realized the cost. *We are critically damaged and Isaac is dying. If he dies while we are bonded, we both will die, and I will not leave him. Please. I cannot do this again.*

"What can I do?" Dani's eyes grew wide and her exhaustion and fear crossed their connection. Steve was not doing well and she was in real danger of being left on the alien ship alone. "I'll do anything you ask."

We need a power source and the resources to rebuild our armor. He directed her attention to the broken control panel beside Tianyi's fallen body. *Nearly everything here is the same metal as our armor and the wiring to that panel will suffice.*

Dani stood with a nod and tucked her hands under their armpits. She dragged their body up the platform and propped them against the smashed control panel.

Bel finished closing Isaac's wound enough that he could risk redirecting what remained of their armor to the panel's open column. The access to power was an immediate relief, and the broken remains of the column and platform would provide more than enough material for them to recover completely.

If they had enough time. Which they did not. Steve's state was still in question, and they all still needed to go home before one of Tianyi's loyal guards decided to seek revenge for their emperor's death. If any loved him enough to care.

"I brought Steve inside so that the guards can't get to him, but can't lock the door." Dani returned, knelt beside them, and rested her hand on their rune. "Timir is *very* dead. He looks like he was caught in an IED blast. What did you do to him?"

We fashioned an IED from our scales. Bel connected to the LAN wires beside the electrical ones and realized he could in fact control the whole ship from there. Helpful once they were stabilized and Steve was attended to. *We can lock the door from the control panel. What is Steve's status?*

"I managed to get the bleeding stopped, but I don't know if he'll make it home." Dani's voice wavered. "Can you help him? When you're done with Isaac, I mean." She swore. "Bel, you can't leave me here alone on this ship."

I do not intend to. He passed relief and confidence across their connection. Isaac's vital signs were stabilizing, their armor was nearly repaired enough to continue healing once he awoke, and Bel had a plan.

Isaac took a deep, shaky breath, and Dani pulled her hand back with an exclamation of relief and surprise.

"Isaac Anderson if you're going to insist on trying to cash in on that insurance policy, you better make sure Steve and

I are off this blasted UFO first." She punched him lightly on his bare shoulder.

"We kinda had to stop the alien monster that was trying to keep us from getting home to begin with." Isaac groaned and tried to sit up. "Dang. I must be alive. Dead wouldn't hurt this badly."

Lie still for a little longer. We are not dead, but we are far from repaired. Bel finished harvesting enough metal to cover their chest and right arm, and sent off a couple commands across the ship's LAN. *We must see to Steve.*

They disconnected from the platform and crossed the room to where Steve lay by the door. The energy they absorbed masked their own injuries with a heady feeling of false vitality. Hopefully it would be enough to get off the flag ship and home to earth.

Steve's skin was a grayish pallor and his breathing shallow as they knelt beside him and laid a hand over the wound. *Can—can we heal him? We took a lot of energy, can't we use it to heal him?*

Belenos hesitated. He'd never tried to heal anyone other than his host before. Tianyi had never suggested it. It would take a slightly different approach since he wasn't bonded to Steve, but perhaps not so different from when he had healed Isaac for the first time. *We can try.*

Keeping their hand over the wound, they prodded gently for any remaining shrapnel, then finding the wound was clear, healed slowly as they withdrew the probe from the wound. Triggering Steve's body to produce more blood to replace the blood he'd lost would be more complicated.

Their own blood supply was critical, and not a match anyway.

"He'll need a hospital when we get home, but he's stable and out of danger." Gemini bent to pick him up in their arms. At least they were healed enough to augment their strength, because Steve wasn't walking out even if he did wake up.

Dani looked doubtful, but didn't argue. "How are we getting out of here?"

"We're taking one of the asteroid hoppers. Tianyi hasn't used the space dilation tunnel yet, so the smaller ship can still get us home." Gemini opened the door to the hall. "It'll be a tight fit but we can make it."

"And... You can fly one of those things?" Dani looked warily into the hall for the alien guards.

"As Prince Belenos, I commanded the entire Vistkian army. We can pilot an asteroid hopper better than Isaac can drive his Camry."

Wow. Thanks, Bel.

"I agree with Steve, that will never stop being weird." Dani laughed out loud. "What about the guards? I doubt they're going to let us just walk out of here." She lowered her voice. "Especially after we killed their beloved emperor."

"Unless things have changed, the guard holds no love for Tianyi. Tianyi was capricious and cruel to both allies and enemies." Gemini led them down another empty corridor. "We also took the liberty of sending them to the other end of the ship before we disconnected from the LAN."

They reached the hanger before they saw any other beings. Steve was getting heavy, and Gemini's wound hurt.

They'd nearly burned through the energy they had taken healing Steve and trying to keep themselves alive. Bel's voice in their head grew silent and each step seemed like plodding to a goal. They were going to face Vistkian soldiers in the hangar, and they were going to need another boost before they did.

They gently set Steve down against the wall beside the hangar door and pressed their armored hand to the control panel. They leaned back against the wall themselves as they absorbed energy, raw materials, and information.

"Are you... Of course you're not okay." Dani huffed. "What do you need? Is there anything I can do to help?"

"We need a couple steak dinners, a couple gallons of water, seventeen and a half pounds of Vistkian Carbide, and a month long coma." Gemini lifted their head from the wall and gave her a weary smile that didn't reach their eyes. They were running on Vistkian tech, Bel's confidence, and Isaac's determination to see his family again. "Short of that, we could really use Steve to wake up and for you to get a weapon. Carrying him is really draining our resources, resources we can't afford to expend in a fight." That wasn't a lie, but it was a convenient cover for the fact that no matter how much energy they absorbed, they were barely keeping on their feet. Once they got into the asteroid hopper, they'd have all the resources they needed to rebuild until they got home.

They just had to get there.

Steve stirred and moaned. Gemini sighed, disconnected, and pushed away from the wall. Getting Steve mobile would greatly increase their odds of survival. They knelt beside him again and laid their armored hand on his chest, taking the time to do a careful analysis and stimulate his body to replace his blood supply faster.

"We're not dead. Yay." Steve opened his eyes and raised a hand for a weak high five.

Gemini responded with his own bare left hand. "Nope, and we'd like to keep it that way. Can you stand?"

"My legs feel like jello, but I think so." Steve grunted as Dani helped him to his feet. He wobbled, but managed not to fall. He looked back at Isaac and swore. "You look terrible."

"Thanks. Two mortal wounds in one day tends to do that to a person." Gemini ran their bare hand through their blood matted hair. "We can repair ourselves once we're home." They looked pensively to the door. "We're really going to need your help to do that, though. If our armor was fully repaired, we could fake our way in. As it is, our best hope is to make for the nearest asteroid hopper and shoot anything that tries to stop us."

Neither Steve nor Dani seemed particularly thrilled with that option – Gemini wasn't either if they were honest. *Steve and Dani are unsuitable protectors. They are neither trained, nor equipped.*

It's not ideal, Isaac agreed tiredly, *but we're the only ones who can pilot the ship. And we still feel like death walking. If they get in over their heads, we can step in.*

"There are three Vistkian life signs inside. Probably just mechanics, since we set off the alarms in the larger hanger we came in at. As far as they know, we don't even know about this one." *Creator, show us favor.*

He has already, or we wouldn't be standing here, Isaac agreed. *I have full faith He will continue to do so.* Bel's surprised joy at Isaac's statement took some of the edge off their tiredness.

"We'll start by bluffing. We'd like to avoid killing noncombatants if at all possible." Gemini steeled themselves and opened the door. They led Steven and Dani in confidently, the glowing electricity crackling in their gauntlet the only show of strength they could muster. *Savior grant it is enough.*

The nearest mechanic looked up from his work, muttered under his breath, and went deeper into the ship he was working on. He shouted in Vistkian to his fellows, "Stupid soldiers picked the wrong hanger."

Another pangolin-like face popped up from behind a tool chest. "Think the Terran slugs killed the monster?"

"We should be so lucky," A third voice called from somewhere deep in the hanger. The three mechanics laughed.

"Huh." Gemini stood down and let the electrical current fade. They shouted into the hanger in Vistkian, "Kindly mechanics. We desire no trouble and only wish to go home. Ignore us and live."

"Oh no, I'm being threatened!" The nearest mechanic mocked in falsetto.

"I'm not dying for Tianyi the Dragon." Tools clattered to the floor by the tool chest. "Lunch break, guys."

Still laughing, the three mechanics stopped working and left for the back room.

"What... Just happened." Dani lowered her blaster and looked around the hanger in bewilderment.

"Tianyi's cruelty worked in our favor." Gemini laughed themselves. "Let's go home."

Chapter 25

"Can I get you anything?" Becca came behind Isaac, laid her hands on his shoulders, and kissed him on the head.

"We're good. Thanks." Isaac coughed and pulled the blankets tighter around him in the recliner he'd barely left since they'd gotten back from the Vistkian flagship. A half-filled bowl of tepid chicken noodle soup and three and a half empty bottles of sports drink sat on the side table to his right. Steve had gone straight to the hospital when they had landed back in Area 51, but even the military had agreed that explaining Bel, alien abductions, and midnight spaceship landings wasn't worth the risk for the minimal benefit a hospital stay would grant Gemini that rest and resources alone couldn't cover. So as soon as they could harvest enough from the asteroid hopper to repair their armor (being careful to pull from areas that rendered the advanced weapons technology useless to the US military), they called for Steve's private jet and slept the whole way home.

It had been immediately obvious a month-long coma was out of the question, so they settled for Alice's pot roast and an extended sick leave.

And promptly got sick, for the first time since they'd met.

"Isaac! You didn't eat anything. How do you expect to heal if you don't eat?" Becca clucked her tongue and gathered up his leftovers.

"Does Alice have any more pot roast?" They needed protein to rebuild their body systems, and the tiny bits of chicken in the soup weren't cutting it. Their armor was nearly repaired, but consciousness had slowed biological repairs and left them open to infection.

"Seriously? You've eaten nearly three whole roasts in the last week." Becca laughed, but fear lurked behind her eyes. "You're going to be made of pot roast."

She's not wrong. Weary amusement threaded Bel's voice. Just as the salvage from the asteroid hopper had been assimilated into new armor, the elements of the pot roast were being assimilated into new cells.

Isaac coughed again to cover his laugh. He'd heard little from his friend since they'd returned, and precious little beyond strict data. His grim focus and determination testified to the critical severity of their injuries.

"It's good to hear you laugh again." Becca perched on the arm of their chair, and leaned into his side. "I almost lost you, didn't I?"

Isaac considered a glib reply, but realized quickly that wasn't quite fair to her or Bel. He blew a slow breath through his lips, wrapped his arm around her, and pulled her closer. "You did. Twice."

Displeasure tightened her lips and the fear in her eyes melted to tears. "Bel saved you?"

"No. He did his best, but as far as I understand it I was too far gone. He could repair my body, but..." He swallowed back a lump that threatened to choke off his explanation. Isaac had been dead for several minutes. While he hadn't even begun processing that, he was fairly confident that trauma was the source of Bel's silence and tireless healing. He tried again with a husky voice. "God had mercy. On me. On Bel. I don't know which, maybe both of us. I was gone, and Bel was prepared to take himself out to avenge me." The memory of Bel's tumble into madness seeped into their consciousness, and Isaac's eyes widened. *How could you keep that from me?*

It is a distraction we could ill afford. Bel's response was flat.

We're going to be dealing with this for a while, aren't we?

There will be plenty of time once you're healed.

Isaac hummed skeptically, wondering if that 'distraction' was what had allowed the virus to take hold, but let it go and went back to answering his wife. "God brought me back, and allowed us to defeat Bel's brother and escape with Steve and Dani. It might be a long road, but we're here now, and we're not going anywhere."

"Until the next emergency, right?" Becca cuddled in closer, sharing Isaac's blanket as she snuggled up to his chest. "It's too much to hope you're retired?"

"Retired, no, but we are on leave." He rested his head on her's. "And I've got the best back up team you could hope for."

"I'm just glad to hear you're back on God's team." Becca kissed his forehead. "I'll worry about you less knowing that."

As will I. Bel's voice strengthened and Isaac's raging fever cooled. His favorite star song hummed in the back of their consciousness for the first time since the battle.

"You can thank Bel and your dad for that." *Thanks, Bel, for everything.*

It's my pleasure. Eternity as a superhero is a far better fate than eternity as a dictator.

Isaac hummed his agreement, but that was all the response Bel got, because, for the moment, Isaac was simply content to enjoy some much needed time with his wife.

About the Author

Alexandra Gilchrist has loved stories of great adventure, deep friendships, and noble ideals since she learned to read. Realizing it was becoming more and more difficult to find those kinds of stories in today's culture, she decided her only recourse was to write her own.

When she's not writing (or wishing the stories were done so she could just READ the blasted things), she enjoys spending time with her husband and kids, deep diving theology at 11pm, watching anime, and cuddling her cat.